Perfect Prey

Also by Laura Salters

Run Away

Perfect Prey

LAURA SALTERS

WITNESS
IMPULSE

An Imprint of HarperCollins*Publishers*

EPub Edition OCTOBER 2016 ISBN: 9780062457554
Print Edition ISBN: 9780062457561

10 9 8 7 6 5 4 3 2 1

To Jack—
to make up for being the most annoying sister
in the northern hemisphere

Chapter One

July 10, Serbia

BELGRADE IS A beautiful city in which to have a panic attack.

Specifically Belgrade Cooperative Building, which is all Art Nouveau architecture and decorative facades and intricately painted glass. In a grand atrium, our group of journalists look down on a mammoth model of how the Serbian capital will look following a Dubai-style redevelopment—lush parks, luxury apartments, sleek shopping malls and the tallest skyscraper in the Balkans.

And I'm about to pass out right on top of it.

"You look hideous," Erin whispers, nudging my shoulder. "Anxiety flaring up?"

"I'm fine," I mumble, sweating with the effort of trying to keep it under control.

"Yeah. And I'm the president of the United States. Let's go outside for a moment."

"Honestly, Erin," I whisper, trying desperately not to draw attention to us. Tim, our press trip organizer, is shooting us dirty looks, which of course makes me three hundred percent sure everyone hates me and thus prompts another bout of palpitations. "I'm okay."

She smirks. "Well, that's good to know, but I'm dying for a smoke. Come with me?"

She's always done this. Ever since we first started interning together in the fashion cupboard of a glossy lifestyle magazine, she's met my episodes with cool, calm poise. Erin Baxter is better than any medication when you're starting to spiral.

Duncan, a gruff Scottish journalist with a knack for asking uncomfortable questions, is in the middle of challenging our tour guide on the supposedly corrupt Arab funding behind the Belgrade waterfront scheme. Nobody notices when we slip out, past marble columns and vaults, grand staircases and terrazzo tiles, flashing our press badges at the bored-looking security guards.

The street is relatively quiet. It's the middle of the afternoon, and most locals are at work, with the exception of a few motorbikes zipping around the roundabout outside the Cooperative Building. Opposite is an old ironworks, which has been transformed into a hive of activity—street food, craft markets and a hip bar, all decked out with fairy lights and art prints. I can smell the homemade lemonade from here.

"What's up?" Erin asks calmly, sparking up a cigarette between her crimson-painted lips. Her hair is dirty blond and Kate Moss–messy, and she has the height and build of a supermodel to match. More tattoos and piercings than your average clotheshorse, though.

"Honestly? I don't know," I say. "Mentally, I'm fine. My body has other ideas." I can feel the excess adrenaline coursing through me, manifesting into stomach cramps, heart palpitations and shaky hands.

"Deep breaths. Cold water. Beta-blocker. You'll be fine."

I groan. "I know. I'm sorry. Last thing I want to do is taint this trip with my insanity."

"Oh, pipe down. I love you for your insanity, not despite it." She grins, hair flapping in the river breeze. Tucks a stray lock behind her triple-studded ear. "Smoke?" I shake my head.

We're on a press trip, funded by the Serbian tourism board. Journalists from across the UK are here to cover a world-renowned music festival from a whole host of angles—me from an economical vantage point, Erin from a fashion reporter's perspective. It's held in a hilltop fortress in the nearby city of Novi Sad, and we're set to travel there this afternoon.

If my tenuous grasp on sanity holds out that long.

I'm about to ask Erin for a swig from her hip flask when her phone starts to ring. She pulls a face.

"Lowe."

Our snooty editor. The one who scoffed when we pitched the Serbia trip—she understands champagne and caviar in Milan, not camping in a field in the Balkans. I remember her sneering over her designer glasses and saying, "But . . . Serbia? Aren't they always at war or flooded or something? You know, if you want a free holiday, I've got a city break to Paris sitting in my in-box. Over Fashion Week. Every fashion intern on the planet would kill to be there. Why on earth would you choose Serbia?"

Erin didn't waver.

"Because no one else is doing it! Think about it. All the top fashion magazines are at the big festivals. They're snapping the celebs and the DJs in their poncho-and-welly combos. They're covering this summer's hottest festival trends. They're sending fashion reporters to Coachella and Tomorrowland. But nobody is at JUMP. And it's quickly becoming the biggest festival in the world. You should see this year's headliners."

Lowe is always giving us a hard time, even when we're out of the country. We're lowly interns, scum on the bottom of her shoe, incapable of everything, including but not limited to: breathing, talking, wiping our own butts. But even she has a soft spot for Erin. It's hard not to.

A horn blasts on the street, a man yells something angrily from a car window and something curdles in my stomach as Erin accepts the call.

"Hey, Lowe," Erin says easily. She's way cooler under pressure than me. Well, way cooler in general. But still.

"Baxter," Lowe barks. Erin has put her on speakerphone, and her piercing tone cuts right through the bustle on the street. "How's Croatia?"

"Serbia."

"Whatever. Did you get my email?"

Erin drags on her cigarette. "Sorry. I haven't been able to find Wi-Fi. What's up?"

"Your feature on the coat designer from Transylvania, that's what."

"Pennsylvania."

"Whatever. It's shit, Baxter. Utter manure. Farmers could spread this on their fields to ensure a fruitful fucking harvest."

Erin laughs. The sound is easy and relaxed. How is she not crapping herself right now? I guess it's no secret that Lowe terrifies me. She's glamorous and cool and intelligent and intimidating. She's Erin in thirty years' time. "You didn't like it?"

Lowe snorts down the receiver. "The angle was too obvious, the quotes were badly laid out and the image selection . . . don't get me started."

"Sorry. Fire over your notes and I'll rewrite." Erin flicks the trail of ash from the end of her cigarette. She has that perfect blend of professionalism and playfulness down to a tee. It makes you feel like arguing with her would be both mean and irrational. I think it's why people, me included, often struggle to say no to her.

Me, on the other hand . . . my JUMP pitch went something like this:

"I—I'm really interested in . . . well, how countries that are known for conflict, how they . . . shake their reputations as dangerous places and rebuild their tourism industries. After the bloody Yugoslav Wars in the nineties, it's fascinating how Serbia is . . . I mean, C-Croatia is now starting to be seen as a hot tourist destination, right? And it'll be interesting to see whether Serbia can . . ."

I wince, a pang of shame at the memory. I pulled it together. Almost.

"But . . . but I think this feature could be really great. I could interview local business owners, get their take on the festival. Try and figure out whether the festival is really doing as much good as they have us believe. Speak to some of the headliners, ask what made them want to get involved in a project like this."

Lowe had made some simpering remark about how *Northern Heart* isn't the *New York Times*, condescension dripping from her words like syrup, but she agreed eventually. That's all that matters. This piece could be my ticket out of the magazine's stuffy fashion cupboard, full of expensive clothes I have no interest in whatsoever.

I'm so busy trying to fan my burning cheeks with a tour leaflet that I don't notice Erin is off the phone. She actually looks a little shaken.

"You all right?" I ask, nudging her shoulder with mine. Smoke curls around her lips.

She stares at the pavement. "Yeah. Fine."

"Really? You look . . . hell, you look like you feel like me. And that's never good." I try for a smile, but it falls flat. "Erin?"

"You ever wonder if you're making a mistake?" she asks, voice thick with . . . something.

I chuckle. "Constantly. Thirty-eight times a second. Hence the anxiety."

A sad smile.

"What's on your mind?" I ask.

Then, as quickly as the strange mood descended, she snaps out of it, stamping the cigarette out beneath her espadrilles. "Nothing. Booze. Let's find a bar?"

So I let it go.

Chapter Two

July 12, Serbia

IF IT WEREN'T for the sheep skulls dangling from trees, donkeys wearing bandanas and the half-naked man singing the Serbian national anthem, it would have been like any other riverfront farm.

When Tim, the organizer of the press trip, had said he was taking us to see some friends of his, we hadn't exactly envisaged hopping into three boats—more like canoes with engines— traveling four miles down the Danube and dismounting next to a field of fly-infested pigs. But by now we've learned not to question anything on this trip. I think Clara, the tabloid journalist, regrets her stilettos by the time we've clambered up the muddy bank and been greeted by a toothless Serbian woman with a sleeping baby strapped to her chest.

There are five people living in this peculiar little settlement, all of whom cheer loudly when they see Tim leap out of his boat. He roars excitedly and embraces one of the aged, bandana-clad donkeys. Two men usher him up the bank, slapping him elatedly on the back, while a little boy—who looks exactly like Mowgli from *The Jungle Book*—is standing at the top, digging a long stick into the sunbaked ground.

We all gather in a wide fenced enclosure, shaded by a canopy of tall trees. There's no stone-built farmhouse, only a rusting caravan with floral curtains, and the hard, dusty ground looks like it's recently been swept—there's a pile of dry leaves at the foot of a thick tree trunk. A couple of mongrel dogs with matted coats chase each other around the caravan, and the boy giggles as he watches them. The toothless woman is now slicing raw meat, her back hunched over a battered wooden table. They all look excited to have visitors. I overhear one of the men telling Clara that they give the donkeys bandanas to keep them cool in the high summer, but Clara's nose is wrinkled in disgust.

It's so far removed from our normal lives that I can't stop thinking about how weird it is that we're here. I think that thought on loop until it's impossible to even be in the moment because I'm obsessing over how weird it is that the moment is even happening to begin with.

The river gushes behind us, the air smells like dried earth and the sun is hot on my bare shoulders. Erin and I take a wander around the settlement, largely at a loss for words. Tim is over by the caravan, still chatting animatedly to the older of the two men, whose skin is so tanned and rough it looks like leather. When we're summoned, the rest of us take seats around a long picnic bench. The woman presents us with the platter of what looks like raw bacon. I look around for a fire or any other evidence that it'll be cooked. Nothing. Nada.

Clara winces. "There's literally a dead animal in front of me."

"As opposed to all the other meat you eat, which is only metaphorically dead," Erin snorts. She's got a sailor's laugh. She glances at her phone. "Of course there's no bloody reception here. Of course there isn't." She looks worried again. Her hair is pulled back into a messy bun, but she's missed a few wisps, which flutter against her tanned face in the light breeze. She's taken her nose ring out for the first time in months.

I nudge her tattooed shoulder. Her bare skin is hot against mine. "What's up?"

"Lowe's gonna kill me if I'm not there to answer her every beck and call," Erin mumbles. She chews her bottom lip. I notice an old bruise lurking beneath her half-sleeve tattoo—patches of yellow and brown underneath the intricate black ink.

"Erin. It's Sunday. She can't possibly expect you to . . ." I trail off when I realize she isn't listening; she's just pressing the on/off button anxiously. I give her hand a squeeze. Her chunky rings dig into my palm. "Hey. Smile. Enjoy your day. You'll never, ever be here again." I wave my hand at the thatched roof above the dining area, the abandoned wooden boats bobbing on the water and the shots of rakia now being poured for a breakfast toast.

She grimaces and tucks her phone away.

Tim clears his throat at the end of the table. He's got mini-Mowgli balancing on his hip, pressing his face into Tim's flannel shirt. His eyes are crinkling against the sun. "I'd like to make a toast," Tim says, accepting one of the glasses of rakia the toothless woman is now handing around. "To Agata—" the woman bows her head "—Djuro and Marin, for welcoming us into their home. To you lot—" we all smile at the recognition "—who make my job thirty times more fun than it would otherwise be, and to the donkeys, who . . . well, who smell like shit quite frankly. To friends, old and new!"

"To friends, old and new!" we chorus. The fruity brandy burns my throat, and I shudder as it hits my empty stomach. The canopy rustles above us and the child chuckles as Tim bounces him up and down. I smile.

My normal life seems a thousand miles away. I wish I could keep it that way.

WE LEAVE THE farm after a couple of hours of eating, drinking and disjointed storytelling in fractured English and Tim's shoddy Serbian. It's after midday now, and the sun is high in the sky as we get back into the boats, salute our drivers—or captains, as they ask to be addressed—and set off even farther down the river.

Sailing into the wind, I feel a little woozy after the fruit brandy and breakfast of raw tomatoes and freshly baked bread. The river is wide and brownish-blue, and either side is thick with acres of dark green trees, wooden jetties and cream-colored houses set back off the banks. We're told it's where wealthy Serbs come to live during the summer months, but we're yet to see another living soul.

Propping my elbows back on the bench, I throw my head back and close my eyes. The sun is baking hot on my face, and the rocking of the boat as it propels forward against the current makes me feel like I could sleep for a thousand years. Partying every night until sunrise for four days is starting to get to me, but I never want the trip to end.

Music reporter Jin Ra's lean thigh is pressed against mine, and I can smell his sun cream. His sharp cheekbones are accentuated by his oversized glasses, and his South Korean skin tone has been freckled by the sun. I catch myself smiling as his arm brushes against mine.

We eventually pull up on a wide stretch of sand in the middle of the Danube. It spreads like a beachy pier from the west bank across two-thirds of the river. The water level is low enough that most of it is exposed, the white sand dry and powdery. A few giant branches of driftwood stick out of the sand, and there are some smooth pebbles scattered around. The only sounds are the scraping of the boats as they're pulled onto the beach, and Erin splashing Duncan with flailing arms windmilling through the cold water.

When my feet touch the sand after jumping out of the boat, I have to throw my arms out to steady myself—I'm as disorientated as I used to get after spinning around and around in circles as a kid. Jin Ra grabs my forearm to keep me upright. My eyes meet his and he gives me a shy smile.

For a while we paddle in the shallow water, take countless Instagram snaps and try to ignore the slate-gray clouds drifting above us, but as they darken, multiply and eclipse the sun, the temperature drops sharply.

Tim smacks his lips, opens his arms and optimistically says, "It'll clear soon. Trust me. I have an instinct for these things."

Almost instantaneously, there's a crack of thunder and the rain starts to fall. I hear it patter over the surface of the river before I feel it, damp and sticky, on my skin. I'm wearing a polka dot sundress with spaghetti straps, and the drops are so fat and heavy they soak me in seconds. We all look at each other, our comrades only just visible through the downpour, and dash back across to the boats.

I try not to panic as a bolt of lightning illuminates the charcoal sky. Is there a worse place to be in a thunderstorm than in a rickety boat on a swelling river? Jin Ra's already in the boat, and his hands wrap around my waist as they hoist me over the side. The rain is warm, but I shiver involuntarily.

We set off with more urgency than before as another roar of thunder claps through the clouds. We sit huddled together on the benches, trying to laugh about our rotten luck, but all inwardly wishing we were safe on dry land. The boat stayed relatively flat this morning, but now it lurches from side to side. I can hardly hear the engine over the plummeting rain smacking the surface of the river.

Crack. Flash.

My earlier calm has dissipated. I'm an extreme person. I'm either superrelaxed or super-on-edge; there's no in between. And I've just swooshed to the other end of the spectrum so fast I have whiplash. Every nerve is on high alert.

That's how I feel mentally. Hyperaware. Of every blinding flash, of every centimeter of damp clothing, of every single raindrop of every single surface.

After a minute or two, the driver swerves over to the eastern riverbank and angles the boat toward a crumbling wooden platform standing below a little wooden hut, which is raised above the water with thick stilts. Before we've even come to a standstill, he's already looping a thick rope around the foot of the platform and leaping out, losing his footing slightly on the wet wood.

I clamber out with not a single ounce of grace, watching as Erin manages the feat with elegance. Her denim hot pants are so drenched they're almost black, and her baggy white tee is almost see-through. Meanwhile, my sodden locks of black and violet hair are dripping water between my cleavage. Shaking like a wet dog, I squeeze some of the moisture out of my dip-dyed mane, but it's no use.

I'm surprised to see there's light coming from inside the hut, and the murmur of male voices can be heard over the roar of the storm. Working our way up the slippery bank, clinging onto overgrown weeds and using jagged rocks as footholds, I start to wonder whether this trip could possibly get any weirder.

The hut has a tiny raised veranda overlooking the river, and there's a little table set up with a burlap runner, thermos flasks and chipped brown mugs. Rivulets of rainwater stream down the slanted roof, but the tiny dining area is largely sheltered. It looks like it's waiting for us. Tim leads the way up the steps wrapping around the side of the hut, me right behind him, and as we reach the top, a man steps out onto the porch.

My mouth hangs open. He's hands down the most attractive man I've ever seen in the flesh. His muscled torso ripples through his wet red T-shirt, and his short, dark brown hair is ruffled and damp, like he's just got out of the shower. His arms are thick, with indigo veins laced over his biceps. Inky black eyes stand out starkly against a tanned, stubbly face, and as he grins, he reveals a row of perfect white teeth.

"Tim! You're here!" he exclaims, embracing Tim with a squelch. He pronounces it "Teem." He turns to me, though I can tell he's already looking over my shoulder at Erin. Nothing new there. He reaches out and shakes my hand.

"Hi. I'm . . . I'm Carina," I manage.

"Hi." Another flash of teeth. "I'm Andrijo."

AN HOUR LATER we're sitting around the tiny table, and the torrential rain is starting to slow. Mosquitoes buzz around our ears, rabbit stew bubbles in a nearby pot and we're on to our fifth or sixth cans of beer. Tim and Borko chat about this year's JUMP compared to the last few, while my fellow journalists are in an intense debate about the political situation in the Middle East. Normally Erin would be straight in there—she's feisty and opinionated and never backs down—but today she is not. Because she's utterly engrossed in Andrijo.

They stand away from the rest of the group, elbows resting on the fence around the veranda, staring out to the river. I hear fragments of their conversation over the raucous debates around me.

She leans into him. "So what do you do in Novi Sad?"

"You're so beautiful. Like the sunset over the Danube in late summer," he replies. She flushes and giggles, sipping from her can while gazing at him. He stares right back.

She has a boyfriend.

Then she asks, "Will you be at JUMP tonight?"

"You are so radiant. Anything for you."

I shiver involuntarily. That's a little intense. He's making my skin crawl, so I force myself to rejoin the conversation around the table.

But not before I hear her say, "So, do you have a girlfriend?"

He holds her gaze. "I have eyes for no one but you."

"I'M GLAD YOU'RE here with me," Erin yells.

I can barely hear her over the pounding speakers in front of us. We're standing right at the front of the main stage—next to twenty security guards, the lead singer's girlfriend and eight eardrum-bursting amplifiers. It's so loud I can barely make out the guitar from the drums, but the view is unrivaled. I can practically reach out and touch the bass guitarist.

She shakes her head and takes my hand, pulling me off to the side of the stage while trying to dodge the endless cables and speakers littered around the backstage area. We lean against one of the portacabins the bands use as dressing rooms. It's still so loud my ears feel crucified, but I can sort of make out what she's saying.

"I mean it, Carina." She still hasn't let go of my hand. "I'm so glad you're here—that we get to share this experience with each other. Imagine if that snooty cow Clara was my only female company out here?" She grins, but her expression has that faux-urgent quality of someone who's drank a little too much and now believes declaring their undying love for people is a matter of life and death. "I'm glad we became lunch buddies. Hell, I'm glad we became friends. And I'm glad we're following our dreams together."

Maybe it's because of the fourth cider I just finished, but I feel a little teary-eyed. The crowd behind us is swaying in time to the slow rock song, filling in the words as the singer holds his microphone in the air.

A strobe light bounces off her silver bangle—the one that matches mine. It's thin and delicate, engraved with an Arabic expression it took us forever to translate: "If you are saved from the lion, do not be greedy and hunt it." When a PR company sent them to *Northern Heart* for a shoot we were producing, we fell in love and bought one each. We always joke that Lowe is the lion.

"You make me feel like I can do it," I tell her, swallowing my usual hesitancy to put myself out there. Again, probably thanks to the cider. "Life. You make me feel reckless, but in the best way possible. I wouldn't be here, in Serbia, writing such an ambitious feature, if I didn't have you by my side."

"Yeah, you would," she says. "But maybe in a decade's time, once you'd finally grown some ovaries and spoken to the lion for the first time."

I shove her playfully into the side of the portacabin and she cackles.

"I'm gonna go pee. Wait here for me?" she asks.

I smile. "Of course."

AN HOUR LATER, the rock set has finished and the crowd is excitedly cheering for the next act—a drum and bass duo who'll surely put the final nail in my eardrums' coffin. But Erin hasn't come back yet, and I'm starting to feel worried.

Has she gotten lost?

She hasn't got the best sense of direction, but the toilets are just around the corner from the backstage entrance. Surely she isn't that hopeless.

I check my phone to see if she's tried to call me, but she hasn't.

I swing around to face Tim. "Erin left to nip to the toilet over an hour ago, but she hasn't come back since. Should we go and look for her?"

He scrunches his face up. "Nah. She's a big girl. Can look after herself. Don't wanna miss this set."

I try to ring her a couple of times, but it keeps ringing out: *"Welcome to the O2 messaging service. I'm sorry, but the person you are calling—"*

"Anyone want anything from the bar?" I ask Clara, Duncan and Jin Ra, but all of them have recently topped up. I flash my press badge at the guard and slip through the gap in the gate that leads to the VIP drinking terrace.

Jostling through clusters of journalists and minor celebrities, I scan the terrace for Erin. She's tall, blond and heavily tattooed, so in theory she should be easy to spot, but I don't see her anywhere.

I frown. This isn't like her. And I don't like the idea of her wandering around lost and alone.

Heavy footsteps pounding against the wooden decking echo through my mind as I try to think of an explanation. Could she have started talking to new people and lost track of time? Or did she decide to go back to the hotel early? Or was she hungry and went to grab a slice of pizza?

All totally plausible explanations, but I know her. She's thoughtful. She would have texted me first, especially after asking me to wait by the stage.

I buy a bottle of water to try and clear my head before heading back to the speakers, where the others are now raving to some obnoxiously intense drum and bass.

She still isn't there.

Uneasiness spreads through me like a fever.

Now it's two in the morning. The walls of the open-air fortress tower over me, but my fear dwarfs them all.

Where the hell are you, Erin?

Bass and blood pound in my ears. A roar erupts from a nearby stage. The crowd goes wild for the last headliner of the night, but the screams and chants are dulled against my mounting terror.

Something isn't right.

I'm running past the same liquor garden I've passed three times now. Why have I never noticed how creepy silent discos are? Limp necks and tense limbs jerk erratically to the sound of nothing. Their eerie shadows ricochet off the crumbling stone walls and white canvas tents. A throng of intoxicated bodies swarms around me like I'm a boulder in a stream.

I wring my sweaty hands together and hit redial for the millionth time.

Dead.

Her phone is dead. Her phone is never dead. It's glued to her hand like she needs it to breathe.

Speaking of breathing . . . how do you do that again?

I jolt to a halt and clutch at my sides, trying, failing, to massage away the sharp stitch. A tux-clad security guard gives me a strange look. My panic-stricken face must stand out like a sore thumb against the hundred thousand other drug-slackened expressions at the festival. I flash my press pass at him, and he steps aside, allowing me access to the backstage tent. The indie band who played the rock stage earlier are propped up at the bar, chasing a row of tequila shots with wedges of lemon.

She's not here either.

She's not raving at the dance stage, she's not necking beer in the Corona tent, she's not on the VIP platform watching the dubstep act on the main stage. She's not back at the hotel—I called and checked. She's not answering my calls, she's not reading my texts. She's not been seen for three hours.

My mum's words of warning dance gloatingly through my mind.

"Serbia isn't safe. You know what happens to beautiful girls in that country."

"You watch too much TV," I'd insisted. "This isn't a Liam Neeson movie."

The men. The men we'd met earlier. There was something too intense about them. Something off.

One more lap. One more lap of the fortress and I'll call the police.

BY FOUR A.M., I'm screaming her name into the night.

I call the police. The woman I speak to on the emergency line tells me a person has to have been missing for at least twenty-four hours before they can launch a search, and that I'm not the first person to have lost a friend at JUMP and thought the worst. She's sure Erin will turn up.

That makes one of us.

THE SUN RISES just after five. Its rays are weak and I'm shivering as I walk across Liberty Bridge, which is still illuminated in blue and pink and green, back into Novi Sad. In the distance, I can almost hear the festival campsite still going like a fairground, but the sounds are drowned out by the gushing Danube below me. It's roaring powerfully with the force of yesterday's summer storm behind it.

Daylight feels alien. Fear is still pulsing through me, but it's somehow not as intense when the sky isn't black and I'm not being thrust around a muddy green by an unruly crowd. The terror is quieter, but it's still there. It's still making my stomach twist painfully and my hands tremble as I walk. My eyes blink rapidly against the sunlight.

I stop in my tracks. The campsite. Of course.

Maybe she's there. Maybe she snuck off with a boy.

I'm about to sprint back where I came from, to run down the rows and rows of tents yelling her name, but my gut tells me that's wrong. She wouldn't do that. She has a boyfriend, and she loves him. They've been together for nine years.

It's wrong.

This is all wrong.

SEVEN A.M. NOVI Sad is waking up.

I wander aimlessly through the streets. The air smells of warm, wet pavement and sweet pastry and Serbian spruce trees. All the buildings are different pastel colors, some sky blue with white gables, some pale yellow with chipped green woodwork and some candyfloss pink with cream-colored cornicing. Shutters are opening and a young waitress is setting up plastic tables and chairs outside a pavement café. She stops and checks her phone. A message makes her smile.

The sight is so normal it seems borderline perverse. My best friend is missing and a waitress is smiling.

I replay the smile over and over in my head to try and keep touch with reality but it's no use.

I'm spiraling.

I'M DELIRIOUS WITH exhaustion and fear and yes, okay, maybe a bit too much cider. But my last drink was nine hours ago, and the whooshing and swirling and plunging in my head feels more sinister than inebriation.

Nine a.m. I've phoned everyone. The other journalists in our group, the hotel, the festival organizers. They closed the fortress two hours ago. There was no one left inside.

I even try the police again, in case I manage to get through to a different operator who's more willing to help. It's the same woman. She tells me to call back once it's been twenty-four hours, but her earlier compassion has evaporated.

I no longer know what I'm looking for in Novi Sad. A flash of blond hair whipping around a corner? A black leather jacket zooming away on the back of a stranger's motorbike? A slender tattooed arm slung around a man's waist? A big billboard that says, *This way! She's this way*?

Jabbing her name on my call log for the thousandth time, I start to feel dizzy, like I haven't eaten in a week, and the pain in my stomach and the lightness in my head are a result of simple hunger. The call takes a moment longer to connect than usual, and for an agonizing split second of hope, I think I might hear a dial tone.

Dead.

Chapter Three

July 13, Serbia

I WAKE UP starfished in the king-sized bed in my hotel room. There's a crack in the curtains, and I can see sunlight blazing through. It's eerily silent, bar the hum of the air-conditioning.

I blink against the confusion. Was it all a dream? I roll over, grasping for my phone on the bedside table. It reads 1:36 p.m. My call log shows me it wasn't just a sordid nightmare. Recent outgoing calls: Erin Baxter (51). I have a message from Tim, the press trip organizer, and a couple from other members of the group, but nothing from Erin. No responses. No voice mail. I hit redial, praying to a God I don't believe in that she'll pick up, and everything will be fine, and we'll laugh about this tonight as we sing along to Rudimental. I'll make her buy me a beer to make up for scaring the living shit out of me.

Dead.

I throw my thumping head back onto the pillow. How did I get to my bed? Why does my head hurt so much? I'm still fully clothed, minus my muddy sneakers. Vague images of a deserted Liberty Square, glimmering puddles and a cloud-pocked sky come back to me. I peel one eye open again to read Tim's text.

We've canceled today's excursion. I don't want you to worry about Erin—we're doing everything we can to find her. Tim

His text was sent two hours ago, and I've had nothing from him since. They obviously haven't found her yet. I take three deep breaths. I refuse to let myself get worked up again until I have good reason.

Focus on what you know. Like the time is 1:37 p.m. and you're in Novi Sad and it's sunny outside and you're too hot and you're thirsty and the duvet is blue.

Reality isn't all that comforting right now.

Duncan messaged me at six a.m.

All right, wee one. Where are you and Baxter? Been looking for you everywhere. Give us a bell so we know you're not in a ditch anywhere, eh?

Clara Fox. Tabloid journalist and gossip columnist extraordinaire. See also: gigantic douche.

Fuck's sake. We've been looking for you and Erin everywhere. They've canceled the winery trip because of you! Where are you?? Cx

My limbs feel like they're moving through molasses as I stumble out of bed to the shower. I feel marginally less panicky after sleeping, but my throat feels dry and scratchy, and my headache is on the blinding end of the migraine spectrum.

This morning flits back to me like beams of sunlight through half-open blinds. Calling the police a third time, talking myself down from a panic attack, staggering back to the hotel and finding an incredibly stressed out Tim in the hotel lobby waiting for me. His crestfallen face when he realized Erin wasn't with me. His assurance that he'd wait in the lobby in case she returned, and that I should go and get some sleep.

Twenty-four hours has never seemed like such a long time. I think of all the terrible things that can happen in that time, and yet the police wait until some bullshit criteria has been met before they'll take action. I know something is spectacularly wrong. I know it deep in my gut. But I have to wait another ten hours before they'll take me seriously.

I stay in the scalding shower until my skin is raw.

PART OF ME is expecting to see panic-stricken faces, endless pacing and frantic phone calls as I take the glass elevator down to the lobby, but already I can see the group lounging on the sofas like nothing's wrong. Clara is typing on her ultraexpensive laptop, and Jin Ra is cackling at Duncan, who's wearing sunglasses inside. Even looking down from the third floor, I can see none of them look remotely worried. Tim is nowhere to be seen.

"All right, kid," Duncan grunts in my direction as I walk over. "How's the head?"

"Sore. How'd you know?"

"The amount you drank last night? Doesn't take a genius." He waves a hip flask at me. Was I really that drunk last night? I can hear from the sloshing of the liquid that the flask is already half-empty. "Hair o' the dog? Sort yeh right out." His light brown hair sticks up in tufts.

My stomach clenches at the thought. I shake my head. "No, thanks." He raises an eyebrow above his aviators and shrugs, taking a swig. "Has anyone heard anything from Erin?"

Clara looks up from her laptop, and her acrylic nails stop

tip-tapping across the keyboard. "Nope. Not a word. Shocking. How can you just disappear without telling anyone where you're going?" She glares pointedly at me. I dig my thumb into my palm. "It's not fair. It's not fair on us, and it's not fair on Tim." Another patronizing shake of the head and she's back to typing up her gossip column.

"Where is Tim anyway?" I glance around. We're the only ones in the glass atrium of the lobby, apart from the middle-aged barman, who's taking great pride in polishing his industrial-sized coffee machine, and the young receptionist, who's coiling the phone cord around her index finger as she chats to a customer in rapid-fire Serbian. It looks scorching outside. The sun's rays are wobbly and the pavements are sizzling as yesterday's rain evaporates into wisps of steam.

"Dunno." Clara doesn't even look up from her screen as she takes a slurp of orange juice. "He's been tearing his hair out trying to get hold of her. He's even called around the local hospitals to see if she's turned up there. You know, I wouldn't blame him for calling the police. This isn't funny."

"I know," I say through gritted teeth. "But the police won't listen. I already tried. I think . . . I think something is very wrong. This isn't like her—"

"Oh, please. She's probably just gone off with those Serbian guys from yesterday. Which is the one she was doing puppy dog eyes at all day? Andrijo?" She rolls her eyes. "She was all over him."

"She has a boyfriend," I point out, but Clara's not even listening. Part of me wishes I had the guts to tell her that not everyone in real life carries on like the celebs she writes her lies about. But I stay quiet. As usual.

Andrijo. That was his name.

There was something strange about him and his friend. They were too . . . friendly? Attentive? I'm never great when meeting new people, and at the time, the uneasy feeling felt no more uneasy than usual. But in hindsight . . . I shake the thought away.

The group's ambivalence makes me feel even more antsy. Why am I the only one filled with dread? I've just started pacing up and down the length of the bar, obsessively checking Erin's social media to see if she's posted anything, when my phone starts vibrating in my hand.

Linda Lowe.

I take a deep breath, but I still tremble as I hit Answer. I can't help it.

"Hi, L—"

"Erin's ignoring my emails," Lowe almost barks down the phone. I wince as her voice rattles through my fragile head. "Really, Carina, the only reason I allowed you both to go was if you'd be on email the whole time. It's deadline day! Does that mean nothing to you? We're trying to sign off a mag—"

"Erin's missing." It's the first time I've ever interrupted her, and I feel guilty almost instantly.

Maybe *missing* was a bit strong, but it catches her off guard. "What do you mean, missing?"

"Missing, as in, none of us can find her. She hasn't been seen for—" I glance at my wristwatch "—fourteen hours."

"Well. Okay." I hear a door slam shut down her end, and the background noise becomes much quieter. She's gone into the boardroom. "Have you tried calling her?"

No, we've just sat here patiently like we're waiting for fucking Godot. "Yes. Fifty-two times."

"And nobody's seen her."

"No."

"Have you called the police?" she says, her voice lower now.

"Yes. We have to wait until it's been twenty-four hours."

There's a silence that neither of us know how to fill. I expect Lowe to yell some more, about how Erin's features aren't signed off and her image selection is shoddy as always and her grasp on the English language is tenuous at best. But she doesn't. She just says, quietly, "Keep me posted." Then she hangs up. I frown at my phone.

A hand touches my elbow and I jump. Jin Ra. He's wearing a slim-fit checked shirt, red braces and a bow tie. "Are you okay, Carina? Would you like something to drink?" His well-spoken accent is soft and slow. I nod.

We each take a bar stool and he orders us two cappuccinos and two still waters. He's one of those people who doesn't just talk for the sake of talking—he and I are the quiet ones of the group. And unlike Erin and me, he's actually at JUMP for the music. We sit in silence for a few moments.

Glancing at his vintage wristwatch, he swallows deeply, his jutting Adam's apple bobbing in his throat. "She'll turn up, you know."

I nod for lack of anything better to do. "I know." No, I don't. "What if she's . . . what if she's passed out somewhere?" I try and remember how drunk she was last time I saw her. "What if she's in trouble?"

Jin Ra slaps a sachet of sugar against his palm. He presses his lips together as he stirs it slowly into the frothy coffee. "But where? There are so many people going around that she'd be found in a heartbeat. And they checked the fortress before they closed it. She's not there."

I know what he's saying is true, but that doesn't help. Because I can't help but feel that being drunk and passed out is better than the alternative.

An alternative I can't even bear to articulate.

I ALWAYS THOUGHT that if someone I knew disappeared, I'd be sitting in the police station within a nanosecond, tracing their last movements and talking to everyone and anyone who could have seen her.

But it's not like that when it actually happens. It's too easy to explain away, too easy to rationalize. Even for the police.

Like house fires and lottery wins, this is the kind of thing that happens to other people. Not to normal twenty-somethings on a fun-filled trip. Disappearances belong safely in the world of CNN and blockbuster movies.

We're journalists. We're used to writing about this stuff, not living it.

TWENTY-FOUR HOURS.

By the time we finally have the attention of the police, all I can think about is how much tragedy can happen in twenty-four hours. A giant earthquake in the ocean can trigger eighteen tsunamis and kill nearly a quarter of a million people. Terrorists can hijack planes, hurricanes can tear cities apart, deadly viruses can spread through countries like wildfire.

Twenty-four hours. It's a fucking arbitrary time limit, in the grand scheme of things. It implies a situation isn't really an emergency if it's only been going on for twenty-three hours.

It's absurd.

What has happened to Erin in the last twenty-four hours?

As the clock changes from 10:59 to 11:00 and we officially reach the twenty-four-hour threshold, I wonder how much that minute really changed anything.

The concept of time is warping and distorting in my mind, like when you repeat a word so many times and it loses all meaning. I do this a lot. I think about things so intensely and for so long until they're not really things anymore and then rational thought processes are impossible and I feel like I'm losing my mind.

The police come to the hotel. This surprises me, because I envisage glaring spotlights, cold metal tables and hot sweat as they question us about every movement we've made over the last twenty-four hours. But they don't appear suspicious of us. Hell, they've only just decided—if only because of the predictable ticking of the clock—that the situation is even suspicious at all.

"At around eleven last night," I hear myself say, "Erin told me she was going to the toilet. She told me she'd be back in a couple of minutes. She never did. Come back, that is."

It seems like an impossibly long time ago, an insane amount of time for a person to be missing, but the police seem unfazed.

"All right," says a young male officer. Detective Ilić, I think he introduced himself as. Thick dark stubble covers his recently shaven head. "Is it possible Ms. Baxter went to go and meet someone?" His English is flawless.

"No. She would have told me," I reply. "She's very responsible."

"So you'd say this was out of character for her?"

"Definitely."

Ilić and I are sitting on the bar stools in the lobby. We've already established that she had no known medical conditions and no history of erratic behavior, and another telephone sweep of the local hospitals comes up empty. Another male detective talks to

Tim and the hotel receptionist, while Duncan, Clara and Jin Ra sit in the same sofas they've been in all day. Even they're starting to look anxious now. A third detective—a middle-aged woman with bright red hair and a mole on her chin—is outside, contacting Erin's family.

"So the two of you are close," Ilić says, but it's not a question. "Had she been acting strangely at all?"

I rack my brains but come up short. "I don't think so. She had the usual work worries, but nothing out of the ordinary."

"You work together?"

"Yes. We intern for the same magazine back in England."

"You're from England?" I see him eye my dark skin and thick black hair with streaks of violet.

Don't bite. "Yes."

"Where are you from originally?"

I grit my teeth. "England."

A cocked eyebrow. "And you say you work with Erin."

"Yes. At *Northern Heart*. We came on the trip together."

"I see. And you say she seemed worried."

I shrug. "Kind of. But just the usual stuff, you know? Like whether our editor would be mad at her for not emailing back right away. It's deadline day. Always stressful."

He nods, scratching his chin with his thumb. The bristly sound makes me shudder. "Can you run me through your movements yesterday? Were you and Ms. Baxter together the entire time—until she left to go to the bathroom?"

"Most of the time. We slept in late yesterday morning, because we'd been up late at JUMP. Around midday, our press trip group went on a boat trip down the Danube, where we were caught in a storm." I'm not sure how much detail I'm supposed to be giving, and I keep thinking of facts I should be including, but I don't know if they're relevant or not and it's perfectly possible my brain might explode before I even reach the point at which she disappeared. "We took refuge with Tim's friend, Borko, who has a residence on the riverfront."

Ilić nods and jots a few things down on a lined notepad. The wrinkled paper is covered in brown rings where he's used it as a coaster for his coffee mug. "Go on."

"We stayed there for a few hours until the storm died down. There was another guy there, in his late-twenties, I'd guess. Andrijo. Erin seemed to be getting on really well with him—they chatted and laughed together the whole time. It looked like they exchanged phone numbers before we left."

"And this was the first time Ms. Baxter had met this Andrijo?"

"Yes."

"Did they make plans to meet again?" he asks.

"I think so. He was talking about coming to JUMP, and wanted to meet up with her if he managed to make it." Even as I'm saying it, I know it looks suspicious.

"I see." He jots down something else. "And what did you think of him? This Andrijo?"

Gorgeous. Intense. Eyes as black as coal. "He seemed nice. They were both very welcoming. I did find Andrijo a little . . . intense, maybe?"

"Intense? In what way?"

I can't put my finger on it. "It's hard to explain. I don't really have any examples—it was more a vibe I got from him."

Ilić cocks his head. "Do you remember finding him strange at the time, or is it just now, looking back?"

My migraine is still pounding and I feel like I'm hearing him from the other side of a very long tunnel, but I try to think. "Just in hindsight, I guess." Really? Just in retrospect? I don't know if I'm being honest with myself.

"All right. Then what happened?"

"Our bus driver picked us up from the hut and we drove back to Novi Sad. We still had a few hours to go before JUMP kicked off again, so I took a nap."

"Do you know what Erin did in that time?"

I shake my head. "We all separated. It was the first free time we'd had since we got here."

"And you didn't ask her what she'd been doing?"

"No." I feel stupid, but how was I to know how important it would be?

I explain how we'd gone to the festival in good spirits, how we'd tried the silent disco, watched some bands, drank some cider and played a game of giant Jenga in the Jack Daniel's garden. Ilić is insistent on knowing how drunk Erin was, but I'm honest and tell him that I was pretty tipsy myself and couldn't really judge her level of inebriation with any amount of accuracy. But I'd guess she was tipsy, too.

With as much detail as I can, I give him rough times of our movements, right up until Erin told me she'd be back soon and to wait by the speakers for her.

"Did anything else seem . . . out of the ordinary?"

Everything. The day itself was so exceptional, so different to our normal lives, but I try desperately hard to think of something, anything, out of the ordinary about her behavior. I can't. I try to think of anything that struck me as odd, besides sheep skulls dangling from trees, donkeys wearing bandanas and the half-naked man singing the Serbian national anthem, but I can't.

Except Andrijo.

He was out of the ordinary.

THE POLICE LEAVE around midnight. After Ilić asks Tim a few questions about Andrijo, the hotel staff let him into Erin's room, where he doesn't find anything unusual. I fight back nausea as they take her toothbrush—they can use it as a DNA sample in subsequent forensic examinations.

Yesterday morning she used that toothbrush as if it was the most normal thing in the world and now they're using it for DNA.

I feel my brain fixating on the toothbrush, but I pull myself away.

Erin's mother is hysterical, but manages to find the composure to give them Erin's bank and credit card details so they can trace any transactions from the last week, plus her cell phone details so they can access her records. I send them a few photos of Erin from the last few days, including a selfie we took next to the JUMP stage—it shows the hot-pink shirt she was wearing last night. I almost break down at the sight of her smile, which already packs such an emotional punch it feels like it belongs to a murder victim.

She'll turn up, I tell myself for the thousandth time, but like any repeated phrase, it's lost all meaning. All I'm left with is lingering dread and an overwhelming sense of emptiness.

The police take all of our contact details and say they'll be in touch if they have any more questions. We agree to get in touch with the British Embassy in Belgrade, and with the Foreign Office back in the UK.

And then they're gone.

Chapter Four

July 14, Serbia

I DON'T SLEEP. The stifling silence in my hotel room, broken up only by the whir of the air-con, leaves too much space for my anxiety to take hold. I can't breathe. I throw off the covers. I still can't breathe. I crank a window open far as it'll go. I still can't breathe.

Grabbing my rucksack, I shove a shaking hand into its depths and pull out the coloring book I'm supposed to use when I feel a panic attack starting. Pen pen pen, there's a pen here somewhere, but I can't find it.

The hotel pen. Blue. It's blue. BLUE IS CALMING.

My scribbles are outside the lines, outside the page, outside this room.

No no no no no.

Erin.

How can doodling help when my best friend is gone?

I hurl the book across the room. It hits the wall and flutters to the ground.

Fuck fuck fuck.

I'm gasping and gasping, but my lungs won't fill. I know what's happening. I can't stop it.

Erin Erin Erin Erin Erin her is name on loop inside my head, faster and faster like a fairground ride I can't get off.

I grab my silver bangle from the bedside table and clutch it to my heart. Erin.

I let her go. I let her go to the toilet alone. I could've stopped it. What have I done what have I done what have I done?

Stupid stupid stupid I'm so stupid.

Over and over and over and over again in my head I replay the scenario. I force it to end differently. Maybe if I think it vividly enough, perfectly enough, it'll change how this ends.

No.

Water. I run to the bathroom and crank the tap on so harshly it sprays everywhere but I don't care. I scoop up handfuls and drink, drench my face, cover my clothes. I'm too hot it's too hot I can't breathe.

The adrenaline is pumping so hard and fast it's like being trapped for hours at a time in that heart-stopping moment you miss a step. Falling falling I'm falling.

I fall to the floor. Gasp for air. There's none.

What have I done what have I done what have I done?

Erin. What have you done?

ERIN IS OFFICIALLY reported missing by the next morning. Medium priority. I wonder what she'd have to do to be upgraded to high. Again, the arbitrary police procedure seems absurd—how can all of this be measured in time limits and quantifiable criteria?

A girl is missing. That's all there is.

The search party is launched in earnest by midday. Her murder victim profile picture is plastered all over lampposts and bins, like she's an old lady's missing cat and she'll turn up in a tree somewhere. The image sticks in my mind, and in my sleep-deprived hysteria, I struggle to let go.

More sweeps of the hospitals come up empty. She hasn't used her phone or bank cards since she went missing, nor was any large withdrawal made from a cash point on Sunday. Her passport hasn't been flagged up at any of the land borders. Police are checking the CCTV from the area around the fortress, but there are so many bodies and so many hours of footage and so much alcohol and, well, she's only a medium fucking priority, isn't she?

It's all I can do not to drop to my knees and beg them to plow every last resource they have into finding my best friend. To me, right in this moment, I can't imagine anything in the world is more important. But I'm sure the loved ones of every missing person feel that way.

I make my way to reception feeling like my mind is full of fog and my eyes have been sprayed with acid. Tiredness has a physical presence; it clings to me. It's heavy.

Today we're all to give our accounts of what happened two days ago. We meet in the lobby, none of the others looking as exhausted as me, and make our way to the police station together. Ilić is there to escort us. He makes idle chitchat about the weather and the headliners at JUMP last night. Absurd absurd this is absurd. How can he talk about the thunder showers when my brain is such a storm?

Tim looks bad, like maybe he hasn't slept either. "Carina. How you holding up?"

"M'fine," I mutter. "Just want to find her." My words are

hollow. After thirty-six hours, what kind of state might she be in? My stomach cramps painfully. I touch my fingertips to the silver bangle. Is she still wearing hers?

The humidity is so thick breathing hurts. Black clouds loom in the distance. There's going to be another storm, but we won't see it. Because we're going to spend our whole day in a Serbian police station reliving one day over and over and over again until we lose touch on what's real. My memories are already warping and distorting, but one thing remains vividly clear: Andrijo.

On the tail end of last night's panic attack I was still too anxious to sleep, and wanted to feel like I was doing something worthwhile. Something that could help Erin. So I picked my coloring book and hotel-branded pen up off the floor, and started jotting down every single detail I could remember about that heart-stopping man with the intense black eyes. Working my way around the outline of a Buddhist mandala, I noted his cleft chin and grin worthy of a toothpaste advertisement, his thick accent and red T-shirt. Then I write down everything I remember him saying, from inane comments about the Danube at sunset to the compliments he showered Erin with. "Beautiful." That word cropped up the most.

The coloring book's tucked into my satchel now. In the cold light of day, my notes look like the scrawlings of a crazy person, obscuring dainty lotus flowers and delicate doves, with angry phrases scratched in blue ink. The words are so slanted and erratic they look like the Arabic on my bracelet. Erin's bracelet.

The bracelet the bracelet the bracelet. I can't stop staring at my wrist, where it's sitting next to my JUMP wristband, wondering if Erin's looking down to the same view. What if she's not, what if—

Pull away. You're falling.

I break the magnetic lure and force myself to focus on what's around me. Hot pavement beneath my feet, a street vendor shouting about fresh donuts, the scent of cinnamon and sugar, the cold sweat coating my skin. Screeching tires. Coughing exhausts. Heat.

Reality.

Novi Sad Police Station is cool and clean. We're here to tell the police everything we can about the day Erin went missing in a bid to find her.

First we're given hot drinks. It's the last thing any of us want when it's ninety-five degrees outside, but they're policemen and it seems impolite to say no. I know the black coffee is a mistake as soon as it scalds my lips. I wanted to wake myself up, inject some energy, but it just makes me even more jittery. My clammy hands shake like my great-uncle's did before he died of Parkinson's.

I'm first. I feel detached from my body as I walk down the corridor flanked by two detectives. Ilić's presence is mildly comforting. Despite the vaguely racist vibe I get from him—"You're from England?"—the familiarity is reassuring. He saw my distress last night. He knows how much Erin means to me.

I take a seat opposite Ilić as he arranges his files across the desk. Another bulky man sits next to him—a translator. Every aspect of the room's design seems aimed at maximizing a suspect's discomfort and sense of powerlessness. The way the desk wraps around the chair slightly, giving the feeling of being surrounded. The lack of anything on the walls, giving a sense of exposure and isolation. All of the light switches and thermostats are out of reach, emphasizing the lack of control the suspect has over their surroundings. I wonder if other people notice these things, too, or if it's just my overactive brain attaching significance to irrelevant details.

And the cameras. One in each corner. Recording everything I say or do.

You're not a suspect, I remind myself. *You should not feel this claustrophobic.*

My throat gets tighter. I sip my coffee. It burns my tongue.

"Okay Carina, let's get started," Ilić says. "Just to let you know that, from now on, I'm going to be talking in Serbian and our translator, Danijel—" Danijel nods "—will be relaying everything to you in English. This isn't to make you feel uncomfortable, it's just so that the recordings can be used and understood in a Serbian court. Okay?"

Court. There might be a trial. For there to be a trial, there has to be a crime. Oh God. A crime against Erin. Rape? Abduction? Murder? It's not a new concept, that she could be hurt, but talking about it so matter-of-factly is like being shocked awake from a hazy nap. Oh God oh God oh God. Coffee and the word *court* twist in my abdomen. I wipe my palms on my jeans. "Okay."

He smiles too big. Starts talking in Serbian. The translator relays, but it's hard to concentrate on what he's saying when Ilić is still chattering in the background. " . . . Great, so our controller has started the recording now, and everything is being recorded like we talked about, okay? Before we talk at all about what happened, there are a few things I'm going to go through with you. The first thing I need to say is the fact that it's about nine a.m. on the fourteenth of July, and we're in the interview suite in Novi Sad. As you know, my name is Jovan Ilić and I'm a detective. Perfect. Now can you please say your full name for me, so that anyone who ever watches this knows who you are?"

I clear my sticky throat. "Carina Corbett."

"Great. There's only our controller watching right now, but the reason we're recording this conversation today is so that you don't have to go through everything over and over again with different people. You just talk about it once with me, and then anyone else who wants to know—who's part of this investigation—can watch this and see what you had to say. So, as you can see, there are cameras there and there—" he points to the small domes in each corner of the room "—and there are microphones here and here." They're little white squares on the walls, the ones I'd earlier mistaken for plugs, with a black fuzzy circle in the middle. "That camera is looking at you, because you're the most important bit, while the other one is looking at the whole room. So everything that we do and everything that we say in this room is being recorded on video and audio, okay? I just want to be sure you understand all of that, okay?"

If he says *okay* one more time I'm in danger of ramming his black marker pen down his throat.

"Okay."

"Now, the purpose of this conversation today is for you to tell me everything you can about the last time you saw your friend Erin. And I just want to be completely clear to you that you're not under any suspicion or in any trouble whatsoever. Your head contains information, perhaps even information that you don't know about, and it's my job to try to capture that information from you. To help us find Erin. That's what this conversation is for, and that's what my role is today. Are you happy you understand everything?"

"Yes," I say, although happy is the last thing I feel.

"Excellent." Danijel's face is devoid of emotion, his voice completely deadpan. I know he's probably concentrating on translating and doing his job, but it's unnerving. I watch Ilić talk animatedly instead. "Before we do get into any of that, I want to explain some basic concepts to you while we're here. First, I want you to know that you can tell me absolutely anything and I won't be embarrassed. I won't judge you. I've heard it all before, okay? You can tell me anything you want in this room, as long as it's the truth as best you know it. And short of telling me you've killed someone, or done something really bad, nothing you tell me in this room can be used to get you into trouble. I don't care if you've been smoking some weed, or taking other drugs, or you got really drunk and slept with someone you shouldn't have. None of us care about that stuff.

"What we need, and what is the absolute most important thing, is that you tell the truth. It's also very important that if I ask you a question and you don't know the answer, please tell me you don't know. Don't try to guess, or make something up because you think it's helpful or you want me to be happy. It's absolutely all right if you don't know the answer to something. I just want you to be honest and tell me that you don't know, okay?"

"Okay." Strangely, the box-ticking monologue he's reeling off is actually helping me relax. Well, as much as I'm capable of relaxing during a police interview with an acute anxiety disorder. I'm the kind of person who needs to know everything about a situation in order to process it, so Ilić's overexplaining makes it feel less alien. I've never been in this situation before, and on TV it looks so stressful. Probably because they edit the box-ticking monologue out.

I gather my thoughts, lining them up in a way that feels logical and helpful.

"Fantastic. And finally, I also want you to remember that I wasn't there, during the events you're going to describe to me. So it's very important that with everything you tell me about, you tell me in as much detail as possible. So anyone listening can close their eyes, and picture in their own heads exactly what you're seeing. Does that make sense? Great. Oh, and also if you need to take a break at any point, you want a drink or you need to use the restroom or something like that, or if you just need five minutes to breathe, then please let me know and it shouldn't be a problem."

"Okay." And it sort of is.

"All right, so, Carina, I'd like you to sit back, take your time, really think, and tell me—in as much detail as you can—everything you can about the last time you saw Erin."

"The whole day?"

Danijel translates. Ilić nods. "The whole day."

Chapter Five

July 14, Serbia

I FORCE MYSELF to sit up straighter. Take a deep breath. Then another. Try to imagine Ilić is just my mum, and I'm sitting at our kitchen table with a cup of morning coffee and telling her what happened on the last day of my holiday. "We got in from JUMP on Saturday night—well, Sunday morning—at around five a.m. Everything was fine. We had a great night, really enjoyed the headliners and had a little to drink. Nothing more," I add, remembering what he said earlier. "Erin's not that kind of girl. Not into drugs, or anything like that."

I wait for him to say something, but he just smiles encouragingly. "We all went to bed separately. Erin was on the phone to her boyfriend, Smith. He's back in the UK but he'd been on a night out, too, I think. They were just chatting about their nights. I was with her in the elevator up to our floor, and she seemed to be listening intently to a story he was telling. We went our separate ways—we had different rooms. She waved goodbye silently and blew me a kiss, 'cause she was still on the phone."

Ilić says something. Danijel repeats. "And how did things seem between Erin and her partner?"

I shrug. "Fine. Like I say, they were just chatting about their nights. They could have argued once she was back in her room, but I have no way of knowing. She didn't mention it the next day, so I assume everything was all right." As I'm saying it, I worry about how vague I sound. *Could have. Assume.* No way of knowing. Is this really how little attention I pay to the world around me? Am I really so caught in my own head I'm utterly detached from my best friend's life?

If Ilić is perturbed by the lack of detail, he doesn't show it. Maybe he recognizes that my ambiguity is founded in genuine lack of knowledge. "Carry on."

"The next morning, we met in the lobby at ten a.m. for our river excursion. Erin was five minutes late—she was applying sunscreen. She'd got a little burnt the day before."

"How burnt?"

"She was pink, not bright red. On her shoulders mainly."

He nods, as if that nugget of information is in the slightest bit helpful. "Okay. What was she wearing at this point?"

"Denim hot pants with flowery pockets poking out the bottom of the hemline. A baggy white tee. Black flip-flops, a rose gold wristwatch."

"Any other jewelry?"

I think hard. "Chunky rings on her index and pinky fingers. Eight earrings in each ear. Her JUMP wristband. Maybe a few straggly hairbands around her wrist." I swallow. "A silver bangle.

The same as this." I hold up my hand and show them my matching bracelet. Tell them the story behind it.

"All right. Then what happened after you all met in the lobby?"

"We traveled to the Danube by minibus. The same one we'd been using all week, with the same driver. It took around forty minutes."

"Can you describe the bus to me?"

I frown. "I don't know. White? Old? Ratty seats with stuffing coming out of the sides?"

"Serbian registration?"

I pause. "Yes. Yes, I think so."

"And the driver. What was he like?"

It goes on like this for ten minutes or so. He never interrupts, but he waits for me to come to natural stopping points before going back on what I've said to ask for more details. I try and re-count the day with as much accuracy as I can, but he always picks on something seemingly insignificant that he wants me to elaborate more on. I oblige as best I can, though sometimes I have to admit I don't remember what color the boats were, or what brand of cigarettes she was smoking with the bus driver.

By the time we reach the thunderstorm, I'm losing focus. But this bit is important. I don't want to break the flow by asking to take a breather. I mentally prepare to share everything I remember about Andrijo and his friend. Picturing the lotus flower and my blue biro scribbles, I try not to think about what could be important and what's irrelevant—I can already tell everything is crucial to Ilić. I like that. The thoroughness soothes me. He really is doing everything he can.

"Just after midday, we left the riverfront farm. We were all in good spirits, even Erin, despite her earlier wobble." I've already explained her worries over Lowe's impending rage. "Sometimes I feel on edge and anxious after a couple of drinks, but the fruit brandy had taken the edge off. I was calm and relaxed, borderline sleepy. It was low tide. We reached this beach island in the middle of the river. Erin was messing around in the water, splashing this guy Duncan. He's on our press trip. You've probably spoken to him?"

Ilić nods and asks, "Had she been spending a lot of time with him?"

I tap the jagged nail of my index finger on the table. "No more than she had been with the rest of us. They did get on well, though. Very similar sense of humor—dry and sarcastic. There was a heated argument between them about politics on the second night, but I don't think either of them even remembered it the next day."

"Heated?"

"Yeah. They're both left wing, but him much more so than her. Accused her of being everything that's wrong with the Labour Party supporters today. She called him a communist. It got a little shouty. I took her away to the bar, and by the time we got back, everyone had forgotten all about it."

He nods. Finds our tangent again. "So you were on the beach island."

"We were. Then the thunderstorm started, and we climbed hastily back into the boats. Thankfully we weren't far from Tim's friends' river hut, so we took refuge there."

"Who were Tim's friends?"

I swallow. "Andrijo and Borko."

He leans back in his chair. "You've mentioned them before."

"Yes." I think of the coloring book, of my manic scrawls and disjointed thoughts, all leading back to him.

"Were they expecting you, or was it a spontaneous visit? Or do you not know?"

An image of the tiny wooden table, set with a burlap runner and chipped coffee mugs, flits into my mind. "They were expecting us, definitely. They'd already made coffee, and there was a massive pan of soup on the stove."

He asks me to describe the hut to me. I tell him every detail I remember. Every sound, every smell, every sight. Every little thing that was so different to my normal life it nearly sent me into a panic attack.

Then he says, through Danijel, "And can you describe them to me? Let's start with Borko. What was he like?"

My memory of him is less vivid than Andrijo, but I force myself to paint in the details. I close my eyes. "Short, stocky. Shaven head. Eyes set close together, a crooked nose. A nice smile, though. Friendly, but quiet. Welcoming. He took pride in the food he made us, and kept making sure we were all well fed and watered. Brought us blankets to keep warm. Towels to dry our hair. Asked us about our journalism work, whether we'd interviewed any interesting people recently. We talked about the founder of JUMP, who we'd spoken to at a press conference the night before. Borko knew him from school; they're both locals." I open my eyes. He looks intrigued.

Another encouraging nod. "This is great stuff. Anything else?"

"Just . . ." I pause. "He had really clean hands. They both did. I remember thinking that was weird, considering they'd been in the forest all day." Is that a ridiculous thing to say? Probably. What kind of lunatic notices people's clean hands? "And . . . neither of them seemed willing to give up anything personal about themselves."

"What do you mean?"

"Well, they were great with us. Really. So welcoming, and like I say, they asked a lot of questions. It was like they were genuinely interested. But . . . but whenever we asked questions in return, the answers were kind of vague. Noncommittal. When I was trying to jot down everything I could remember about their lives, I realized I knew nothing. And I think they wanted it that way."

"I see." Ilić leans forward now, steepling his fingers in front of him. "Can you give any examples? Of times they dodged questions, or gave strange answers?"

I press my lips together. Try to sort through the jumble in my mind. I can feel the thoughts starting to swirl out of control, shimmery strands of memory slipping through my fingers as I try to grasp them.

Shit, I'm going insane. I'm not Albus fucking Dumbledore. My brain isn't some weird bowl of memories I can dip my nose into. *Pull it together, Corbett. Focus.*

Okay. Examples. Examples, examples, examples. "Erm . . . at one point, Erin asked Andrijo where he worked. He said 'in a café,' but when she asked him where, he just told her he'd love to take her out for coffee sometime." Even as I'm recounting the exchange, I know my logic is tenuous. He was probably just being flirty.

But no. There's a gut feeling growing more and more intense. He was different. I'm drawn to him. And that has to mean something.

I push on. "She asked him where he grew up. He was vague. Said here, there and everywhere. She asked if his dad was in the

army, as they tend to move around a lot. He just asked what Newcastle was like. That's where we live," I add hastily.

"Okay."

"And . . . and this happened in every conversation. He was
noncommittal about the music he likes, the places he's visited, his
hobbies. Every time Erin asked him something, he batted it back
unanswered. I think she was too blinded by his beauty to notice."

"So you noticed this based on interactions between Erin and
Andrijo? Not your own conversations with him?"

I swallow. "Yeah. I'm kinda awkward, socially. Not the best
with strangers." I hold up a clammy palm. The strip lighting illuminates the thin coat of sweat. "See?" I try for a smile, and am
grateful when he reciprocates.

"You're an introvert," he says. Danijel stumbles over the words
as he translates, and I think of how beautifully it mimics the way
I stumble through life. Fucking poetry.

"You could say that."

"We like introverts. They're good observers." Another friendly
smile. It's probably all a ploy—to build rapport and gain my trust
and hope I spill some game-changing secret—but I still appreciate
it. Just like I appreciate how he doesn't find it weird that I spend a
lot of time watching Erin, enraptured. "Let's move on to Andrijo.
Can you tell me about him?"

The way he phrases questions makes it seem like he knows
nothing about the investigation, like he's never seen or spoken to
the people involved. It makes sense. The open-ended questions
allow for me to elaborate far more. Besides, whoever listens to this
tape might not know the ins and outs of the cast of characters.
Like a jury. I shudder.

"He's . . . he's a looker." I blush. My cheeks are hot, like an idiot schoolgirl. Because that's totally the kind of thing I do. "Muscular. Short, dark brown hair, ruffled and damp from the storm. Black eyes, like pools of ink. Tanned, stubbly face, with one of those cleft chins you could stick a coin in. Perfect white teeth. He wore a red T-shirt, blue jeans and white, muddy Converse."

I omit certain details. I know I shouldn't, but so many of the details etched on my memory are borderline creepy. The kind of things no normal person would remember. But I do, because I'm either hyperaware or completely disengaged. Usually depending on whether I've remembered to take my meds.

No normal person would remember the way his dark veins were a road map on his bulging arms. Or the way his eyes, blacker than the thunderclouds, kept darting to Erin. Or how, when he handed her a flask of coffee and their fingers touched, he snapped his hand back like a static shock had passed between them.

I imagine them labeling me an Unreliable Witness: withholds information in a futile attempt to disguise her own insanity.

"He complimented her a lot," I blurt out. "Andrijo. Erin. Said she was beautiful, like the sunset over the Danube." I remember the burning jealousy I felt at those words. I remember not knowing whether I was jealous of Erin because of them, or jealous of Andrijo for having her attention. "Maybe that's a Serbian thing. European men tend to be more forward than Brits. But still . . . it was quite intense."

"Intense how?"

"Like . . . by the fourth or fifth reference to her beauty, she looked a little uncomfortable. Maybe just because it was happening in front of everyone else, which would make anyone feel a little awkward. Not that she isn't used to the attention . . ." *Stop, Carina. Remove that ugly bitterness from your voice. She's missing. She's in* trouble. *Now isn't the time to resent her.* I stare at my hands. "Or maybe it was the intensity in his eyes. Like he was a predator and she was perfect prey."

"Some men are strange around beautiful women," Ilić says. It's a throwaway comment, but the warmness that was building between us rapidly vanishes. His tone leaves me cold. *Don't,* I want to snap. *Don't make excuses for it. Erin is nobody's prey.*

Except maybe she is.

Chapter Six

July 17, Serbia

I'm a Significant Witness.

It's because I'm the last person who saw her, mainly, but also because I'm the person in the group who knows her best. The paranoid part of me also wonders if they've clocked on to the fact I'm holding back. That my brain is clinically diagnosed chaos.

We were supposed to fly home yesterday.

If you buy into the parallel universe theory, I'm sure there's another world out there, a world exactly like ours, in which we all boarded the 10:28 a.m. plane to London Heathrow via Vienna. All of us, including Erin.

I read up on it once. The multiverse theory. When I couldn't sleep and felt like having my mind blown. The idea is this: space is so big that the laws of probability imply that surely, somewhere else out there, there are other planets exactly like Earth. In fact, an infinite universe would have infinite planets, and on some of them, the events that play out would be virtually identical to those on our own Earth. But we don't see these other universes because our cosmic vision is limited by the speed of light—the ultimate speed limit, in a way. Light started traveling at the moment of the big bang, about fourteen billion years ago, and so we can't see any farther than about fourteen billion light-years.

Many physicists would argue that somewhere in our infinite universe, Erin is still safe. I try to take comfort in that fact, but I can't. Because I'm not a physicist. And because that world is not the world I'm in.

Tim and I are staying in Novi Sad for another week. Because I'm a SigWit, and because I guess he feels responsible. In my moments of anger, I think about how dismissive he was of my concerns. "Nah. She's a big girl. Can look after herself. Don't wanna miss this set." He has clout with the festival organizers. He could have had a message sent to the security on the fortress entrances, made sure they looked out for her leaving. But he didn't.

Is that suspicious? I'm losing track. I don't think so. He was just drunk and lazy. His concern since he realized the magnitude of the situation has been sincere, without a doubt.

We remain in the same hotel. This morning Tim and I eat breakfast in near-silence. We have nothing in common except this monumental tragedy that sits beside us like a third person at the table, a devastating black hole sucking away our conversational energy.

It's late morning. We're the only people in the hotel restaurant; all the JUMP-goers have gone home, and the businessmen are all away to important meetings and conference calls in the city. A young waiter is standing, hands folded around a tea towel, not so subtly checking his phone. The buffet smells of smoked sausage and burnt toast.

I push the rubbery scrambled eggs around my plate with a fork. The chinking noise is like nails on a chalkboard. Tim's staring at his phone. It's been flashing all morning.

I clear my throat. He doesn't look up. "What do you think happened to her?" My voice is barely a whisper. Yesterday I was anxious, jittery, hyped up. Today I am low. A deflated balloon.

He puts his phone down carefully on the table. It's faceup, the screen still on. He's sending an email. "Honestly?" He sighs through his nose. "I'm not sure I want to think about it."

"We have to," I say, still murmuring. "We're part of the investigation now. We have to think about it. It's all we should be thinking about."

His eyes flit down to his phone, then back to me. "It's only been three days. She could still turn up unscathed."

"Yeah."

He stabs a sausage with his fork. Shoves it in his mouth. Chews. "You don't remember anything that could be a clue?"

I shake my head. "She was there. Then she wasn't."

"Maybe that's a good thing. That there was no sign of violence. Nothing suspicious."

Not nothing. Andrijo.

"What if . . ." I put my fork down. Force myself to look at him. "What if she was trafficked?"

He raises an eyebrow. "Trafficked."

"Yeah. You know. She's beautiful. Probably worth a lot."

"You've been watching too many movies, kid."

"I'm serious."

He sighs again. Flicks his phone screen off. Rubs his mouth with his hand. "So am I. Think about it. When it comes to trafficking—which I'm not denying does happen—locals are much easier targets. It makes no sense to abduct western girls, 'cause there'd be international pressure to actually look for them. Nobody gives a shit about poor people in poor countries, and traffickers know that. And if we're being realistic, homicide—with or without sexual assault—is way more common than abduction and trafficking."

"Yeah. Totally makes me feel better." The words *homicide* and *sexual assault* ring in my ears.

A pained expression. He shuffles in his chair. "I know this looks bad, Carina. Trust me, I know. I'm not trying to dodge around that. It's bad. But please don't go jumping to radical conclusions."

It's a radical fucking situation, I want to say. I don't. I say nothing. Story of my life.

THERE'S ANOTHER POLICE interview today. I'm not as nervous as I was last time—I know Ilić now, and I know he's thorough. He'll get what he needs out of me, even if I'm not sure what exactly that is.

First he takes me shopping. He drives. I had no idea that happened, really, but apparently the police like to look after their Sig-Wits, especially if they're away from home. Makes sense. I wasn't equipped for a long-term stay in Serbia. I buy some food to keep in my room, a few toiletries, a book to read. Then he takes me to a launderette—I'm running low on clean clothes. Even buys me a coffee while we wait.

The whole time, he's friendly and professional. Tells me a little bit about himself and his personal life (he's just got married to his high-school sweetheart; they're expecting their first kid in a couple months), asks me about other places I've traveled. It's all amicable, but there's a certain distance I can't quite put my finger on. It's like he's taking care of an elderly person for the day, and even though he's happy to make conversation, there are a web of personal lines he can't and won't cross.

He doesn't mention Erin once. I guess he doesn't want me to say anything significant—there's that word again—off the record, and he can't really be giving away anything from their end. I've probably not been ruled out as a suspect yet. I remember a phrase from an incredibly dry police procedural my mum used to watch: "Trace, Implicate, Evaluate." It's used on everyone involved in a big case like this. Basically it means they take someone like me, find out everything they can about them, and compare that to all the other info they have, searching for any reason at all to make them a suspect. And then they evaluate how likely that is. Essentially everyone is a suspect until proven otherwise, even though they're not formally declared as such. That's a big deal. Even I know that.

As far as I know, there are no official suspects. There've been a few dead-end leads—calls put into the station, a couple of supposed sightings. None of them have been viable. People seem to forget CCTV exists. I have no idea what'd compel someone to put in a fake call in a situation like this. Maybe they're just bored. Maybe they're just looking for their moment of glory. Who knows.

After we've run our errands, he takes me to a small bungalow on the outskirts of Novi Sad. It doesn't look official from the outside—there's a small porch with benches and plant pots, flowery curtains in the windows and a tiny but neat garden. Only the security gates and ID passes give the game away.

Ilić shows me around—the interview room, control room, bathroom and a minuscule kitchenette—before leaving me in the waiting room with a cup of tea while they set up. It's homely but sterile—IKEA furniture, nothing personal, professionally cleaned. It's so quiet I can hear my watch ticking. I still feel hollow and empty, which is actually easier to deal with than hyperanxious.

Next thing I know, I'm in the interview room with Ilić and Danijel. They do a sound check. Ilić asks the controller to bang the wall if he can hear us, and the steady thump comes a second later. The controller sticks his head around the door, says he's ready to roll and the recording has started. Ilić gives me the official spiel. Again, I feel soothed by the monotony of the protocol. It's reliable. It's safe.

"Okay, Carina," Danijel translates. "Today we'd like to start with your relationship with Erin, and what you know about her as a person. For us, it's really important to understand her, and as one of her closest friends, you're well-equipped to help us with that. Now, as you know, the last few times we've spoken it's become clear there's an hour-long gap in your knowledge of Erin's movements on Sunday the twelfth of July—the time in which you took a nap at the hotel. What happened in that time may or not be important to the investigation, but we still need to fill it in as best we can. We are checking CCTV and tracking down anyone who could possibly have any information about that window, but in the meantime, it'd be extremely helpful if we could try and understand her mind-set at that point. Is that all right?"

"Sure."

"So, in your own words, it would be fantastic if you could tell me a little about Erin's mood that afternoon. Nothing is too trivial or too silly. The more detail, the better." A smile. "Whenever you're ready."

I'm silent for probably too long. This is hard, harder than recounting the actual events. Because anything Erin said or did that implies a certain mood is filtered through my mind, through the layers of friendship we've built up over the last year. But there are still holes in the filters. Black spots in my knowledge—hundreds of them, thousands, things I don't know about her and now I maybe never will. I don't know enough about her love life or her family or her upbringing to apply any context to her behavior.

Oh God. I'm overthinking it. But I can't stop.

This is too much pressure. Too much weight for one girl to carry. Anything I say right now is going to somehow influence their investigation. What if I get it wrong? What if I fuck it all up?

Like a morbid mother pulling her drowning child from a lake, anxiety lifts me from my comfortable depressive lull. I gasp. The fresh air is toxic. Everything is heightened. I'm plugged into the waves of crippling fear and sparks of paranoia and overwhelming sense of impending doom.

Breathe breathe breathe breathe remember how to breathe. In, out, in, out. Ignore the morbid mother hugging you too tight, the morbid mother who saved you from drowning when you didn't want to be saved.

Lake lake lake. Plunge back underwater.

I reach for depression, for my kinder aunt, but my mother won't let me go.

Depression is feeling too little. Anxiety is feeling too much. I never win.

I'm losing it.

I'm lost.

EVENTUALLY, AROUND SEVEN at night, they calm me down enough to talk. The brown paper bag does fuck all, but the Xanax works a treat. It's my last one, but I try not to think about that or I'll spiral again.

"I'm sorry," I say, back in the interview room. Danijel looks a bit pissed off—he probably wants to get home. If Ilić is irked, he doesn't show it.

"That's no problem, Carina. I understand this is an incredibly difficult time for you. Just take your time, relax and start again when you're ready." I think of his heavily pregnant wife back home and can't fight the surge of guilt. Last thing he needs is to be stuck here dealing with a nutcase all evening.

"Okay. Erin." Inhale, exhale. Think of Ilić's wife. "She acted pretty normal on the way to the farm. It was only once we were sitting around having 'breakfast—'" I act out the air quotes with my fingers "—that she started to get a little worried."

"Can you define *normal* for me?"

I rack my brains. "Chatty, witty. Dirty humor. A sailor's laugh. Fiery at times, 'specially when she gets worked up about something. Like the politics argument with Duncan. She always dresses pretty casually—not really a girlie-girl—but I was a little surprised she'd taken out her nose ring. I hadn't seen her without it in months." I wonder where it is now, whether the police found it in the hotel room. "Oh, and she has one of those smiles that just makes guys fall in love with her." A beat. "Like Andrijo."

Ilić doesn't react to the name the way I want him to. "All right. So what changed when she got to the farm?"

"It happened when she realized there was no phone signal. Even though it was a Sunday, she was paranoid our editor wouldn't be able to reach her if there was a problem with one of her pieces. Lowe often goes into the office and works on weekends, and will text or call us if she needs us. I don't think she fully believes in time off. So, yeah, Erin was on edge. Kept pressing the home button on her phone. Went quiet, too. Didn't really participate in the group banter."

"Why would she be this worried over her boss not being able to reach her? What's her attitude toward work like?"

I think about this for a moment. "She's one of those people who acts really laid-back, but deep down is very driven. A fashion intern, but not content at the bottom of the ladder. She wants to move up quickly—she's impatient like that." I have to force myself to use the present tense. "I know she struggles financially, and picks up bar shifts on evenings and weekends to pay her rent.

"So I guess she didn't want Lowe thinking she was irresponsible or didn't care about her job. When we first pitched the feature idea, we were met with some resistance about jetting off to another country over deadline week. Erin was desperate to prove herself, to show it wouldn't be a problem and that she's capable of keeping all her plates in the air."

"Plates in the air?" The expression is lost in translation.

"As in, she wants to prove she can juggle lots of work at once."

"Ah, I see." Ilić thinks for a minute. "How heavy was her workload generally? How was she coping at work?"

"I mean, we're all superbusy. We produce a three-hundred-page magazine and two supplements every month, and there aren't enough hands on deck most of the time. She seemed to deal with it better than the rest of us." I remember a joke she once cracked on our third day of overtime in a row. "Although she did once say to me that she's like a swan. It's all elegant and graceful on the surface, but her legs are kicking like mad underwater, trying desperately to stay afloat. I thought she was kidding. Maybe I should've paid more attention."

"Don't beat yourself up," he says in English. Danijel looks at him, confused. "Often, the people who seem to be doing the best are fighting the hardest battle with themselves. Success isn't easy."

I smile. "That's true. From the outside, I probably look like I've got my shit together. But, well, you've just witnessed firsthand that my shit is, in fact, fucking everywhere."

He laughs, genuinely. Not his elderly-relative laugh, but one that comes from his belly. I'm grateful to have him onside.

Danijel coughs, and we both snap back to attention. Ilić clears his throat. "Okay. So how did her mood—"

"Wait," I interrupt, suddenly remembering a small detail that could be important. "I just . . . I just realized I didn't tell you something. About . . . well, not about her mood exactly, but . . . she had a bruise. On her arm. An old one, by the looks of it."

A cocked eyebrow. "A bruise? Can you describe it to me?"

I swallow, close my eyes. Try to picture it. "Yellowish in color, which is how I know it was old. Just starting to fade. It was hard to make out the shape because of her tattoos. But . . . I think it was pretty small, and round like a coin. On the inside of her upper arm."

"Were there any others?"

I shake my head slowly. "Not that I saw. I'm sorry."

"And she never mentioned how she got this bruise?"

"No. I don't think so."

"Right. Thank you. Thanks for remembering that." He nods, looking deep in thought, then continues. "So, how did her mood progress over the next few hours?"

My mind's still reeling over the bruise, but I push on. "She perked up a bit. I gave her a pep talk, which seemed to help. And like I say, by the time we reached the beach island she was laughing and splashing Duncan in the shallow water. I didn't think it was all an act, but maybe . . ." I shrug. "Maybe I don't know. Maybe we never do."

A warm nod. "Go on."

"It changed drastically as soon as she met Andrijo. It was like she'd been sleeping all day, and was suddenly awake. A spark in her eye, like I've never seen before. Not even when she talks about her boyfriend," I add, wanting to make them aware it's unlike her to flirt with other guys.

Ilić purses his lips. "And . . . this was definitely the first time they'd met?"

Woah. I hadn't even considered that they could have met before. "I thought so . . . I mean, they were introduced as if it were. But . . . I don't know. She could've met him at JUMP on one of the other nights. I don't remember seeing her talking to a guy, but . . ." I trail off. My skin's getting prickly again, thinking about him.

I think Ilić notices me starting to get worked up. I rub my arms, blink quickly, try to get rid of it. He steers me away. "What happened once you left the hut?"

"He's like a flame," I say with such ferocity it's like I'm suddenly remembering critical information. "I couldn't look away. Neither could Erin. She was like a moth, when usually she's a butterfly. She lost her flair, her sass, when he was around. She seemed to lose herself in him. That's what creeped me out. It was like . . . it was like she would've followed him anywhere."

Ilić doesn't respond. I think he wants me to go back to the question he just asked, but I can't. Because I just made sense of it. I just put my finger on the thing that's been bothering me for days, and the moment is so equally relieving and terrifying it takes my breath away.

I lean forward on my seat, gripping the table with my hands. They're shaking. "You have to talk to him. You have to. Have you talked to him?" I don't wait for a response. "You have to talk to him again, again, again, until you get him. It's him." I'm out of breath. "Did you talk to him? Is he a suspect?"

I despise the pity in Ilić's eyes. Like he really does think I'm insane. Slowly, he says, "We have spoken to him. We've spoken to everyone who saw Erin that day."

"And?" I demand. Did you feel it? Did you feel him burning?

He shakes his head. "I'm sorry, Carina. We can't discuss any specifics of the case with you. It'd be bad practice."

I thump my palm on the table so hard I startle myself. "I don't care about bad practice. It's important! It's him." I know I sound like a whiny child, especially in the context of my breakdown earlier. But this seems so pressing, so urgent, so inexplicably crucial, that I can't bear not knowing. "Please," I whisper. A pathetic afterthought.

Ilić sighs, starts talking. I'm shaking as Danijel translates. "I appreciate it's frustrating that I can't tell you certain things, but our priority is to find Erin. This kind of investigation is very sensitive, and to have the best chance of finding Erin we need to make sure that investigative information is kept confidential from everyone. I know that's difficult to hear, but sharing information can have unintended consequences that we can't even think of yet, and that could make it harder to find Erin, which neither of us want."

He rubs his eyes then. He looks tired. He's not as clean shaven as he was a couple of days ago. "Plus, the reality of police investigations is that we follow many, many lines of inquiry, the vast majority of which lead absolutely nowhere. Getting your hopes up with every little thing that we do would not be constructive. So I know it's hard, but you just have to trust we are exploring every avenue, making every inquiry and trying our hardest to find Erin. And we're very grateful for all of the information you've given so far."

My cheeks are burning, but still not as hot as the image of Andrijo made them.

Chapter Seven

July 20, Serbia

THE DANUBE PARK is all immaculate pathways and arching trees, huge patches of thick grass and unkempt bushes spilling onto the pavement. Hazelnut trees smell nutty and spicy, interspersed with bursts of red Japanese quince. The park is lush; it's life.

Nature is unfazed by human tragedy. Is it weird to wish I was a tree right now?

Yeah, Corbett. It's weird.

Tim and I sit on a memorial bench in front of a small pond. In the middle is Đorđe Jovanović's nymph statue, spouting streams of water from her hands and feet. The drunken clock bongs in the background, just across the river. We each have a gelato cone—mine pistachio, his dulce de leche. He takes big bites, not flinching as the freezing ice cream hits his teeth, whereas mine is slowly melting down the side of the cone and onto my hands.

"You've got sticky fingers." Tim chuckles, gesturing toward my cone.

"That's what your mum said last night," I retort, but there's no joy in the comeback. Normally I live for innuendo, but today I'm just trying to focus on not throwing up in the water nymph's stony face. The nausea feels never-ending. I can't even remember what genuine appetite is like.

It doesn't help having to spend so much time with Tim—a near-stranger. The beauty of anxiety is that when you're alone, you get trapped in your own head and started obsessing over things, but when you're with other people, you get worked up over the complexities of social interaction.

Does he think I'm an idiot?

What if I say something stupid?

Will he laugh cruelly at me?

What if he says something and I don't hear him the first time?

Will I just have to pretend I did and hope for the best?

Is this a heart attack? My arm is numb.

I can't call an ambulance. They'll judge me.

Is he judging me? Oh God. He's judging me.

What if I have a panic attack in front of him?

How will I ever recover from the shame?

So you add that underlying fear to something like a missing-person investigation and it's amplified a thousandfold. Because the fear is actually legitimate, for once. Something I say could irrevocably fuck things up. It is an actual matter of life and death, not just a hypothetical one.

Great times. I love being me.

Shit, he's been talking for about twenty seconds and I haven't listened to a word he's said.

" . . . think you're handling this so well, considering. You must be a very strong person."

Ha! Ha-ha! I want to laugh in his face. I fight back a scoff. "Yes. Thank you."

Yes. Thank you? What are you doing! You sound like you think you are a strong person now. Quick, say something else. Anything else. Not a "your mum" joke or an inane reply that makes you sound more arrogant than Simon Cowell.

"How do you know Andrijo and Borko?" I ask Tim, before I can talk myself out of it again.

He doesn't flinch or otherwise visibly react. He probably expected me to ask that at some point. "I've known Borko for years. We met in 2005, I think, the first year I did the JUMP press trip. He was working for the Serbian tourism board at the time, and we became good friends. Bonded over rakia and women." He flashes a seedy grin I try to ignore.

"And Andrijo?"

He shrugs. "I met him for the first time last year. Seems nice enough."

"Erm . . . did you . . . have you spoken to Andrijo recently?" I stammer, forcing myself to lick my gelato before it forms a puddle on the pavement. "Or Borko. Either of them, really."

"A little. How come?"

I shrug. I try for nonchalant but it comes off as erratic mental patient jerking against her restraints. "Just wondering. Have the police spoken to them?"

He looks like he's measuring his words. Probably because it looks like someone's put a cruciatus curse on me, and he doesn't want to make things worse. "Yeah. They've both been interviewed."

Calm. Down. For crying out loud. My heart's thumping like a jackhammer against my rib cage. "What happened?"

"Think they were initially quite suspicious of them actually. Especially Andrijo, probably cause he and Erin were getting on so well that day." He takes a huge bite of his cone. It sprays everywhere from his lips as he continues. "But they checked his phone records, and there was nothing between him and her. And he can account for his whereabouts from just after we left the hut to well after the time she went missing. Was at work with his boss. Kasun. He's a respected figure in the area." He shrugs. "They've told him they'll be in touch if they need to ask anything else, but thankfully it doesn't sound like they're really concerned about him. Or Borko, for that matter."

Thankfully? I'm shaking. No. This can't be happening. It . . . it has to be him.

I was so convinced.

But he has an alibi. And no real motive, in the eyes of the police.

Maybe I latched on to him because it was easier to hate an evil with a face.

From Boom to Blood and Back Again: How One Music Festival Plans to Resurrect Serbia from the Ashes of Its War-torn Past

By Carina Corbett

My cursor has been blinking at the end of my byline for nearly an hour. I'm alone in my hotel room, air-con whirring on full blast. It's midnight, and I can't sleep. So I'm trying to write through the rising wave of anxiety I have no way of suppressing.

Laid out in front of me are my interview transcripts from last week. After the gelato with Tim—blood pumping and throat tightening—I went to a local internet café, armed with my trusty dictaphone, and transcribed the interviews I'd managed to squeeze in before Erin went missing. The festival founder, a couple of local business owners, a disgruntled taxi driver, a spokesperson from the Serbian Embassy in Belgrade, where they're running a multi-billion-dollar redevelopment scheme to revamp the country's beat-down capital. I have some great quotes and fascinating insights, but when I try to think about how to arrange them in my piece, my brain swims.

My angle is solid. I know it is. Because of its geography, the country has been fought over for many millennia, and as a result the Petrovaradin Fortress has been occupied by the Celts, Romans, Byzantines, Bulgarians and Turks. I want to explore the beautiful poignancy in the way that fortress is now used as the setting for a music festival, a way of bringing people together. Where travelers from around the globe gather to celebrate one shared passion. And celebrate is what they do.

I want to do a brief history of Serbia, from its glory years while the Serbian Empire flourished, to the way its people suffered as serfs of the Ottoman Empire. A summary of the last hundred years, and the myriad ways in which the century has been a disaster for them. The Balkan Wars. World War I. The Yugoslav Wars. War, war, war. Endless bloodshed.

And now: a party.

But how can I do such a huge feature justice when I can't even remember what I had for breakfast? When I can't remember what it's like not to be plugged into an endless surge of adrenaline?

I'm angry. I'm angry and I'm frustrated at this stupid fucking illness. If I had a visible ailment—a broken bone or a chemo-bald head—people would understand. They'd understand why everything seems so much harder than it used to. But not even an X-ray would show the shitstorm that is my brain, the clusterfuck of thoughts and fears determined to bring me to my knees.

I'm ambitious, dammit. And I'm smart. I'm capable.

I can do it, except I can't.

The relaxing album I was listening to on Spotify ends. A siren wails outside on the street. My curtains are open, and the fire truck's blue and red and white lights illuminate my desk. I feel it, the familiar pressing on my chest. The air-con is too cold and not cold enough. I'm burning and I'm freezing and I don't know which hurts worse.

Spiral spiral spiral it's starting. No. Please no.

I sob, a gasping, racking sob that takes my self-pitying breath away. Drop to the floor, grab my satchel.

Fumble, fumble, fumble, find it.

The empty Xanax packet is a death sentence.

I can't breathe I can't breathe I can't breathe.

Erin.

Erin.

My trembling hand grabs the bangle, our bangle, like it's a buoy in the ocean. Maybe she's touching hers now, wishing she could get a message to me, a message that she's okay.

But no no no she's not okay nothing is okay nothing will ever be okay.

I'm howling now, animalesque wails punctuated with gasps for air, air that will never come.

This is bad this is bad this is a bad one.

I can't call an ambulance. They'll judge me.

Erin Erin Erin.

I grab a pen. Get out get out get out of my head, I need these thoughts out of my head.

The coloring book. I fill it, page after page after page of words, they're all connected, everything is connected, Andrijo and the fortress and the bangle and the gelato and the drunken clock and the sheep skulls and the storm and Erin.

What does it mean? Paper runs out. I can't find the hotel notepad. No no no no no. Yes! My arms, my legs, I can write on myself, notes notes notes. My thighs are maps of Petrovaradin and my forearm is Erin's final words.

"Wait here for me?"

It's all connected. It has to be.

But how?

I FIND A half-full packet of beta-blockers in my wash bag. They bring my heart rate down enough that I can catch my breath, fill my lungs, stop feeling my blood pump through my veins like it's acid.

Limbs akimbo, I lie flat on my back atop the duvet covers, eyes glued to the ceiling fan. I've scrubbed the ink from my limbs in the lukewarm shower. Got myself a glass of water; it's not cold enough, but it'll do.

I pull myself into the present. Feel the hard mattress on my spine, the steady beat of my heart. Flutter my eyes closed against the pink sunrise peeking through the curtains. The room smells of hotel chain soap and foreign detergent from the launderette. I'm so tired my bones hurt.

But I made it through. I made it through.

I think I'm in a half-dreaming state, like when you're falling asleep on public transport and are kind of still aware of your surroundings, but you're starting to hallucinate, too.

Except what I'm hallucinating is real.

It's a memory, really. A memory of Erin—one of our very first.

We'd interned together for three weeks. Up close and personal in the fashion cupboard, sorting through endless packages from endless PR companies for endless magazine shoots, and we fucked up all the time. Got yelled at all the time. It was like some *Devil Wears Prada* hellhole. I upped my meds dose in the first week, and again in the second.

Thing is, we were both the same combination of excited and terrified when we first started. Me, because I'm a lunatic, and because my mum didn't approve—the arts are no way to make money, don't you know?—Erin, because she'd dropped out of the law program at a prestigious London university—after spending her undergraduate years studying history—to pursue her dream of working in fashion. She was stone broke. Student finance needed her loan back since she was no longer attending school, but she'd already spent it on rent and a shiny new domain name to start up her shiny new fashion blog.

It was mainly exciting, though. We shared the giggly terror, the surreal "how are we here?" feelings, the panic over getting Lowe's coffee order wrong. I was in awe of her then, though that never really went away. I didn't find her draining to be around, which is saying something considering I'm more socially anxious than your average house elf. She glowed, but not in a way that made you feel dull. She brought you up to her level, helped you shine with her. She was the sun.

The physical beauty was one thing. But it was her intoxicating personality I found the most enthralling—dark sarcasm, a deep drive, a steely glare when it was needed. Take-no-shit badassery. I loved it. All I wanted to do was watch her in action.

So like I say, it was three weeks after we first started. I was miserable in the work, constantly on edge, but a little part of me woke up every morning looking forward to seeing her. People talk about the high when you meet someone romantically and they change everything, but sometimes you get that in a friendship, too.

She brought me a coffee that morning. Went to Starbucks early. It was the run-up to Christmas, and we'd been talking for ages about those syrupy lattes that give you more of a high than a gram of cocaine. Gingerbread, extra whipped cream. I still remember how it tasted—warm and sweet and spicy, like my new friend.

I went out on my lunch at noon. Nowhere in particular, just to grab a sandwich, get some fresh air and pick up some gloves, because it was freezing out. I came back, desperate for the toilet, so I dashed into the restrooms. One of the two cubicles was locked. And even though I'd never heard her cry before, I knew the sobbing was hers.

Smith, her high-school sweetheart and long-term boyfriend, had given her hell for borrowing money from her uncle. Told her he no longer respected her after she dropped out of law school, how he used to see her as an equal, but now she's just some dumb fashion bimbo like the rest of them. He's a newly qualified architect. Dreams of a big house and a fancy car and a well-stocked liquor cabinet. And she'd taken that dream from him by following hers.

I hated him, in that moment. Watching her mascara dribble down her cheeks, her eyeliner smudged along her brow line, I fucking hated him. In the months afterward, when he came to meet us on work nights out, I couldn't hide my resentment.

She clawed the cubicle walls like an animal. I wished she'd

claw his face like that. The worst part was, her hurt and anger were directed at herself. She blamed herself. Blamed herself for putting her happiness above his.

She was back to burning brightly by the next morning. But it scared me, that moment in the toilets. Because her sadness was so raw, so deep, it was like she wasn't her anymore.

Chapter Eight

July 22, England

FLYING HOME FEELS like a betrayal.

Boarding the plane feels like a betrayal.

Ordering a grilled cheese sandwich feels like a betrayal.

Laughing at a joke feels like a betrayal.

Breathing feels like a betrayal.

How dare I carry on living as normal when my friend is gone? How dare I get to go home to my family when my friend does not? How dare I walk back into that magazine office and write features and design pages and interview public figures when my friend cannot?

The seat belt around my waist and the rattle of the catering trolley and the emergency exit signs and the smell of duty-free perfume . . . they're all lies. None of it is real. It's all a nightmare. And I can't believe the details or I'll start to believe the tragedy.

So I stay detached.

I sit next to Tim on the plane. I go through phases of barely being able to move or speak or breathe. I feel like someone has locked me inside my mind and thrown away the key, and I have to get out or I'm going to explode. So I do something perfectly ordinary, like order peanuts, and then I'm crippled by the sheer ordinariness of it, which was the whole point of doing the thing to begin with but it sets my mind off-kilter once again.

It's exhausting.

Tim's saying something, but it's like he's underwater so I have to ask him to repeat himself.

"How are you feeling?" he asks.

"I'm fine," I hear myself lie.

But there are things I want to ask him. I take a drink of water, stuff some peanuts in my mouth and swallow hard. I once read a book on how to be present. Mindfulness, I think the concept's called. You have to focus on your five senses, on how everything around you feels. So I try. Salty peanuts, cool air-conditioning, citrusy sweet perfume, roaring engines and all-gray everything. I haul myself back into reality like I'm pulling my body back from a cliff edge.

After three more days of police interviews, in which it became very clear they are not interested in Andrijo in any way, we were given the okay to fly home. Neither of us are suspects. I'm a SigWit, but they've got all they can out of me. "All they can" mostly comprising panic attacks and the occasional nugget of genuine information.

It scares me, how the time's passed. Nine days. It's been nine days. Surely she can't still be alive and well? Wouldn't we have heard from her by now if she was?

When I first considered the option, trafficking seemed to be the worst possible explanation. But now it feels like the only one in which she could still be breathing.

"Tim . . . I want to ask you about Andrijo. Don't you think he's a little . . . intense?" I ask. I know I've phrased it poorly, and my old journalism lecturer would be horrified at the inherent bias in the question, but what can I say. I'm traumatized. I'm off my game.

"Mmm. Maybe. A lot of Serbs are like that, though. They're very passionate people."

Passionate doesn't seem like the right word. It was more like he was trying to be soft and smooth when really he's all sharp and fierce. Like a lion dressed as a sheep. He didn't fit.

He was calculated.

But the police spoke to him, Tim told me. He's clear. Looking back, it's easy to overthink Andrijo's importance in events. I guess it's easy to overthink anything in retrospect. You have enough distance from the situation to weigh up explanations and make judgments, but sometimes that's not a good thing because you lose that natural instinct somewhere along the way. You attach your own bias.

Like right now, I get the sense that Tim is weighing his words carefully. Maybe tomorrow I'll look back and find that odd, and noteworthy, or maybe I'll look back and think it's just a result of the surreal situation we're in. It's impossible to tell what perspective the distance will give me.

"He and Erin seemed to be getting on well," I muse aloud. I'm trying to sound natural but there's nothing natural about it.

"True. Though he gets on well with a lot of women." Tim tries for a laugh. "A real ladies' man. And Erin is . . . beautiful."

"Do you know if he came to JUMP that night? The night Erin disappeared?"

He shakes his head slowly. "No, he didn't. Like I say, his boss accounted for his whereabouts. He never even mentioned the possibility of making the trip to me."

"Huh," I say, leaning back in my chair. My knee is bouncing up and down spasmodically and keeps bashing against the folded-down plastic table. "I'm sure I overheard him tell Erin he might see her later that night. But he didn't say that to you?"

Tim furrows his brows. "No. I don't think so."

Strange. Unless Tim's the liar, in which case . . .

And Andrijo's boss could be lying. People do that.

Scenarios rattle through my brain. Andrijo arriving at JUMP, texting her while she's at the bathroom and asking if she'll come and meet him. Kind, unsuspecting, beautiful Erin seeking him out in an empty nook of the fortress.

You have a boyfriend you have a boyfriend you have a boyfriend, I try and tell past Erin, as if I can transcend the space-time continuum and somehow stop this from happening.

Him taking her.

I picture the fortress in my mind. Is there a side entrance he could have used to sneak her out? The main gates are always packed with guards and festival-goers. If he was trying to abduct her, there's no way he could have done it inconspicuously. But if he and Borko have been coming to JUMP since 2005, there's every chance they could know about another way in and out.

I dig around in my backpack for a pen and paper. My hands find the coloring book, but I shove it farther down into the bottom. I don't want Tim to see my crazy firsthand. Pulling out a tattered Sudoku book, I turn to one of the easy pages, already filled in with my scrawly biro handwriting, and start jotting down some notes.

Find layout/blueprint of fortress.

"What's Andrijo's surname?" I ask Tim.

He looks over his shoulder at my notes. Frowns. "I'm not sure. Sorry."

Look up Andrijo using Facebook networks, e.g., Novi Sad, JUMP.

"What about Borko's?"

"Zoric."

Look up Borko Zoric (and check his Facebook friends for Andrijo).

Feeling like I'm being proactive helps calm my mind, so I keep scribbling until I run out of ideas. I want to investigate other disappearances in the area, especially at JUMP, and whether those people were ever found again. I want to know everything about the people we met that day. I want to write down every single little damn detail I can remember yet again because who knows what's relevant or not in a situation like this?

Then I complete four fiendish difficult Sudoku puzzles, eat the rest of my peanuts and promptly fall asleep. I'm emotionally, physically and mentally exhausted.

I dream of sheep skulls, inky black eyes and Erin's murder victim smile.

MY MUM MEETS me at airport arrivals, which she would never normally do, and throws her arms around me. I picture the alternate universe in which Erin's mum does the same, but it's so painful I feel like someone's digging a knife into every pressure point in my body. I can feel in the desperation of my mother's embrace that she's thanking the universe for sparing her daughter and taking someone else's instead.

Our relationship is tumultuous at the best of times. My workaholic father died when I was eleven, and my mum has never recovered. He left behind a newborn baby boy—my brother, Jake, who's now fourteen—and a woman who was so depressed she quit her job, sold my father's business and let her world fall apart.

Not that Erin's family life was any easier. Money was always tight, even though her father worked offshore—still does. When Erin left high school at eighteen, her parents both assumed she'd get a full-time job and money wouldn't be so tight for once, but after a year of slogging away for sixty hours a week as a health-care assistant, she secretly sent off an application to Northumbria University. She got accepted onto the History program, took out a student loan and didn't tell her mum until the day before the first semester started. She changed to night shifts at the hospital, gave up sleep for three years and graduated with first-class honors. All her family cared about was her getting back to work full-time. Erin didn't even go to her own graduation ceremony.

So you can imagine how well it went down when she left law school and took on an unpaid internship at a glossy lifestyle magazine.

"Following your dreams is for rich kids and retired old folk," her mum told her. "Reality doesn't work like that. Write when you're sixty-five and have a government pension to pay your bills."

Erin almost listened.

When I arrived on my first day at *Northern Heart*, I expected to be making tea and doing a lot of photocopying, at least in the first few weeks. My heart sank when I saw the fashion cupboard, where all the new season clothes sent by PR companies are stored. Fashion is not my forte. I nearly quit after a week, but two things kept me there: the fact interns could pitch and write features . . . and Erin.

"Oh, love," my mother coos in my ear. "I'm so sorry. I know you and Erin were great friends."

"Not were, Mum," I mumble, but the sound is muffled as my face presses into her shoulder. Her wild afro tickles my nose. "Are. She's not dead."

At least, that's what I keep trying to tell myself.

People go missing all the time. A quarter of a million Brits are reported missing each year, and ninety-nine percent of those cases are solved. The odds are in Erin's favor.

Right?

THE BURNT-RED BRICKS of Northumbria Police Station on Newcastle's Forth Banks are vivid in the July sun. Sheets of sleek glass and polished chrome insistently convince the public that this building is something other than a center based around crime and violence and tragedy and suffering. It's not just a police station—it's modern design blended with traditional northern architecture. It's a work of art.

An officer stands outside, puffing desperately on a cigarette. A train thuds down the railway line right next to the station, wheels clanking on tracks and brakes squealing against the friction. I get caught in the juxtaposition. To my left is a building full of interrogation rooms and cells and criminals and detectives, and on my right are eight train carriages full of people who are probably wondering what kind of sandwich they fancy for lunch and which shop they should go to first on their shopping trips.

I know which world I'd rather be a part of, but I'm way past the stage of having a choice. Erin is the ball and chain tying me to the one on the left, and I feel guilty for complaining because God only knows what she's been through in the last week and a half.

I'll probably have a BLT for lunch. I try the thought out, wondering if I can still fit into the world of the train carriages.

Nope. The thought feels foreign in my brain. Like the smell of someone else's house on your clothes.

It's too weird being home. Being in Serbia was like being stuck in a nightmare, an endless time vacuum where everything slowed down and sped up and warped before my eyes. I was there forever and just for a second. My world ended in that vacuum. And now here I am, out of the nightmare, back to my normal life in my normal city.

But Erin is not. She's still there.

I pop a Xanax and a beta-blocker just to be sure. My pharmacist was the first place I visited this afternoon. I feel deliciously numb.

Focus. Back to the police station.

I'm here to meet Paige Tierney, the family liaison officer who's handling Erin's case through Interpol. The Serbian police force are responsible for the search in Novi Sad, but there's an FLO here to deal with Erin's nearest and dearest, plus a charity trust that's going to help with publicity and media coverage. The word *publicity* tastes vulgar, like this is some PR campaign for a new cosmetics line.

The FLO has been communicating with Erin's family, my mum says, making sure they're kept well-informed and supported. They keep people up to date with the police investigation, introduce them to Victim Support and inform them about other resources. If an inquest or court case is likely, the liaison officer also prepares them for that. They also help with practical matters, such as recovering relatives' belongings.

And as I am a SigWit and Erin's closest friend, Officer Tierney is extending her umbrella of compassion and care out to me, too.

Plus, I've been doing my research. It seems the FLO is important in building a solid relationship with the family, gathering material from them in a manner that contributes to the investigation.

They gain confidence and trust, making the family feel like they can confide anything in them.

Anything. Like a confession? Or am I too cynical?

I'm willing to bet it's happened before.

Having tried to make sense of the gibberish in my coloring book, I've brought more sensible notes to show Paige. I've laid out the timeline of Sunday, July 12, and filled it in with every single little detail I can remember. For a moment, self-preservation kicks in and I worry this makes me look suspicious—apparently liars always give too much detail. But finding Erin is the most important thing, and I don't care if I accidentally implicate myself in the process.

I know I'm innocent.

The cigarette-smoking officer holds the door open for me. The reception is all curved white walls and blue plastic chairs illuminated by fluorescent strip lighting. I tell the receptionist I'm here to see Officer Tierney, and he ushers me toward a seat. Paige is just finishing up with another family and will be with me shortly.

My fingers fumble absentmindedly with my notepad as I wait. There's something about being around policemen that makes you want to appear unsuspicious, and apparently that involves sitting as rigidly as a plank of wood—with about the same level of facial expression.

Again, my mind floats to Andrijo. I've pictured those coal-black eyes so many times now that they're imprinted on my frontal lobe. When I was writing my timeline, I tried to note down everything I remember him saying on that day, and again I fixated on the same strange pattern. He gave no personal details. He didn't talk about his friends or family, his job or his hobbies, his musical tastes or what food he likes to eat. Every comment he made was about the events of that day—the storm is settling and there are so many thunder flies swarming around and isn't the Danube so moody and beautiful when the sky is overcast?

Everything he said was an observation. And that's weird. Why would you be so careful and guarded during conversation that you give away absolutely no personal details whatsoever?

Unless you have something to hide.

Fortunately, Officer Tierney—"call me Paige"—doesn't take long and descends down an übermodern glass-and-chrome staircase to greet me. She's relatively young with smooth, dark skin like mine, black hair combed back in a neat bun, and she's in a tailored gray suit rather than a police uniform. Chatting away about the weather and other mundanities, she leads me upstairs, past a school-like cafeteria and down a corridor to a small interview room.

I take a seat opposite her as she arranges her files across the desk. We start chatting, and it's wonderfully informal compared to the interviews I did with Ilić. But for some reason I find myself missing the stilted soliloquies about protocol—the firm guidelines made me feel secure. Nevertheless, Paige is warm and chatty, and seems to take a huge amount of interest in Erin as a person. You assume all police officers will be solely focused on the cold hard facts of the investigation, but Officer Tierney is sensitive and considerate. It's not that she tiptoes around me, but she never pushes me for more, and offers a sympathetic smile whenever appropriate. She's more like a shrink than a detective. And I'm pretty familiar with both as this point.

I keep talking for nearly an hour. We cover a lot of the same ground as I did with Ilić, and the same buzz phrase keeps coming up—"out of character."

I'll say yes, yes, it is out of character, then I wonder if it really is. I'm thinking too hard about Erin's character, and now it's like when you're waiting for your suitcase on an airport carousel and you're so sure you know what it looks like until you're faced with all these other options that could just as easily be yours. And is it definitely gray not black? Does it really have wheels? Is it shiny or matte or metallic? And now you have no fucking idea what your suitcase looks like.

Who is Erin Baxter?

I find it hard to explain how Erin's identity is warping and shifting in my memory, but I try and put across that she's protective of her friends and responsible. I try and emphasize that this is not normal behavior for her. I try and define her character so I can prove this is out of it.

But as soon as I land on a particular trait, I remember instances that contradict it. She's logical and rational, but her common sense seems to evaporate after a glass of wine. She's considerate, but she often called in sick to work and left me to deal with deadline week hell alone. She's self-assured, but she cries over what her misogynistic boyfriend thinks of her. If you try and pin down her personality, you'll go around and around in circles until you're seasick.

Erin is a perfect contradiction. Everything and nothing is out of character.

"How are her parents doing?" I ask Paige, wondering if I'm overstepping my mark.

"Her mum's a mess, understandably." A grimace. "It's horrific enough when your child goes missing on home turf. She must feel even more helpless and afraid when it's overseas. I believe she's flying out to Belgrade soon. We're helping cover the costs."

"Makes sense," I say. "What about her dad? Is he flying out, too?" I remember Erin telling me her father works offshore on the rigs. She doesn't see him very often.

Sadie gives me a strange look. "Her father's in prison. Domestic abuse. Four years and eleven months through a five-year sentence."

My stomach drops.

Something else I didn't know about Erin.

She's honest, but she lies.

HER DAD WAS in prison.

Domestic abuse.

Against her? Her sister? Her mum?

The bruise. She had a bruise, an old one.

It was round, like a coin, and quite small. On the inside of her upper arm.

A . . . thumbprint?

Ilić asked me if she had any others. Was he thinking of four more fingers on the back of her arm?

Grab marks?

My mind spins.

But he's in prison. Nearly out, but . . .

Was she scared? Of him being freed?

What if she went to visit him?

What if he attacked her?

But why? Why would he attack her? That could prolong his sentence. And . . . and she's his daughter.

How could he attack Erin—Erin, who's gone?

Chapter Nine

July 24, England

I HAVE TO get out of the house.

My mind is spasming like an overexerted muscle, and I'm going stir-crazy. I consider calling my mum, but she doesn't really "get" anxiety, and has long since given up on trying. So I've given up trying to explain. Sometimes I want to scream at her: "You spent my adolescence in a state of chronic depression and left me to fend for myself!" It wouldn't achieve anything, though. So I bite my tongue. Now is normally when I'd call Erin and go do something fun. Her absence hurts.

So I set off on the four-mile walk to town. I live on a cheap estate in the student area of Newcastle, and while normally I'd get the bus, I could use the fresh air. Plus, I'm not exactly feeling flush right now.

I applied for a paid job last night. Junior Crime Reporter at the *Daily Standard*. I'm qualified, thanks to my degree, and I have publishing experience. And I'd be reporting on something that mattered. Plus, it pays a decent wage. But I'm not getting my hopes up. Hundreds of journalism graduates are after the same job.

It's overcast and cold for late July. The British summer heat wave we were promised never really materialized, but I'm kind of glad. Extreme temperatures don't suit me. The kids I pass playing football on a patch of cracked concrete don't look at me, even when a rogue strike nearly decapitates me. I roll my eyes and throw the ball back at them, trying to quiet the ridiculous thoughts of "What if I throw it wrong what if they laugh at me what if what if what if . . ." They're kids. Why do I even care?

I think about Erin's dad as I walk.

Part of me gets why she wouldn't tell me. I've watched enough soaps to know that domestic violence victims often feel ashamed— that they didn't speak up earlier, that they couldn't stop it, that it was somehow their fault. Erin probably wanted to keep it in the past, to bury her shame along with her pain and move on.

But he's getting out. Next month. August 11—that's his release date. Surely she was stressed about that? What if he was planning to seek revenge on her family for pressing charges? What if one of them gave evidence in court he'd made them swear not to?

And the bruise. Old, yellow, the perfect thumbprint.

It can't possibly be linked to what happened in Novi Sad, and yet . . .

And yet it seems too much of a coincidence not to be.

I FIND A grand total of nothing about Erin's father's trial on the internet.

I'm in Newcastle City Library. Sprawled open next to me, spines cracked, are a couple of psychology volumes, in which I found more info about the emotional and mental effects of prolonged domestic violence.

But I don't know his name. I try the search terms "Baxter" and "domestic violence" and "Newcastle Crown Court" and "five-year sentence" in all different combinations, but nothing comes up. The surname is too common, as is, sadly, the crime. Maybe he wasn't tried in Newcastle. Maybe his sentence was originally longer and they let him out early for good behavior. For whatever reason, it's not showing up.

My stomach growls for the first time in ten days. Maybe being back on home turf has renewed my appetite. I grab a Snickers and a cup of crappy filter coffee from the cafeteria, then slump back into my chair, sighing so heavily the homeless-looking student next to me jumps. I'm at a dead end. The notes I made on the plane have proved fruitless; there's no readily available information on the fortress layout.

Like a homing pigeon, my brain is drawn back to the same thing it always is when I'm thinking about Erin: Andrijo. Trafficking. Darkness.

I remember what Tim said: "Think about it. When it comes to trafficking—which I'm not denying does happen—locals are much easier targets. It makes no sense to abduct western girls, 'cause there'd be international pressure to actually look for them. Nobody gives a shit about poor people in poor countries, and traffickers know that. And if we're being realistic, homicide—with or without sexual assault—is way more common than abduction and trafficking."

It makes all kinds of sense. I'll readily admit I'm clinging to false hope—other than her voluntarily running away, trafficking seems like the only scenario in which Erin's heart is still beating.

Sweet, sweet endorphins follow my first bite of Snickers. Better than any antidepressants, I shit you not. Typing tentatively, I do a Google search for other Brits who've gone missing in Serbia.

Nada. Just a ton of official embassy sites, some articles on World War I casualties and a *Daily Fail* column on how Kim Kardashian is stealing her hairstyles from a Serbian pop princess.

Again, I try some different terms, but it's no use. I find some immigration figures, a story about two newlyweds who died after their yacht capsized off the coast of Montenegro and another *Daily Fail* conspiracy theory about Winston Churchill being the secret love child of the king of Serbia. There's a small piece about a young British woman called Brodie Breckenridge. She went missing in Croatia eight years ago, but that doesn't help. Because she was never found. The mystery was never solved. She just vanished.

Crumpling up my empty Snickers wrapper and tossing it in the trash can near me, I start a search in the library's digital archive: "sex trafficking, Serbia."

A handful of titles appear. I make a note of their reference numbers and hunt them down in the library. They're spread over a couple of floors—some filed under international politics, some under law and criminality—and some are missing, but I find a couple that seem like they might be useful. I flick open the first. Its cover is a sordid close-up of a woman's crouched-over silhouette.

In Transit:
European Trafficking Via the Balkans

According to research conducted by Dr. Norman Williams in 2012, Serbia is a source, transit and destination country for women and girls trafficked transnationally and internally, primarily for the purpose of commercial sexual exploitation.

Disturbing statistics compiled by Williams earlier this decade showed that not only are foreign victims transported to Serbia in the interim, but internal sex trafficking of Serbian women and girls also continued to increase as of 2007—comprising more than three-fourths of trafficking cases in that year.

However, local and national Serbian law enforcement bodies can only despair: Williams found that efforts to shut down known brothels only served to prompt traffickers into better concealing victims of trafficking.

I lean back in my chair, taking a swig of the coffee. Granules float on the surface, bitter and grainy. Delicious. The student next to me, dressed in one of those hobo cardigans and sporting extremely unwashed hair, keeps clicking her pen on and off, over and over and over. I press my eyes shut. They still sting with tiredness. I can't remember the last time they didn't.

This paper seems to corroborate Tim's theory. Locals are easier targets, and account for over seventy-five percent of reported cases. But what about the other twenty-five percent?

I flick through a few more essays, one on the ineffective and often lenient prosecution of traffickers, another on the reintegration of the victims.

I'm not sure how long it takes for the reality of what I'm researching to sink in. Whether it's the dry academic terminology used in this dark, dark world of exploitation, or the way my eyes keep dropping to my bangle as I read about one victim who committed suicide just a month after she was rescued.

I gulp down more coffee, but it's no use. Hot tears sting my eyes. This can't be real. It can't be. My beautiful, kind best friend cannot be gone. I cannot be delving deep into this terrifying looking glass in a desperate attempt to convince myself she's alive.

It's the first time I've felt real-human sad, not manic-anxiety sad or gaping-depression sad. One tear slides down my cheek. Another. The lump in my throat is sharper than the iceberg that sunk the *Titanic*.

Whatever happened twelve days ago, she's been hurt. She's scared.

She's dead, or she wants to be.

Chapter Ten

July 27, England

THERE'S NOT ONE single part of me that wants to go back to work today.

Erin was the only redeeming part of that hellhole—Erin, her laugh and the promise of something better. But my *NYT*-worthy article is still half-written on my USB drive, and my best friend isn't coming back.

I swear, if Lowe gives me one ounce of sass today, I'll . . . well, I'll probably cry and pop a forty-seventh Xanax of the morning, but I like to think I'd tear her a brand-new asshole to bleach.

Turns out sympathy is worse than sass. The smarmy receptionist who calls everyone "hun" throws her fake-tanned arms around me, smelling wonderfully of burnt biscuits and cat piss. Almost everyone on the design team grimaces and nods once, in that way they assume means "I'm so sorry" but actually just makes them look like those toy dogs that sit in the back of cars and bob their heads out the rear window.

Hardly any of the advertising team have made it in yet—why would they? It's before nine a.m.—but the editorial department is ready for my arrival. There's a biscuit tin on the empty desk next to the men's editor. Someone's baked cookies. They've saved me a copy of the mag that hit shelves last week, something they always forget to do because I'm a lowly intern. I don't want to open it because Erin's name will be in the imprint, which is stupid because she's probably dead.

Dead. It's not quite onomatopoeic, but it feels it. Flat. Short. An unapologetic full stop at the end of a sentence.

And Lowe's face, dear Lord. It's like she's trying to twist it up in an elaborate show of sympathy, but the Botox hasn't quite worn off yet so she slightly resembles Helena Bonham Carter in full-blown villain mode. I really want to ask her why Tim Burton doesn't need her on set today, but my jokes are always wasted on her.

"Sweetheart." She swoops me up in a hug, all cashmere cardigan and musky perfume. "I'm so terribly sorry. I should never have agreed to the trip, knowing what I do about those kinds of countries." I don't ask what she means by that, because I doubt she even knows herself. "Shall we have a chat in the boardroom?"

Everyone watches as I trail behind her like a lost puppy. I'm still carrying my satchel, weighed down with the book I checked out of the library last week. I planned to read it on my lunch. She grabs us both a cup of water from the cooler and shuts the door behind her.

"Thanks for giving me the last few weeks off, Lowe," I start.

She waves a hand at me. "Nonsense. You'd've been no use to me anyway. The police needed you, and besides, it's important to grieve properly. How are you feeling? Poor dear. You must be in terrible shock. Was is traumatic? Are you traumatized?"

"I'm okay," I lie. "I didn't see anything, really. She just ... didn't come back." I swallow.

She's paler than usual. She drops her voice to a murmur. "I can't believe it."

"Me neither." Stupid real-person tears threaten to pour again.

She sniffs, pushes back her chair. "Well, let me know if you need anything, okay?"

I'm grateful for the brevity. I think she's in danger of getting emotional, too, and neither of us wants that.

"Thanks, Lowe."

She squeezes my shoulder. "Take care of yourself. And get me a coffee." She winks, though, and I can't help but smile. I think she's all right, beneath it all. And I like that she doesn't bother telling me it'll be okay, or that Erin will turn up, or that the police are doing all they can and they'll find her eventually. She's an intelligent woman. She knows neither of us believe that. She knows I know how black the world can be.

The fashion cupboard feels like a house left empty after a divorce. If you associate a place closely enough with a person, one without the other seems impossible.

Her stuff has been tidied up and I hate it. The reusable coffee mug with a bespectacled owl, the polka dot umbrella she keeps here in case it rains on a coffee run, the sleek black-and-gold pencil case with the posh fountain pen Smith bought her for starting law school. It's all been put in a shoebox and tucked away to the side of the room. I can't even look at it. The only belonging I've seen of hers since she went missing is her toothbrush, taken away by detectives to use for DNA sampling. I don't think my fragile mind could handle fixating on a quirky owl or a sparkly pen or a funky umbrella, all so quintessentially her.

I flop to the ground. There are no chairs in here; there's no room. Just a fraying blue carpet we've spent hours and hours and hours cross-legged on, surrounding by postage labels and compliments slips and clothes we could never afford. We were a good team. She had the eye for fashion, I had the knack for organization. I try and bring order to my own mind every minute of every day. A glorified wardrobe was no challenge.

Deciding to start sending back the A/W lines we've already shot, I get to work, losing myself in the monotony of folding and labeling and franking. Every time I want to make a wisecrack comment about a ridiculous product name (Hobo Camel Dungarees are set to be big this season) or an overly enthusiastic PR pitch ("I just super-duper absolutely think *Northern Heart* will totes adore this fabulous clutch!"), I have to catch myself. I have to remember I'm alone.

Still, I'm getting through it; I've almost made it to lunchtime. But then I find it.

Her leather jacket. It's somehow gotten mixed up among the branded clothing, and I'm so wrapped up in my routine I barely notice until I realize there's no tag. I hold it away from me and gasp; the flood of emotion is overwhelming.

Black with chunky zips and an androgynous cut, all sleek edges and cool angles. She loved this jacket. Splurged on it one lunch break a few days after the fight with Smith. Her very own brand of "fuck you, I do what I want." I loved her for it. We went to a creepy old churchyard after work and I photographed her wearing it for her blog.

It still smells of her. Chanel No 5, coconut shampoo and the occasional cigarette she sneaked at particularly stressful times and thought nobody noticed. I drop it. Press the heels of my hands into my eye sockets. *Don't cry don't cry don't cry.*

No use. The tears come anyway. Clumps of watery mascara cover my palms. I pick it up again. Hold it close to my chest. Erin.

I squeeze the fabric harder, but something rustles in the inside pocket. A receipt? No. It's more like a plastic wrapper—Haribo? She loves jelly sweets.

Careful not to jam the zip, I slide the pocket open, but inside it's just a plain white packet with a simple black code. A corner is missing. It's been opened.

Nausea sweeps through me, cold and sudden. I know what these are. I've used one myself, after a drunken slip with a guy in my journalism class.

Pregnancy tests. There's one missing.

Think, think, think.

I have no idea how long they've been in there. We've been at *Northern Heart* together for nine months, and she bought the jacket three weeks into the internship. It could've been any time.

But it wouldn't have been. The packet is bulky and it rustles—she wouldn't have carried it around for so long.

I try to remember the last time I saw her wearing it. It was pretty warm before we left for Serbia, one of those random weeks of actual sun we rarely see in the North East, so she'd have baked liked a jacket potato in thick leather. Maybe late June? Early July?

It's just a stab in the dark and I know it. I can't remember when she last wore it, had no idea it'd ever be important.

How little attention we pay to those we love.

Again, I'm thrown that she didn't tell me. We had—or at least I thought we did—one of those beautifully candid friendships borne from both proximity and a genuine, soul-deep bond. She never hesitated to tell me about her bowel movements or the kinky things Smith asked her to do in bed. There was no such thing as too much information.

Maybe she spouted off about the little stuff so I wouldn't notice the big stuff. A jittery Erin before meeting her father in prison, a nervous Erin before taking a life-changing test, a hurt Erin after someone grabbed her. All hypotheticals, but all founded in fact.

It must have been negative, though. She was drinking in Serbia. Not as much as usual, but I just figured that was because money was tight. And she didn't look pregnant. I know girls with a petite frame like hers don't really show until later on, but surely I'd notice? I think back to her outfits in Serbia.

Baggy tees. Every day.

No, this is ridiculous. She wasn't pregnant. She couldn't've been.

But there's a scenario, flashing through my head. One that fills me with horror.

Erin, falling pregnant by the man who resents her for following her dreams.

Erin, panicking, not knowing who to turn to.

Erin, confronting her dad, him grabbing her.

Erin, full of fear, screaming at him to get off her, because she's carrying his grandson.

Him. Grabbing her harder.

I have to know. I have to know if she was pregnant.

SMITH LOOKS LIKE hell.

I had his number saved in my phone, from the time Erin's ran out of battery and she needed to keep him updated on what bar we were in so he could meet us. My last outgoing text to him was *See you soon baby zxx*—obviously sent by her. It killed me to read it.

He wasn't surprised to hear from me, he said. Agreed to meet me on my lunch hour. Suggested a coffee shop, but I needed somewhere nobody would eavesdrop. Besides, I've had too many public breakdowns lately. Preemptive action seemed necessary. We're in the churchyard down the street from my office, sitting on a memorial bench, surrounded by gravestones.

My memory of Smith was a clean-shaven baby face, perfectly styled brown hair, expensive suits and a watch you'd assume to be fake if you didn't know his family. Too much aftershave. Eyes that never quite focused on anything in particular; he's too good to listen to you, too good to pay proper attention.

Today, he's the more disheveled of us two, and that's coming from the girl with a mascara-stained face and fading streaks of violet in her coarse black hair. His top button's undone, the knot on his tie is too small; he hasn't shaved in a few days. I smell deodorant, lots of it, but no aftershave. His eyes are red and puffy.

"I miss her," he murmurs, voice hoarse. He's staring at a gravestone, engraved with the words Loved by All, Taken Too Soon.

"Me, too."

"Tell me about it," he says. "Tell me about the last time you saw her."

I tell him. The music, the humidity, the emotional conversation, the offhanded goodbye. Not goodbye. *"See you in a minute."* I'm still waiting for that minute to end.

"Was she happy?"

That catches me off guard. What a morbid question. It's like asking, "Did she die happy?"

I shrug. "I think so. She always lets you know if she isn't." I throw the word *always* around pretty loosely. "Anyway, Smith, that's kind of what I wanted to talk to you about. I . . . there's something I have to ask. About Erin. In the last few months."

I study his face for a sign he might know what I'm talking about, but as usual his eyes are vacant. The placid expression has gone, though. In its place is a frown carved in cement. His pain is written in his hunched brow and tensed jaw.

"I . . . found this." I pull out the twin pack of pregnancy tests. "One's missing. Did you . . . was she . . . ?"

"The fuck is that?" He snatches the packet. Pulls the other one out. Goes white. "What the—"

"You didn't know."

He looks at me now, for the first time. Gapes. "Was she?"

I shake my head. "I don't know. That's what I wanted to ask you. She didn't mention it?"

"No, she . . ." He trails off as his voice catches in his throat. "No."

I don't know what to say. I rest a hand on his shoulder, but he jerks as if I've shocked him. "You all right?" I ask tentatively.

His head drops into his hands. "I just . . . we had it all in front of us, you know? Our future was so fucking bright, a future we'd worked for since we were sixteen. I'd be a successful architect, she'd be a partner in a law firm. We'd have three cars and a nice house, kids we could afford to send to private school. A dog. Were things rough when she changed her mind and dropped out of school? Yeah. But we were getting through it. We were. And now . . ." He pounds the bench with his fist. "Fuck. It's all just gone to shit, hasn't it?" A bitter laugh. "She's gone. Vanished off the face of the earth. How am I supposed to live now? How the fuck do I carry on breathing when everything I wanted in life has been taken away from me?"

I'm kind of not loving the self-involved way he's voicing his heartache, but I do feel for him. Still. You'd think his main concern would be her: what she's been through, where she is now, whether she's hurt beyond repair.

Whether she was carrying his child.

"In the last few weeks, before we went away . . ." I start. "Was she herself? Or did anything seem off?"

A silence—too long. Maybe he's trying to decide whether I know about her dad. "She, uh . . . she had something coming up. Something she was worried about. But beyond that . . ." He shrugs helplessly. "I mean, how do I separate one from the other? Like, yeah. She was worried. Who wouldn't be?"

I let my silence tell him I know what he's talking about.

"She was drinking. In Serbia." I dig some dirt out from underneath my fingernail. Flick it onto the churchyard path. A raven watches us from a tree. "And . . . well, she didn't look pregnant. I never saw her out of a baggy T-shirt, but I don't think there was a bump." I shudder. "I don't know. Fuck."

"Yeah." He nods. "Fuck."

Chapter Eleven

July 28, England

AT FIRST I'M not sure whether to tell Officer Tierney about the possible pregnancy. It just seem so uncertain. A game-changing prospect we have no way of proving.

Unless . . . unless the police can access her medical records. I think they can in serious cases like this. I remember once reading a comment piece in *The Guardian* on how police want unconditional access to such information, because when they're answering a 999 call from a vulnerable individual at three a.m., they need the right details there and then, not during office hours once they've finally got the proper permission from the relevant department.

So I'm assuming they can . . .

But if Erin really was pregnant, would she even have gone to see a doctor? It depends. On whether she wanted to keep it, on how far along she was, on whether she'd told her family or Smith—which it sounds like she hadn't.

Andrijo. Father. Bruise. Baby.

Each tangent I find myself latching on to feels so pressing, so fundamentally crucial to the investigation, and yet they can't all be relevant. And even then, the only thing I know for sure is that her father's in jail, soon to be released. My feeling about Andrijo could just be a feeling. My hunch about the bruise could just be a hunch. My fear over her carrying a child could just be a fear.

I'm sitting where I always am at nine-thirty on a Tuesday morning—cross-legged on the floor of the fashion cupboard. Erin's jacket has been folded carefully into the box with the rest of her stuff. I don't even remember whether it was me who did it.

The card Paige Tierney handed me at the end of our chat is already dog-eared around the edges. I jammed it in my jeans pocket, and now it's gone soft like cotton.

She told me to contact her if I needed anything, or if I thought of anything else I needed to tell her. She even said I could get in touch about Erin's work belongings, and she'd liaise with the family about having them picked up.

That's it. I'll arrange a meeting, citing the jacket and other miscellany as a reason, then also happen to bring up the test. Or I could put the test back in the pocket, pretend I never found it and hope Paige checks the pockets and reaches her own conclusion? No. Too risky.

Why am I so scared to tell her? Because it's probably irrelevant, and definitely won't help the Serbs find her. And maybe she'll think I'm stupid, think I'm wasting police time, think I'm a paranoid little girl with nothing better to do than . . .

Enough. I need to stop this cycle of obsessing over what people think. I'm pissing myself off in the way I use anxiety as a crutch.

This is important. This is Erin.

Imagine this was the one thing that could help her? That could make a difference in the search? They could understand her state of mind. Understand her rationale—or lack thereof.

An image comes back to me, for the thousandth time since I half-dreamt it at sunrise in Novi Sad.

Erin, devastated, clawing a cubicle wall like a lion who'd lost her cub.

Sadness was so raw, so deep, it was like she wasn't her anymore.

What could an unwanted baby do to her?

Or . . .

Another thought chills me to my core.

What could an abortion do to her? Could it unhinge my best friend entirely?

Shaking pathetically, I pull out my phone, check Lowe isn't about to charge in, pull the cupboard door shut and type out a poorly worded text to Tierney.

At this point, I have nothing to lose. But Erin does.

In fact, Erin might have already lost it.

I'VE SPENT MORE time in police stations in the last few weeks than in my own bed.

"And you have no idea how long the tests could've been in her jacket?" Officer Tierney asks, peering at the ripped-open twin pack over her glasses.

I shake my head. "Nope. No receipt either. I checked."

Her expression is grave. "And the police think she had her wallet on her when she disappeared, so there's no way of checking for a receipt there. I'll have them scan her bank statements, see if there's a transaction at a chemist or pharmacy which could fit. Hard to tell, though. They aren't itemized, bank statements."

I look at the bar code—it contains an abbreviated reference to the firm who produce them. "It's a well-known brand," I say. "I'm sure the RRP wouldn't be difficult to find. Then you could cross-check that."

"True. But if she picked it up at a supermarket with her bread and milk, the price would be skewed. It's a long shot."

I must look downtrodden, because she adds, "You did the right thing bringing it to me, though, Carina. Really. Thank you. This could help."

I force a smile, even though it's the last thing I feel like doing. "Will you tell her mum?"

She chews her bottom lip, smeared with rose-colored lipstick. "I'm not sure yet. It could upset her more, and until we're certain . . ."

"Will you ever be certain?" I ask.

"Maybe not. But if there's nothing on her medical records and we can't find a match on her bank statements, it'd probably do more harm than good to bring it up."

"But she might know something," I point out. "And there might be something in the house. Like . . . the other pregnancy test."

She looks deep in thought. "I'll see how the other checks come back and take it from there."

"Is there anything else I can do to help?" I ask. Probably a stupid question. I'm no detective. I regret asking as soon as I do.

"Just look after yourself, sweetheart." A warm, maternal smile. "And get some rest. You look exhausted."

That's one word for it.

IT'S WELL OVER an hour by the time I get back to the office from the police station, and even though Lowe peers down from her mezzanine, she doesn't say anything. Just nods. It's a weird moment.

Normally I'd be hung, drawn and quartered for taking too long on my lunch break.

I pause before I turn down the mini-corridor to the fashion cupboard. Psyche myself up. Turn, head up to Lowe's mezzanine.

She looks utterly alarmed. I've never had the guts to enter her space uninvited.

It's a clean, urban space. Apparently the company who rented the office space before *Northern Heart* had a peace-and-love hippie of a CEO—she lit incense and invited all her staff to meetings on beanbags surrounding her desk. Lowe did away with all that non-sense. Now it's all quirky ladder bookshelves, oversized floor lamps and a huge desk piled high with back issues of *Vogue* and *Tatler*.

There are two sleek blue-and-silver chairs—the most uncom-fortable on the planet—in front of her desk. She gestures to one. Before I can change my mind, I hastily grab one and plonk myself ungracefully down.

"I, uh . . ." *Oh, for goodness' sake. After everything that's hap-pened, you're still afraid of your dragonness editor?* "Erin's stuff. In the shoebox. I wanted to take it back to her mum. Is that okay?" I don't mention the jacket. Paige has that now.

She looks surprised. Proactivity in the face of tragedy prob-ably doesn't seem like it'd be my strong suit. "Sure. You know her mother?"

"I met her once." It's not a lie. Erin had a bad stomach flu around Easter, and though she tried to stick it out at work, I made her go home at lunchtime when she nearly passed out on me. Called her mum on her behalf, waited with her outside, piled her into the ancient tin can of a car. Explained how I'd already cleared it with Lowe, which was a lie. Like I say, I've always been scared of her. Anyway. Karen Baxter was grateful, and Lowe got over it.

Lowe purses her lips. "I wonder how she's doing. Poor woman. I can't even imagine . . ." Her voice catches. "If one of mine were to . . . I just . . . I don't know what I'd do." She's staring at her hands, shaking her head slowly. Clears her throat. "Anyway. Yes, that's fine. Do you need to leave early?" I swear her eyes are shinier than normal.

"No, it's okay. Thank you, though."

A gentle nod. In a soft voice: "I hope they find her."

"Me, too."

I guess she is human, underneath it all. I imagine her going home tonight and hugging her kids twice as hard as usual. And in that moment, I'm no more scared of her than I am my own reflection.

Grief is a leveler. A reminder we're all the same, deep down.

ERIN'S HOUSE IS like her, full of inconsistencies. A small but perfectly mown lawn, unruly flower beds. Open windows, drawn curtains. Endless clutter filling the rest of the space, bikes and toys Erin and her sister have long grown out of. A small terraced home, fraying around the edges.

Erin hasn't lived here for years. She's draining her savings renting her own one-bedroom flat on the city's quayside, desperately clutching at the threads of independence her decision to intern nearly stole from her. She suspects Lowe is on the cusp of offering her a paid position, so she keeps sticking it out, keeps saying no when her mum begs her to move back in.

"I'm twenty-fucking-five," she told me, every time it came up. "I'd rather live on the street with my pride intact than live with my mum and sister again."

I get it. This house in front of me must have been the stage for countless acts of violence at the hands of her father. What did these walls witness? I picture pillows muffling sobs. I picture blood seeping into carpets and Erin's mother scrubbing them with bleach before her daughters saw. I picture screams and yells drifting up through the chimney, loosening soot and ashes, sending the nesting doves fluttering away in fright.

I shudder as I walk up the drive. Nearly trip over a dog's mangled tennis ball and a tooth-marked chew toy. Their Labrador died months ago.

This family was falling apart long before Erin disappeared.

The familiar wave of nausea ripples through me as I knock. My rational brain—which I'm surprised still works, if I'm honest—says, "Karen Baxter is a grieving mother and frankly does not give one single shit how you behave today." Anxiety brain says, "DANGER DANGER RUN AWAY BEFORE YOU MAKE AN ARSE OF YOURSELF." I grip the shoebox of Erin's belongings. The owl on her coffee mug gazes up at me.

Tears prick my eyes. When I was a little girl, I genuinely believed my teddy bear had a soul. I kissed it before I left for school every morning, because God forbid a stuffed animal felt unloved, and I made sure he was always sitting comfortably on my bed with a perfect view of the room. I'm twenty-six now, and he still feels like more than stuffing and synthetic fur in my arms.

That's what Erin's things feels like: more than things. They're pieces of her.

The door opens. "Carina. Come in, come in." Karen hugs me, and I don't care that it's far too familiar from someone I've only met once, because she smells like her. She smells like Erin.

The whole house does. White lily detergent and stale coffee and something a little more human.

We go to the kitchen. She offers me tea, and even though I'd kill for a cuppa, I say no, because I'm British and thus polite above all else. I slide the shoebox onto the oak table, but don't take a seat. Because . . . British. "How are you doing, Karen? Is there anything I can do?"

"I'm all right, pet." She flicks the kettle on despite the fact I declined. Gets two mugs out, and a packet of chocolate biscuits. "Money troubles, as usual. County court bailiffs banging down my door. Repossessing everything I own to pay for everything I don't. But I'm trying to keep busy. Not lose hope. Talk to the FLO as much as I can. Lovely woman. You've met her, haven't you?"

"Paige? Yes. She's great. She mentioned you were planning to fly out—Saturday, she thought?"

Her hands tremble as she scoops sugar into the mugs. She swallows, hard. "I was planning to, yes, but the detective leading the investigation over there said it might be too upsetting for me at the moment. I'm going out next Saturday instead. I keep thinking . . . w-what if she's found before then, and I'm not there to be with her? She'll be scared, so scared. God knows what she's been through. And her silly old mother is too fragile to even be in the town where she vanished. I—I . . . I don't want her to be alone."

I read the subtext: What if she's found before then, and she's dead, and Karen didn't even have the courage to go to her? Would she even be able to board a plane and fly out there now, knowing she'd be met with her daughter's body?

I wouldn't be strong enough either.

"She won't be alone," I say softly. "And if they find her, I'm sure you can catch the very next flight out there. Be with her in a matter of hours."

She nods. Stares at the kettle as it bubbles. I wonder what she's thinking, whether she genuinely believes that's something that might happen. That Erin might be found alive. "It makes me question whether I knew my daughter at all."

I frown. That's not what I expected her to say next. "What do you mean?"

A heavy sigh. She tucks a loose lock of dyed-blond hair behind her ear. "They ask all those vague questions, right? About her acting out of character, about whether she was happy, whether she was troubled. And you think you know the answers, but over time, you become less and less sure of yourself. Was she really happy? Did I miss something? Did I . . . d-did . . ." She chokes on her words. "Did I fail? As a mother? As a friend?"

If I had the slightest ounce of social skills, maybe I'd go to her, hug her shoulders, reassure her. She didn't fail. She's a wonderful mother.

But I don't. I stand there, awkward, secretly relieved I'm not the only one who's losing my grasp on Erin's true identity. "I feel the same," I whisper, so quietly she might not have heard. "Everything's distorted in my memory. Like when you're trying to remember a dream, and at first you're sure of what happened, who was there, where it took place . . . and then you realize actually it wasn't your mother, or your daughter, or your schoolteacher, but someone who looked nothing like them, acted nothing like them. It wasn't your home or your office, just a place that felt remarkably like it. The details slip away. It's all abstract, in shadow."

Karen's shaking. The kettle has boiled. She ignores it. Keeps staring at the mugs, her hands gripping the counter so hard her knuckles are ghostly white. "Deep down . . . in your gut. Do you think she was happy?"

I know what the kind answer is. I also know what the honest answer is. They are not the same.

But what good is a kind lie at a time like this? Nothing can ease the pain of a missing child. So I say it.

"No."

I expect her shoulders to slump. I expect her to howl. I expect her to implode.

"Neither do I."

We both stand in silence. Through the gap in conversation, a heavy-metal track bellowing about the injustice in the world floats down the stairs. Erin's teenage sister.

"How's Annabel coping?" I ask quietly.

Karen snaps out of her daze. Pours the water into the mugs. Stirs, for far too long. "Angrily. The way she copes with everything."

I think of her abusive father, about to be released from prison. Treading carefully, I say, "Understandable, I guess. It's a lot to deal with, especially at that age. And the timing . . ." I watch for a reaction. None. "I guess she has a lot on her mind."

Flatly, Karen responds, "You know about Simon."

"I do."

That's when her shoulders sag. "I should have done more to protect my babies. I should have left him long ago. I should have . . . shit. Five years seemed so long. Long enough for us to move away, far, far away, and start a new life. That was the plan. It always was. To bring the bastard down, and then to run. But when it finally happened, when we finally convicted him . . . running away just felt like the coward's way out. Like we were letting him win."

She's still stirring. Erratic. Angry. Metal clashing and scraping against china again and again. "To tear Annabel and Erin away from their lives . . . surely that would cause more harm than good? I kept agonizing over it. Kept saying I'd make a decision tomorrow, next week, next month. And now here we are. He's getting out next month, and Erin is gone."

I'll confess. When I first learned of Erin's father—and the fact he was about to run free—my initial reaction was one of shock. That Karen hadn't taken them all away from this town. Somewhere he could never find them again. But that's fucked up. Internalized victim blaming. Now, hearing the guilt in Karen's voice, I want to drag the shame from her heart and set it on fire. It. Is. Not. Her. Fault.

"Is that the main reason you believe she was unhappy in the last few months?" I ask. Or was there more? The pregnancy test is at the back of my mind. "Fear?"

"She was always the least forgiving of him. Every time I took him back, believed him when he said he'd change, I'd immediately try and continue as if nothing had happened. Thought it was the best way, you know? Tried to keep him happy, relaxed, neutralized. Normal. For them. But she could never forgive, never forget, and I don't know how I ever expected her to. A part of her died every time he lashed out, and so a part of me did, too. Even after he went down, those perished pieces of her never did come back. Because he was still her dad. She still loved him. I know she did."

My heart's aching for Erin. "Did she ever visit him?"

"A little. Not for a while, but once the emotional scars started to heal, she did try. It was hard for her, seeing him like that. But she persevered. Annabel never did."

"Why?" I mumble. I can't wrap my head around it. "Why would she ever want to see him again after what he did?"

"Because the same person who beat her is the same person who taught her to ride a bike. For the first fifteen years of her life, he was her hero. He worked away a lot, but whenever he was home, he treated her and Annabel like princesses. Took them to theme parks, movies, petting zoos. Bought them a telescope, spent hours teaching them about astronomy. Did silly puppet shows to cheer them up whenever they fell on the playground and scraped their knees. He was an amazing father." She messily wipes away a tear with the heel of her hand. Passes me my tea. "Until he wasn't."

"What changed?"

She drags a chair back, takes a seat. Gestures for me to do the same. Annabel's angry music is even louder now. "His whole world. When his mum got really sick, he couldn't cope. Turned to drink. Her prognosis was terrible." My expression is blank. "Erin's grandmother had a rare genetic disorder. Aubin's syndrome. Manifests later in life, like Parkinson's. She was an empty shell. Simon adored that woman, and he couldn't cope with her demise. Then the financial crash happened, and we just about survived, but that sense of stability was gone. He started drinking even more. And the drink, coupled with the grief, is what ruined him."

"I'm sorry," I whisper.

"She was a wonderful lady, Simon's mother. I miss her hugely. The way she was with the girls . . . before it all went downhill . . . it was exactly how Simon was with them. Pure, unadulterated love. She'd have done anything for them."

"She died?"

"A few months after Simon went to jail. I always thought it was the shame that killed her. She thought she'd raised a monster. She blamed herself. We women always tend to do that." She takes a sip of tea. Flinches at the heat. "Erin especially. Whenever something goes wrong in her life, Erin lashes out. Not at the world, but at herself."

Chapter Twelve

July 29, England

IT TAKES AN eternity for noon to drag around, but it does. I've arranged to see Officer Tierney again. She sounded stressed when I called—her caseload is probably impossible—but agreed to meet me at the station on my lunch break. We're in her tiny office, not the interview room. There's a dead orchid and a stack of old newspapers on her desk. The *Daily Standard*. I still haven't heard back about my job application.

"So you didn't ask directly about the pregnancy," she says. Her lips are deep red today. "That's good. Thank you."

I shake my head. Try to smooth my crumpled shirt I didn't have time to iron this morning. "Just tried to hint at it. Leave openings she could fill. But I definitely don't think she knows anything about it. We pretty much focused on her father. And his impending release."

"We've talked about that a lot, too. Poor girls." She chews her full lip. "If there's anything to the pregnancy scare . . . well. It's just . . . it'd be a lot to cope with."

"Yes . . ." I say slowly. Is she insinuating something? Or am I reading too much into it, as usual?

She swivels in her chair. Turns to look out the window, down the river. Raps a biro on the plastic arm. "I'd just . . . I would worry. If I was the detective on this case."

"That she did something to herself?" I retort. "No. She wouldn't."

Silence.

"Did you hear anything back about the checks you were running? Her medical records? Bank statements?" Desperation stings the back of my throat like bile.

"Not yet. I only relayed the information yesterday afternoon. These things take time."

Her voice is distant, like she's mentally gone somewhere else. It's pissing me off that she has her back to me. Is she trying to subtly imply I should leave? Am I annoying her? My knee starts bouncing up and down. Chest tightens. I don't want her to be mad at me. I need her on my side; I need her to care like I do. I thought she did, but . . .

"Have you ever heard of Brodie Breckenridge?" she asks, so quietly I almost miss it.

"No." A pause. "Wait. Yes." Where have I heard that name? I riffle through my recent memories, searching for the needle in the haystack.

I find it. My library research. I stumbled upon a short article about her when I was searching for Brits who've gone missing in the Balkans.

"She disappeared in Croatia," I say. "She was young. British. Ten years ago? Twelve, maybe?"

"Eight. And yes, you're right. She was young, British. Vanished into thin air in Dubrovnik in 2007." She turns slowly back to face me. Her neck is so narrow she's almost bird-like. "A reporter. She was on a press trip."

I sit up straighter. I hadn't read that far into it. How could I have missed it? My brain begins whirring. "A press trip like ours?"

"A press trip very much like yours, yes." She squints at me, or maybe just past me, like she's looking over my shoulder for an answer to a burning question. "In fact, it was almost identical. Because it was led by none other than Tim Halsey."

I swear the temperature drops ten degrees.

"Tim?" I gape at her. "The same Tim?"

"The same Tim."

My stomach twists. "How did the Serbian police miss this?"

"They didn't." She shrugs, but it's anything but nonchalant. "In both cases they've interviewed him extensively. Put him through the ringer, as far as I can tell. He's clean as a whistle. He's never been made an official suspect, but he's on standby to fly back out there if they need him again. Isn't supposed to leave the UK. They say they're likely to need to speak to him again at various stages of the investigation . . . I guess they're going to try and find any other parallels they can between Erin and Brodie."

"It . . . It can't just be coincidence. It—" I shake my head violently, trying to get the furious thought-jumping to stop. I keep settling on one. Andrijo. "Tim says he met Andrijo in 2014. What if they could prove that's a lie? Find something that links them before then? Would that be enough of an inconsistency to label him a suspect? Or at least to dig further into his past?"

Her eyes widen. She grabs one of the old newspapers and scribbles something down in biro. "Great thought. Can you remember when he told you it was 2014?"

I cast my mind back. I remember the conversation well—I've replayed it in my mind so many times, scrawled various versions around Sudoku puzzles and Buddhist mandalas. It was on the plane.

"I've known Borko for years. We met in 2005, I think, the first year I did the JUMP press trip."

"And Andrijo?"

"I met him for the first time last year. Seems nice enough."

"Wednesday twenty-second of July," I say. "A week ago today."

I relay the conversation to her. She keeps jotting down notes in the newspaper's bleed.

"Do you know anything about how Andrijo and Borko were interviewed? Were they treated as suspects?"

She shrugs. "Not officially. But the police view everyone as a potential suspect, and evaluate them accordingly. Inconsistencies in that phase are huge, so the information you've just given me could help enormously. Thank you."

I nod. She's being open with me, and so even though the self-preservation part of my anxiety-riddled brain is screaming at me not to, I ask, "And do you know what their alibis are? Where they were when Erin disappeared?"

Pressing her lips together, she looks torn. But her professionalism wins out. "I'm sorry, Carina. You know I'm not at liberty to discuss sensitive information like that."

I want to scream, *But you just told me about Tim's involvement in Brodie's case!*

It's probably different, though. That case has been closed for years, I'd imagine, so it's no longer "sensitive information." Still . . . it sort of pertains to Erin's investigation. Has she crossed a line? The anguish on her face certainly suggests so. I also get the sense there's more she wants to ask me, like whether I found Tim strange or suspicious. But she can't, because this isn't an official interview, and she isn't a detective.

"Thanks for stopping by, Carina. And for treating Karen with kindness and respect. I truly appreciate it, and I promise you, we really are doing everything we can to find your friend."

MY LAPTOP MOANS as it whirs to life. I've had it since my first week of university eight years ago, and even then it was a largely useless piece of crap. I make another cup of tea while it almost gives itself the computer equivalent of an aneurism trying to connect to the Wi-Fi.

As I see the new email notification, my heart thuds. Helen Hammond from the *Daily Standard*.

I got an interview. Friday.

A grin breaks out across my face for the first time in nearly three weeks.

Yes.

Yes.

And then I burst into tears.

How can I still feel joy? How is that possible? The guilt is overwhelming. Erin is gone. No matter what the outcome, she's been through something unimaginable, and maybe hasn't even survived it. And I'm smiling about a job application. I grip the bangle, our bangle, and try to stifle the racking sobs. Bury my face in the duvet.

Is this how it's going to be for the rest of my life?

A dark part of me understands Smith's selfish concerns about his own future. Because yes, Erin is the victim, but we're collateral damage. None of our lives will ever be the same again. Karen, Annabel. Even Lowe—touched by this grief so raw anyone can see it and hurt.

Is it completely and utterly fucked up to celebrate a small victory?

Am I grieving right?

Am I even supposed to be grieving at this point?

Exhaustion drags my limbs into the mattress. Medication is dulling my mind. There's no energy left; it's been sapped by heartache and pain. The interview is a glimmer in a dark, dark night. A night I don't think will ever end.

The house is silent—my brother Jake's plugged into his Xbox downstairs, headset in full play. Mum's asleep. I crawl into bed. Prop up my pillows behind me, switch the lights off so all I can see is the glaring screen.

Type into the search engine: "Brodie Breckenridge."

This time, it pulls dozens of articles from the cyber ether.

It's not as high profile as I'd expected, but she vanished in May 2007—around the same time as Madeleine McCann. Pretty much all the major news coverage was assigned to Kate and Gerry's pleas for their daughter's safe return, and Brodie slipped under the radar. Still, I find enough information to get a grasp on her case.

Brodie Ellen Breckenridge. Twenty-eight years old. A journalist with a major British broadsheet. A press trip with the Croatian tourism board. Went on a night out with some locals in Dubrovnik on May 18, and was never seen again.

Tim doesn't appear in any of the coverage, but why would he? At the time he was nothing more than a SigWit. I doubt my name crops up in any of Erin's PR. I still can't bring myself to look.

After a few weeks, the articles fizzle out, make way for a fresh wave of international disasters. From what I gather, the case was never solved. There were no promising leads, no significant suspects, no reported sightings with any real credibility.

Please don't let history repeat itself.

As strange as it sounds, it's the picture of Brodie that chills me most. It's not that she looks creepily like Erin, just enough so that it's noticeable: blond hair, red lipstick, big smile. She was beautiful. Maybe this is all as simple as sexual assault gone bad. Maybe there's no big conspiracy. Maybe Erin and Brodie were in the wrong place at the wrong time, and their beauty got them in trouble with male predators. I don't want to believe the world is that vulgar, but things happen every day to prove it is.

There's another similarity between them, one too obvious to ignore. They're both journalists. Did someone have a vendetta against reporters? Did Tim?

The police investigated him. He's clean as a whistle. And even I can't deny seeing him in the VIP bar at the time Erin went missing.

Plus, there are eight years between them. He's led countless other press trips in that time, ones probably involving dozens of other beautiful blondes, all which have occurred without incident.

Unless Andrijo is the real connection.

Beautiful face. Coal-black eyes. Intensity so sharp it cuts through you.

Where was he on May 18, 2007?

Chapter Thirteen

July 30, England

"I HURT HER."

Smith is a mess. Not even wearing a suit—he hasn't been to work in days. Puffy eyes, part-hangover, part-grief. It's raining in the churchyard. He doesn't notice as beads of water run down his forehead, dripping off his brow and into his eyes. My umbrella is doing nothing to keep me dry.

I want to console him. I do. But the image of Erin in that toilet cubicle, clawing the walls, howling like a wounded animal, is too powerful to forget. *"He used to see me as an equal, but now I'm just some dumb fashion bimbo. Like the rest of them. I've taken his dream from him by following mine."* I hated the shame she carried with her in the weeks after he apologized. She couldn't forget it. She felt like less, when really she's so much more.

Karen. *"Whenever something goes wrong in her life, Erin lashes out. Not at the world, but at herself."*

And that's why Smith's self-indulgent remorse falls flat at my feet.

He takes my silence as an invitation to continue. "I should've supported her. I should've . . . I should've done everything in my power to make her happy. To keep her safe. I'd give anything to go back and do over. I . . . I love her, Carina. I really do. You probably think I'm a total bastard. I wouldn't blame you. I've fucked up. There's no denying that. But the thought of anything bad happening to her . . ." He drops his head into his hands. His gray jumper is soaked through. "Fuck."

I force myself to say, "It's not your fault." Because even though he's right, and I do think he's a total bastard, his douchebaggery really is not to blame for her disappearance.

Despite my animosity, I agreed to see him again because I needed to do more probing about the possible pregnancy. He may not have explicitly known about the test, but surely he can look back on her behavior over the last few months and figure out whether she had an inkling? They spent so much time together. Was she drinking? On work nights out, she's always stuck to vodka, lime and soda. She could easily have skipped the vodka and none of us would've been any the wiser. But on their date nights and family events, it would've been harder to hide. Or was he so wrapped up in himself he didn't notice? It wouldn't surprise me.

And her mental state. I know it's tough to separate the possible pregnancy from the turmoil over her father's release, but they've been together nine years. He should know her well enough by now that something so huge could never slip under the radar. Should.

Her body would've changed, too. She's tall and slender, so even though a bump probably wouldn't show up that fast, I hear boobs swell like crazy in the first trimester. Smith's a guy. If he's gonna notice anything, it'd be that.

Something twists in my stomach. The idea of Erin, pregnant, going through all of this, a half-formed child in her womb, is too much. I almost don't want to know. Because if it was true, it'd be too horrifying to even comprehend.

A baby. Erin.

Both dead.

The familiar tightening in my chest brings a rush of dread.

No. Not here. Not now.

Inhale, exhale, inhale, exhale.

Just breathe. Keep breathing. Don't stop breathing. It's the only thing you can control.

Smith's talking but he's far away, near a gravestone, on top of the steeple, buried underground, somewhere I can't hear him.

The umbrella clatters to the ground.

This isn't real this isn't real none of this is real.

She's fine. Erin is fine. Her baby is fine.

I can't tell where my anxiety ends and my grief begins.

I cannot survive this. Neither can Smith. We are collateral damage. We are broken.

Swallowed in this gaping black hole, this hollow darkness, the absence of light between stars.

The loss of her.

I collapse into him, and sob until there's nothing left.

Chapter Fourteen

July 31, England

LESS THAN THREE weeks after she vanished, I'm already trying to forget her existence.

It hurts too much to think of her. And I can't afford to be incapacitated by grief.

As painful as it is to forget Erin, it's nowhere near as agonizing as it is to remember. And so, with a dream job and my own sanity on the line, I double up my meds and embrace the delicious numbness. Much as I wish I didn't, I need to survive.

I'm using my hour-long lunch break to go to my job interview. The *Daily Standard* offices are only a few hundred meters from *Northern Heart*, and hopefully Lowe won't question the fact I'm dressed far more smartly than usual.

My morning in the fashion cupboard is spent in a state of med-induced relaxation. I brought a list of possible interview questions to rehearse as I steam clothes for a shoot, as well as a ton of information I found about the publication's history. But my brain is too quiet. Nothing sticks to the peaceful white noise. A drug-induced haze. It's fucking great. For the first time in too long, nothing hurts. I'm no longer navigating a battlefield of emotional land mines and traumatic open fire, where the bullets are memories and my subconscious is holding the gun.

In fact, I feel so calm I could curl up and sleep. There's a huge fur coat we were sent for our A/W shoot . . . it'd make the perfect blanket. My eyelids start to droop at the prospect. Nothing has ever felt more alluring than a nap in this very moment. Slumber pulls me under. Maybe if I sleep for five or ten minutes, I'll wake up superrefreshed for my interview.

I'm asleep before I even hit the ground.

"CARINA!"

The piercing shriek wakes me. I barely felt the hands on my shoulders, shaking me frantically.

"Wha . . . ? Lowe?" My throat's impossibly dry. Why am I on the floor of the fashion cupboard? Curled up in a fur coat like Cruella fucking de Vil?

Lowe's outline is blurry, but I can sense the panic.

"Jesus, Carina, you scared the hell out of me! What the . . . ?"

Okay, maybe not panic. Anger.

"I—I'm . . . sorry . . . I just . . . what time is it?"

"I almost called an ambulance, sweetie. What happened? Did you pass out?"

"No," I say, suddenly unsure. "No, I just . . . I got really tired. I'm sorry. I upped my dose of medication, is all. Maybe too high. I'm . . . m'sorry."

She shakes her head, impatient. "Stop apologizing. Are you all right? Did a doctor authorize your new dosage, or did you self-prescribe?"

My silence tells her all she needs to know.

A sigh. Not patronizing, but not far away. "Listen, Carina. I know you've been through a lot. This must be incredibly difficult for you. Anybody would take this hard, and I know you have a more fragile disposition than most." I grit my teeth. "Maybe it's best if you take some time off. Time to clear your head."

Something's fighting through the haze, but it's dressed in shadows. "Really, Lowe, I'm fine. That's not necessary. I'll see my GP. Sort out my dose. I'll be fine, I swear." I gulp back the lump in my throat. "I need this. It's all I have." A sympathetic head tilt. "Besides. You need me here. Have you seen the state of this place?" I try for a joke, but my words are so slurred it's just kind of tragic.

"You're right. I should've sacked you a long time ago." Her joke is funnier than mine, but I still can't smile. "But really. Don't worry about that, love. We have another intern starting next week, to replace . . . well, she's starting next week. So we could cope without you for a while."

That cuts through the fog. I tremble. Push myself up onto my elbows. "You . . . you're replacing her already?"

"Well, we have the fashion supplement coming up, and we need as many hands on deck as we can. And . . . well. Even if Erin does come back, I doubt she'll want to jump straight back into work. She may have been through a lot. It makes sense, Carina."

The buzz of anger is unfamiliar. It's not usually my default reaction, but this feels so callous, so hasty. "You've given up on her. After everything she's done for *Northern Heart*, you're giving up."

"Listen—"

"No. This is just . . . it's so disrespectful. I'd have thought even you would—"

Now she snaps. Climbs to her feet. Purple-painted lips pucker in anger. "Even me? Who do you think you're talking to?!"

I'm too weak to stand, my legs folded pathetically under me, but I still find some venom to inject into my words. "You didn't even publish her fashion reports on the site. Did they not uphold your demanding standards? Even after she potentially lost her life on that trip, you still can't find it in yourself to publish something less than perfect?" I snarl. I don't know where the rage is coming from, how it's even piercing my cloudy mind, but it feels strangely good. "She was killing herself for you, Lowe. She would've given anything to graduate above intern level. You know what? I think you were intimidated by her. By her beauty, her passion, her gift. Her youth. I bet you're glad she's gone."

She stabs a finger at me, hand trembling with anger. "She never sent me any reports. Too busy having a grand old time to do any work, I assume. Was I pissed? Hell, yes, I was. But to insinuate I'm glad she could be dead? Don't you dare. Don't you fucking dare, little girl."

The numbness shatters.

I WAS FIRED. And, as I was leaving the office with my tail between my legs, the clock chimed three.

I lost my internship, and I slept through my job interview, and the depression is so heavy I don't even care.

None of it matters. None of it matters in this cruel, cruel world.

The sadness swallows me whole. I let it.

I STOP BY my mum's house on the way home. She's washed her hair, and is actually blow-drying it back into a neat ponytail, rather than leaving it to puff up into an unmanageable afro like she usually does.

"Working tonight, Mum?" I drop my keys into the bowl by the front door. She's picked up a job at a pub down the road. The money from selling my dad's business isn't running out just yet, but it's good for her to get out. Meet people, earn a few bucks.

"Yeah. Five 'til close. Payday weekend, too. Town'll be mobbed. You have any plans?"

Crawl into bed and never leave again because what's the point? "Nah, nothing. Might see if Jake wants to catch a movie or something. There's a new Marvel film out he wants to see."

She lays down her hairbrush on the vanity chest we picked up at a thrift store. We painstakingly painted it duck-egg blue, stenciled the drawers with white rose appliqués. That was one of her good days. She turns to face me. I try to hide my surprise at how old she looks. Fine lines wrinkle her eyes. Jowls have settled around her jaw. "I appreciate you, Carina. Really, I do. How strong you are. How you care for us."

I want to cry as she walks over to me, still standing in the doorway, and cups my face. "I know the last few years have been hard for you, since your father passed. And I know I haven't always been the best mother . . . I've relied far too heavily on you, and that was unfair of me."

I'm about to speak, to tell her it's okay and that she doesn't have to worry about me and that I'd do it forever if I had to, but she presses a thumb to my lips. "But now . . . now you're going through something very hard. And it's time for me to step up and be a mother. A real one." Her eyes are glistening. So are mine. She swipes one of my tears away. "You're so special. So bright. This internship is just the beginning for you. I feel it in my bones."

She pecks a kiss on my forehead, and I dissolve. Tears come thick and fast.

No, I want to scream at her. I failed. I fell apart. I met with disaster and it destroyed me.

THE MORE THE medication wears off, the worse I feel. The shame comes first. Hot, burning shame over the way I spoke to Lowe, after she's been so great the last few weeks.

"You know what? I think you were intimidated by her. By her beauty, her passion, her gift. I bet you're glad she's gone."

I cringe, curling myself up in a tight ball in my bed, wishing I could scrub the ugly, ugly words from my memory. Shaking, I press my fingers into my eyes until kaleidoscopic spots appear.

I don't even deserve a job.

And what kind of idiot sleeps through the job interview of a lifetime? I tried to numb myself to the pain of losing Erin, but I opened up a whole new world of regret. I cry even harder, huge, rasping sobs, when I imagine coming home and telling my mum I finally made it. I finally got a job.

Instead I have nothing.

Even through the tears, there's something niggling in the periphery of my mind. Something demanding to be seen. Lowe said something today, something that mattered, and I can't quite . . .

I freeze. Stop crying abruptly.

That's it.

Erin didn't submit any fashion reports.

Why?

We were so focused on that day. The day she disappeared.

What happened in the days before? What happened to stop her doing the job she loved more than anything?

I sit bolt upright in the dark room. Grab my laptop from where I left it on the floor after my last research session. As it fires up, I riffle through my handbag for the coloring book and a pen. Start jotting down as much as I can remember from the Friday and Saturday of the trip.

Friday. She definitely said she was going to an internet café to work—the hotel Wi-Fi wasn't fast enough to upload high-res photos to the *Northern Heart* Dropbox account. Did she have problems once she got there? Was the broadband still not good enough? I'm sure she would have mentioned that to Lowe, though. This doesn't make any sense.

Why?

Pulling my hair into a bun, I prop myself up in bed. Clean my tearstained face with a dried-up makeup wipe. Bring up the remote access email server for *Northern Heart*. Log in to Erin's account.

We all have a variation of the same password. Hers is NHBaxter1014. Mine's NHCorbett1014. NH, surname, the month and year we joined.

There are dozens of unread emails. Nobody's been checking her account in her absence, probably assuming that an intern has no important correspondence to check. They'd be right. It's mainly press releases from fashion brands, beauty e-letters and invites to design graduate fashion shows in London. The odd email chain with pushy PRs asking if she liked the pashminas they sent, and whether they'd be making it into the next issue. All unanswered.

Her sent box is pretty unremarkable. Some of the dates do match up with the time we were in Serbia, but they're mostly just PR inquiries she's forwarded to the fashion editor to deal with. The only accompanying text from Erin is *Sent from my iPhone*. So they weren't accessed from the internet café.

I'm about to log out when I notice the bolded folder on the side panel: Drafts (1). I click.

There's something there: 10 July 2015. Linda Lowe in the addressee field. I open it.

> To: editor@northernheartmagazine.co.uk
> Subject: JUMP fashion report, day one
> Date: Fri, 10 July 2015 14:05:21 +0200
> From: e.baxter@northernheartmagazine.co.uk
> Hi, Linda,
> Hope all's well at *Northern Heart* HQ!
> Please find attached the first draft of my day one fashion report from JUMP—hope it's all right. If the subeditor has many changes, feel free to fire them over and I'll make the amendments down this end.
> Currently uploading the accompanying images to Dropbox, so

And then it cuts off. It was never finished, never sent.

What the hell happened at five past two in the internet café? Why did she never send that email?

It's too weird. Until now I've had problems defining "out of character," but this certainly is. My heart thuds. The world seems to think Erin was raped. Left for dead. Sexual assault gone bad. After all, that's how most missing girls turn up.

But this proves—or at least hints—that something was awry at least two days before she disappeared.

Doesn't it?

Exhaustion clings to my body like cigarette smoke, but I'm mentally alert.

Think, Carina.

I'm not the greatest technology whizz, but I try to find some kind of location stamp on the draft. An IP address. Anything.

Nada. If I could narrow down which internet café she was in, maybe it'd help. I don't know how, but I'm running out of ideas. If only her laptop used location services, like her phone—

Like her phone.

I grab mine from under my pillow. Open the messaging app we use to spam each other with pointless crap. Our ongoing conversation is full of funny memes, tales of public transport woes and messages along the lines of *I'm grabbing a Starbucks before work, want the usual?* It physically hurts to scroll through and read, like someone's plunged a knife into my heart. But I know what I'm looking for.

That Friday afternoon, while Erin was working, I was in a pavement café with Jin Ra and Clara. We had pancake stacks bigger than our heads, and I sent her a picture saying: *Me and my leaning tower of awesomeness wish you were here!* She pinged back saying, *OMG! That's just cruel. I'll be here crying into my laptop. SAVE ME SOME. Bitch.* Sent at 14:01:57 +0200. I swipe the message to the side, praying she enabled in-app mobile location.

Bingo.

Povezivanje Kafe, Novi Sad.

They don't have a website, but I pull it up on street view on my laptop. I vaguely recognize it—it's on a side street off Zmaj Jovina, the main drag with pavement cafés and pastel-colored buildings, some sky blue with white gables, some pale yellow with chipped green woodwork and some candyfloss pink with cream-colored cornicing.

I screenshot the shopfront, try to imagine Erin sitting in there working. It doesn't fit, but it must have happened. What could have stopped her working so abruptly that she didn't even send her email?

What do I know so far?

I riffle through the pages of my coloring book. My God, I really am nuts. There's a beautiful lotus flower illustration utterly destroyed by my biro scrawls. The publisher who prints the adult coloring books—claiming they're excellent for inducing a sense of relaxation and calm—would have a seizure if they could see my copy now.

I find a new page to ruin. A dainty dragonfly. Scribble *Povezivanje* at the top, underline it twice.

Okay. First, she could have been pregnant. Cramps? Some kind of pain in that general region?

A panic attack about her situation? They're sort of my area of expertise, but anyone could fall down the anxiety rabbit hole in that predicament.

After a moment's pause, I also jot down what Karen told me, and what I've ascertained myself: when things go wrong, Erin blames herself. Lashes out. Loses her touch on rationality. That could be relevant, or it could be nothing.

Next, her father. Did she receive a phone call from him? From the prison? From her mother or sister fretting about his release? I jot down the exact time the email draft saved, unsent. Make a note to tell the police to cross-check it with her phone records.

And the bruise. How could that tie into this? Maybe it wasn't as old as I thought. Maybe she sustained it on that day. Did somebody grab her in the café? Freak her out enough that she left, work unfinished, Lowe unanswered?

I make another note: tell police to check CCTV in the café at that time. Look for anyone approaching her, talking to her, touching her.

Andrijo? No. Even I know that's a huge stretch. No matter how potent his intensity.

Still. I write down: check Andrijo was at work on Friday, July 10. I forget his boss's name—the one who gave him the alibi—but I'm sure they can contact him again.

I zoom out of street view a little. What else is around Povezivanje Kafe? More shops and cafés, mainly. Liberty Square. The cathedral. Danube Park, where I sat and ate pistachio gelato with Tim, pretending not to be clinically insane. Digging for information about Andrijo.

It'd help if I knew where Andrijo worked—so I could see if it's near Povezivanje. Did Tim say he was with the tourism board? With the council? I rack my brains, but I don't think he ever mentioned it. I rub my temple—a tight tension headache is forming. Anxiety med withdrawals. Just what I need.

I tap my forefinger on my bottom lip. It's likely that if Erin visited this café on Friday, it could be where she spent the blank hour on Sunday. Though no one has come forward, as far as I know, with any reported sightings of her—surely a member of staff or another customer recognized her? You don't miss people like Erin. She's never faded into the background in her life.

For lack of anything better to do, I zoom out even farther. Flick from street view to map and back again. Frown. A few hundred yards away from the fish market, there's a big building site taking up almost an entire block—like all the houses have been demolished, the ground flattened, and they're starting again. But on the map view, the plot has a name: Bastixair Distribution Center.

Maybe the street view is out of date, and they haven't had a drone on the area in a while?

It's absolutely huge, whatever it is. I do a search for Bastixair— it's a veritable giant of a pharmaceutical company, employing thousands of workers across Serbia. I search for Andrijo's name, but they don't have all of their employees listed—only heads of department. There are a ton of news articles praising its scientific research and celebrating its job creation after the bloody Yugoslav Wars, plus a few excerpts from medical journals I have no hope of understanding. I'm about to click off the tab when a phrase catches my eye: *Aubin's syndrome.*

I gasp.

Erin's grandmother died of Aubin's syndrome.

Chapter Fifteen

July 31, England

THIS HAS TO be relevant.

"Erin's grandmother had a rare genetic disorder. Aubin's syndrome. Manifests later in life, like Parkinson's. She was an empty shell."

I do a quick internet search. According to the NHS website, it's a very rare illness. Only around one case in every 100,000 people in the UK.

"She was a wonderful lady, Simon's mother. I miss her hugely. The way she was with the girls . . . before it all went downhill . . . it was exactly how Simon was with them. Pure, unadulterated love. She'd have done anything for them."

There's no way this is a coincidence. Erin's grandmother, whom she loved dearly, suffered from a rare genetic disorder. Four years after she died from said disorder, Erin went missing within a few hundred yards of the Bastixair Distribution Center in Novi Sad. Bastixair, known for its research into Aubin's syndrome and easing its unpleasant symptoms.

Definitely not a coincidence.

I scan the NHS entry.

No cure.

I rub my tired eyes again. Think, think, think. How does this fit?

Maybe Erin was looking for a cure. For a way to ease the symptoms.

But why? Her grandmother is already dead.

Does her father suffer from it?

I freeze.

Does Erin suffer from it?

Does her baby?

It's late on a Friday night, so it's not like I'm surprised when Officer Tierney doesn't pick up, but a rush of disappointment floods me anyway. I leave a shaky voice mail—something about being told to leave a message after the tone unnerves me—and hang up.

Have the police uncovered this link yet? Maybe not. I only know about Erin's grandmother through talking to Karen at her kitchen table. I'm sure the detectives have spoken to her in great detail, but would an ailing grandmother, dead years ago, have come up?

Even if so, they may not have context for the piece of information, like I didn't until five minutes ago. Bastixair is right on their doorstep, but would they really know what medical research the pharmaceutical giant is carrying out? I'm undeniably ignorant when it comes to knowledge of what scientific discoveries are occurring in my home region. Why would they be any different? Besides, Aubin's might not have been mentioned at all.

I feel my heart beating: palpitations. Anxiety attacking me with vengeance after I tried to quell it with drugs. Coupled with fear over what I've just potentially discovered . . . the dose of adrenaline feels near-lethal.

Aubin's syndrome. Time to do some research.

Government health websites tell me all I need to know. It's a degenerative genetic disorder with harrowing symptoms. They start physically—muscle weakness, slow movement, difficulty walking and talking. The mental deterioration comes soon after. Dementia, depression, insomnia, behavioral changes. Sensory confusion. Emotional detachment.

My heart aches for Erin, watching her beloved grandmother become a stranger. Personality atrophy that'd soon drive her father to alcohol and violence. Cramps seize my chest.

I keep reading. The disease tends to manifest most commonly in old age, with most sufferers being over the age of seventy, but several cases of early onset Aubin's have been reported in the UK this year.

Was Erin one of them?

My mind goes a million miles an hour, a high speed chase between fear and curiosity. Physically, she was the same as always. Elegant, strong. Capable. Mentally? The words *depression* and *behavioral changes* leap off the screen.

I look for information on how the symptoms of early onset Aubin's differ, but find nothing.

Tugging my ridiculous coloring book out from under my pillow, I'm about to start making yet more notes when the blaring of my phone cuts through the darkness. Squinting at the screen, my stomach flips: Paige Tierney.

"Hello?" I say. My voice cracks. I grab my glass of water, sip thirstily.

"Carina? I got your voice mail. Is everything okay?" There's genuine concern in her voice. Either she's a great actress or she really does care. "You said it was important."

"I . . . guess." I clear my throat again. It's full of sawdust. "I was just . . . just calling about the case. Erin's case." Swallow. "I found something."

"In what respect?"

I almost say "a clue" before I remember I'm not in a Scooby Doo cartoon. "Just . . . something. Her grandmother. She died, a few years ago."

"Yes, Karen mentioned that. Erin was heartbroken. Who wouldn't be?"

Palpitations are getting more erratic. "Yeah. She, erm . . . she had an illness. A genetic disorder, called Aubin's syndrome. Did Karen mention that?"

A pause. I can hear a TV talk show on in the background. A studio audience laugh uproariously. I wonder if she's alone. Eventually she replies, "I'm not sure. She could have. I'm sorry, Carina, I don't have my notes in front of me."

Notes. She needs notes in order to remember the details of the case. Sometimes I forget other people don't think about Erin every second of every day.

"Right." I know my words will have much less impact now, but I persevere. "Well, Aubin's is a genetic disorder. No cure, but there's one pharmaceutical company in Europe who produce medication that eases the symptoms. It's based in Serbia."

More riotous laughter from her TV show in the pause that follows. "Oh. Okay. That's . . . interesting."

"It is," I insist, as if I'm trying to convince her of something terribly obvious like the sun's surface being hot. "Called Bastixair. And there's a distribution center just a few hundred yards from the internet café she was using in Novi Sad." My words are muddling together. "That can't be coincidence."

The silence that follows is painful. "When was the last time you slept, Carina?"

This afternoon, when I passed out at work for hours and was shaken awake by my boss, who promptly fired me.

"I . . . what? What does that have to do with anything?"

"I know this is very tough for you. Please tell me you're looking after yourself?"

"Yes," I mumble, suddenly a shy schoolgirl meeting a new teacher for the first time. My cheeks burn. She's dismissing me.

"Good. It's late. Go and get some rest. We can talk tomorrow, if you like?"

Paranoia tells me she knows. She knows how badly I fucked up today, and she's being all sympathetic and maternal, but also disregarding everything I'm saying as a symptom of insanity.

I don't want that. I want her to listen to me.

But after we hang up, I'm far less sure of the importance of my discovery.

I've messed with my meds and now I'm losing my mind.

Chapter Sixteen

August 1, England

I HAVE NO job, no friends, no life outside my desire to find Erin. But I can't do that in England. Not with a FLO who thinks (knows) I'm insane, and nobody else I can talk to about it.

Well, not nobody. Karen.

So when I call her, and ask if I can come with her to Serbia . . . I'm really hoping she'll say yes.

I want to go, and I want to slot all the little pieces of the puzzle into place back where it all began—or ended, depending on how you look at it. I want to prove to myself that my fear and my anxiety do not control me, and that I can overcome my problems when it really matters. Even without Erin.

So I hoped Karen would say yes. And she does.

She wants the company, she says, and she knows how close Erin and I am. Since her daughter started working all hours at *Northern Heart*, some of her university friends had started drifting away, and a lot of her high-school friends fell out a long time ago. Annabel refused to come. I'm the only one who bothered to visit Karen in the aftermath. I feel terrible when she says that—I had an ulterior motive. But still.

I ask about Smith, whether he'd want to come, too, but she tells me he's going off the rails. That does not surprise me. I think of the two of us sobbing in that graveyard, of how grief had swallowed him whole.

Karen picks me up. We talk mindlessly on the way to the airport. She's jittery with nerves about what's waiting for her in Serbia. Erin doesn't come up in conversation once, and somehow that's more awkward than discussing her. I imagine her in the backseat, listening to us dodge around her disappearance by talking about the weather and her new lipstick and how beautiful Belgrade's waterfront supposedly is. She'd probably find it hilarious, knowing Erin. She always had a morbid sense of humor.

Not had, I correct myself. Has.

I'd be lying if I said I'm not relieved we can't get seats together on the plane, since I booked so last minute. I appreciate the alone time on the flight, even though I just read the same page of my book over and over again and try to resist the drinks trolley as it clatters down the aisle. Alcohol is not a good move right now. Not when so much hangs in the balance.

I lean back in my seat, and sigh deeply. The morbidly obese man next to me, who smells of unwashed hair and dairy products, gives me a filthy look. Probably just for being a black girl and daring to exist in such close proximity to him. He eyes my purple dip-dyed hair with disdain. I can't even bring myself to react.

I press my eyes closed, though I'll never manage to sleep over the din of the airplane cabin. When we reach Novi Sad we're getting a taxi from Belgrade, because it'll be late. Karen and I will probably just check into our hotel and get some sleep. Tomorrow, though, I want to meet with Ilić again. Tell him everything I've discovered, even if none of it means anything. The baby, the disease, the café. He should know it all.

Then I want to visit the café myself. Scope it out. Ask the staff if they remember anything. I know I'm no detective, but I can't stand learning all this stuff, passing it over, then just hoping everyone else is good enough at their jobs to explore the avenue fully.

It's the paranoid control freak in me. She's hard to silence.

KAREN HUGS ME goodnight as we go to our separate rooms, and a wave of sympathy crashes down around me—the magnitude of her loneliness and grief is hard to comprehend. Her husband, a violent alcoholic, is in prison. Her oldest daughter is missing, feared dead. Her youngest daughter won't even leave her room; she tells her mother every day how much she hates her. Karen Baxter is losing everything, and right in this moment, I'd do anything to save her.

Still, I'm glad for my own space. I prop myself up in bed, surrounded by fluffy hotel pillows and goose-down duvets, and work on transcribing my coloring book scrawls into legible notes. Ilić may well laugh in my face, but I have to do it. I have to put myself out there.

For Erin.

Chapter Seventeen

August 3, Serbia

RAIN RICOCHETS OFF the cracked pavements. Puddles pool in the dips of the street. Liberty Square is drenched, and so am I. Wrapping my pristine notes in my scarf so they don't get ruined, I shuffle my squelching feet. Ilić is late.

It's Monday morning, and I'm seeing a different side of Novi Sad to the tourist-filled JUMP city of earlier in the summer. It's a city whose economy and industry is experiencing a welcome resurgence after the state-imposed trade embargo of the nineties. Men in suits talk into smartphones and women in pencil skirts flip through folders and sip from paper cups as they march to work. There are very few teenagers with backpacks and henna tattoos or world-traveling students with dreads and deep tans.

The change is disconcerting. The city has moved on since I was last here. It's like a different place, and yet Erin is still missing. She has been for three weeks.

Can she really come back from this?

In my lowest moments, when I truly believe she's gone forever, I cling to the idea that maybe she wanted to disappear. There was so much theoretically going on in her life that anyone might want to run away from. Maybe she wanted to vanish into thin air. Maybe she needed to get away. When Officer Tierney first suggested it, I'd been horrified. But there's something comforting in the idea that maybe it was her choice.

It'd be selfish, sure. Leaving her family and friends and boyfriend irrevocably devastated in the aftermath.

But her sadness was so raw, so deep, it was like she wasn't her anymore.

And Karen said it herself.

"Whenever something goes wrong in her life, Erin lashes out. Not at the world, but at herself."

It's a thin theory, but it gives me hope that she's not suffering.

Ilić eventually rounds the corner, red umbrella shielding him from the rain. I start toward him, and he stops to wait for me to meet him. This irks me and I'm not sure why.

"Morning," I say, false-brightly.

"Carina," he greets me, holding a hand up in a half-wave. "Hi. Good to see you again. Sorry I'm a little late—I have another case that's taking up so much time." He rubs his drooping eyes emphatically. "Anyway, let's get inside."

Gratefully, I follow him to the police station, but him telling me about his caseload has rubbed me the wrong way. Made me feel like Erin is no longer a priority—that other cases are more important.

We walk in silence, mainly because it's impossible to hear each other over the pounding rain. I'm soaked through, fabric clinging to my damp skin. He doesn't offer me the umbrella. Again, it irks me. Am I just supersensitive today?

Once we reach the station, we go through the whole interview setup and spiel again. At first I'm surprised our conversation is going to be recorded, but I suppose they can't risk me saying something crucial and them not having it on tape. What if I arranged this meeting to confess? They can't take chances. I get it. But suddenly my notes seem so infantile in the cold light of the recording equipment.

With the box-ticking monologue and never-ending admin complete, he asks, via Danijel, "So, Carina. Why don't you start by explaining a little about why you wanted to schedule this chat today?"

I'm hyperalert, like I was the day of the thunderstorm. Every sensory experience is amplified: the cold wetness of my soggy feet, the faint hum of electrical equipment at work, the smell of Danijel's espresso, the tiny pink blood vessels snaking over the whites of Ilić's eyes. The scratch in my throat and the pound of my heart massaging my rib cage.

"I, um . . ."

Good start, Corbett. Really solid. Way to sell your theory.

Awkward silence.

"No need to rush, Carina. Take as long as you need. And remember: you are not in any trouble. Anything you tell us at this stage can only be a help."

I can't quit thinking about the way Paige dismissed me on the phone on Friday night. Attributing my theories to lack of sleep. I've since wondered whether she's skeptical because my information didn't fit either of her theories: voluntary disappearance on Erin's part, or a connection to Brodie Breckenridge, who disappeared hundreds of miles away.

Ilić isn't like that, though. He'll listen. I remember our painstaking initial interviews, the way he wanted to know what brand of cigarettes she smoked with the bus driver, the color of the boats we hired, the ingredients of the soup Borko cooked for us. He'll want to know this. I'm sure of it.

My notes swim in front of me. I snap my attention back to him. I don't need my notes. I've gone over this stuff in my head endlessly over the last few weeks—I can do it from memory.

"Well, firstly," I say, relieved I've said anything at all, "I found a twin pack of pregnancy tests in her jacket pocket back home. One was missing. Did Officer Tierney pass that on to you?"

"She did, yes. We're very grateful for the information." Smile. But no further questions.

"Right. Okay. Well, that was one of the main things I wanted to discuss with you. I know Paige mentioned cross-checking the purchase against her bank statements—was that fruitful?"

Another smile, but tighter this time. "You know we can't discuss details of the investigation with you, Carina. But you can rest assured we're still doing everything we can, and following every lead we're given."

I blush furiously. Why do I feel like I'm being dismissed again? I shake away the paranoia.

Although I want to bring up Andrijo, the last shameful time I did is imprinted on my mind. Anxiety on top of panic on top of fear on top of frustration.

"You have to talk to him again, again, again, until you get him. It's him."

"We have spoken to him. We've spoken to everyone who saw Erin that day."

"And?"

"I'm sorry, Carina. We can't discuss any specifics of the case with you. It'd be bad practice."

Fucking bad practice. Everything's bad practice.

I want to bring up her dad, too, but I really have nothing new to add, and I know I'll be met with a firewall if I try to probe, try to gauge how seriously they're considering that fact about Erin's life.

"Have you heard of Bastixair?" I ask.

They exchange a glance. Ilić frowns. "Of course. It's one of the biggest employers in Novi Sad."

"Right. And there's a distribution center near Zmaj Jovina. Near the internet café she visited on Friday, July 10—Povezivanje?" I stumble over the pronunciation.

"Okay." Ilić is looking blankly at me, and I'm about to explode with frustration, until I realize I've omitted the key link.

"Erin's grandmother," I blurt out. "She had Aubin's syndrome. It's a pretty rare genetic disorder, and she died four years ago from it. And Bastixair . . . a lot of their research is geared toward the disease. They currently offer medication to relieve some of the symptoms, but I believe they're researching a permanent cure."

I'm still met with baffled expressions. They don't know what to make of this information.

Am I insane? Am I actually insane to believe this is important?

My breathing was ragged with excitement, but is now slowing with disappointment. "Erin was sending an email, on that Friday afternoon. To our boss. But she cut it off halfway through, and it saved to her drafts. Something interrupted her."

"How do you know this?"

I lower my head. "I hacked her work emails. And tracked her location at the time using the messenger app on our phones. She had location services enabled."

Ilić's eyes widen. Have I just told him something he didn't

know? "Okay. Is there any chance she could've visited the same café in that blank hour on Sunday afternoon?"

I shrug. "I guess. Although she didn't get in touch with my editor by email after that. Lowe—our boss—says she never heard from Erin the whole time we were there."

Something else occurs to me. Why would Erin have been panicking about her lack of cell reception on the riverfront farm if she'd had ample opportunity to contact Lowe all weekend—and hadn't bothered to do so?

Ilić lands on the same plot hole. "But you said she'd been worried about your editor being mad at her for being uncontactable."

I nod slowly. "Right. And . . ." I hesitate. There's still a trace of condescension in his gaze, like he's dealing with a psychiatric patient. "And doesn't the fact she cut off an email halfway through writing it, a whole two days before she disappeared, suggest there was something amiss before she vanished? Coupled with the lack of explanation for her worried demeanor?"

Silence.

"And doesn't that mean," I continue, "that she's unlikely to have been sexually assaulted and left for dead, as the whole world is assuming? Because unless she was being targeted prior to her disappearance—unless she was being stalked—and she was worried about that . . ."

I trail off as I notice Ilić sit up straighter.

Have I touched on something they hadn't previously considered?

Was Erin being stalked?

HEAD THRUMMING, I leave the police station with a plethora of different ideas all demanding my attention. A thousand puzzle pieces from different jigsaws, none of which will ever fit together. One from a battle scene, one from a fairground, one from a seascape and one from a city at night.

Bruises? Abusive father? Unborn baby? Brodie Breckenridge? Aubin's syndrome? Andrijo and Tim? Stalker? Suicide?

I try to slot them together in different combinations, like I'm playing that old Mastermind game where you have to work out the pattern of the colored pegs based on what you've already discovered in earlier rounds. Abusive father and Aubin's? Bruise and stalker? Unborn baby and Andrijo?

Nothing fits.

Ilić and I talked for a while longer. They're going to take second looks at her social media and phone records, in particular at apps like Messenger and Snapchat, to see if there's anything that could raise alarm bells. Anything that smacks of stalking.

Once I'd gained their respect again, I also mentioned the discussion I'd had with Paige about Tim's tie to Brodie Breckenridge. I made it clear I'm not insinuating they're incompetent, and I don't expect them to share any aspects of the investigation with me, but that I just wanted to share some ideas I had.

For instance, I brought up the fact that on July 22, Tim claimed to have met Andrijo last year, so anything linking them before then would be enough of an inconsistency to question both men again. They didn't sneer at me this time.

Karen is on her way into the police station as I'm on my way out—it'll be the first time she's met the Serbian police in person, despite the numerous phone calls over the course of the investigation thus far. She's dressed immaculately in a cornflower-blue sweater and pristine white jeans, but her hair has a kink from where she's slept and forgotten to brush it out, her foundation hasn't been rubbed into her skin properly and her mascara-painted eyelashes have the clumped-together quality of someone who's recently cried.

She greets me with a hug, asks me how I slept. I lie and say well. She lies, too, I guess. Overpowering perfume wafts off her, like she thought she could mask her misery with floral notes. Being here must be agonizing for her. Up until this morning, the city in which her daughter disappeared was just an abstract image in her mind—a towering fortress and pounding music and dark tunnels leading nowhere. Now she's here; she can feel the pulse of the place, feel the energy of the people that live here, feel the absence of her daughter.

We agree to meet for lunch when she's finished with the police, but she looks to be on the brink of shattering, and I'm not sure she'll survive the morning without her heart splintering.

Somehow, being around Karen makes me feel closer to Erin. The same way her belongings felt loaded with sentiment, her mother is a living piece of her. A connection to the girl who felt everything so deeply she almost lost herself every single day. Because our souls are never truly contained within our bodies; they're in the art we create and the things we buy, in the choices we make and the promises we break, in the people we love and even the people we hate. Everything and everyone Erin has touched remembers her. I feel slightly less bereft at the thought. She's still here, even if she's not.

She's here in Karen, in her polka dot umbrella, in her blog, in Smith, in me. She's here in the fashion cupboard at *Northern Heart*, in her falling-apart family home, in the fortress in Novi Sad. She's here.

Or maybe I'm delirious.

I wait until Karen's gone inside, then pull out my phone and punch the Povezivanje into the maps app. Because Erin was there, potentially more than once. And now I need to comb the café for any last traces of her, for the pieces of herself she left behind two days before she vanished.

POVEZIVANJE ISN'T FAR off Zmaj Jovina, the main street of shops and pavements cafés. On my way there I pass leather shops and Converse outlets, delis and cocktail bars, trash cans and wooden benches and streetlamps, and with every new thing I spot, I think of Erin walking past them just three weeks ago. Has it really only been three weeks and one day? I think of the Carina of three weeks and two days ago, when the biggest disaster I could imagine in my life was running out of Prozac or making sure my mother remembered to eat. Those problems felt so heavy, so urgent, so life-threateningly serious. Now they are dwarfed.

It also feels foreign to picture Erin as a living, breathing person going about her daily life. Sure, I'm forever remembering fragments of memories of her laughter, of her tears, of her pain, but imagining something so ordinary as her walking down the street seems unspeakably obscure.

It's then I realize my concept of Erin as an organism has shifted from present to past, from living to otherwise. I can't pinpoint when I started to consider her gone, but right now she seems so far detached from my current reality that her existence feels a sheer impossibility.

And so, when I make it to Povezivanje, I'm breathless with guilt. I never meant to give up on her. I've done everything I can to keep her alive in my mind, explore so many possibilities that her survival is conceivable, and yet my subconscious has betrayed me regardless. Grief has a way of doing that, pitting your heart and your head against each other.

Povezivanje screams: "Look at how modern I am!" Lime green beanbags and purple sofas, all smooth edges and deeply uncomfortable cushions. Silver light fixtures, cheap and cheerful laminated menus, white linoleum floors polished to within an inch of their plasticky lives. Behind a bored barista, there's a spaceship-sized coffee machine, in front of him a fully stocked cabinet of sterile-looking cakes, lifted straight from their wholesale boxes and arranged carefully behind the glass to look somewhat appetizing. A row of computers on an extended counter along the back wall, purple bar stools with Z-shaped legs perfectly lined up in front of them. Five in total.

For an exhilarating second I imagine searching the browser history on each to cross-check the contents with Erin's dates, but then I remember she had her own laptop. The police seized it after she disappeared, and there was nothing remotely suspicious to be found. They wouldn't have even considered questioning the unsent email in the drafts folder. Maybe now, in light of the stalker theory, they'll reexamine the device, trawl through the trash folders and backup drives with a fine-tooth comb.

Or maybe, the paranoid part of me insists, *they were simply humoring your outlandish theories so you'd leave them alone.*

My heart's pounding like a drum at a parade, and the guilt over my lack of faith in Erin's survival still sticks to my lungs. I'd intended to go straight up to the counter and ask the barista whether he recognized my beautiful friend, but I'm still fundamentally terrified of talking to strangers. So I pull up a zigzag stool, boot up a PC, and when he asks me how many credits I'd like to buy, I swallow my fear and request twenty minutes of Wi-Fi and a cappuccino.

I'm convinced I must look mentally unstable, but one big perk of black skin is nobody can tell when you're blushing. So I just face the screen, stare at the log-in page and wait for him to bring me the code. The hotter-than-the-sun cappuccino has too much foam and too little cocoa powder, but I can barely taste it anyway. The barista smiles at me, and there's something strangely attractive about him and his hipster beard, eyebrow piercing and deep blue eyes.

Did he hit on Erin while she worked? Is that why she stopped writing the email and never started again? Are the flirty undertones in his half-smirk something more sinister?

Jesus, Corbett. Get a grip.

He's harmless.

As subtly as I can, I search the corners of the ceiling. No cameras. Damn. There's no way of seeing what exactly Erin was up to on Friday, July 10, 2015 at 14:05:21. I hope the police can pull up some worthwhile footage from the street outside.

Like most people in their twenties, I'm an expert at wasting time on the internet, so I kill the twenty minutes no problem. I try to check my *Northern Heart* emails, but find the account has been deleted—fair enough—and there's nothing in my personal in-box from the *Daily Standard*. Again, no surprise. I'm on the verge of typing Erin's name into Google, delving into the dark world of the police-orchestrated media campaign, but I know I wouldn't be able to stomach it. I log on to Facebook instead.

After scrolling through my feed for a few minutes—succumbing to a few clickbait articles my friends have shared, liking a second cousin's engagement announcement—her name crops up regardless. Mary-Kate Johnson, one of the salesgirls from *Northern Heart*, has used her as clickbait, or likebait, of her own.

Miss you every day, Erin Baxter. Praying you'll come home soon <3"

I fight back the nausea. I don't think Mary-Kate ever acknowledged Erin's existence, beyond the flesh-searing jealousy she fired Erin's way when she first joined the intern team. The status has eighty-six likes and dozens of well-wishing comments, all sending their love to Mary-Kate in this difficult time. The wave of anger catches me off guard.

Then I can't resist any longer. I click onto Erin's page.

The gut-wrenching feeling never comes. Maybe I'm numb to it after all that's happened, but her quirky profile picture of her own shadow doesn't evoke any stabbing grief. She rarely updated her status, so most of the posts on her feed are posts she's been tagged in by others. There's not much to get upset about in comparison to my real life memories of her.

My coffee is still roughly the temperature of liquid magma, so I scroll down a little farther.

Erin Baxter became friends with Robyn Ward and two others.

Robyn Ward is a girl from *Northern Heart*, and I assume Barbara Baxter is an aged relative judging by her profile picture. But Kieran Riddle? I don't recognize him.

Something twists in my stomach. Are the police looking at the same profile right now? Questioning whether or not he'd been stalking Erin?

His profile is private, and we only have one mutual friend. But a quick scroll through his friends list shows that most of them are women. Beautiful women. There are the obligatory family members—I assume Brian and Helen Riddle are his parents—but the rest resemble an amateur modeling portfolio: nightclub photography featuring fish pouts, hair extensions and false eyelashes. He's listed as a University of Lincoln alum, but doesn't have a current employer on his profile.

I really have no idea what I'm looking for. He's never posted on Erin's wall, and I have no way of knowing if they've private messaged.

In a bolt of inspiration, I remember one of the notes I made on the plane home, scrawled in the margin of a fiendish Sudoku puzzle, and never acted on. *Find Borko Zoric on Facebook.* Hands trembling, I open a new tab and type his name into the search bar.

Bingo. Third result down. Borko Zoric, Univerzitet u Novom Sadu. Novi Sad University.

But it's not Borko I'm interested in. I click on his friends list, type "Andrijo" and watch as two profiles come up.

The first has an F1 car as its profile picture and is in the Leskovac network—a quick glance at a map of Serbia shows me that's a city in the south, whereas Novi Sad is in the north of the country. I discount him. Mainly because the second profile, Andrijo Marković, is clearly him. I'd recognize those inky eyes anywhere.

Damn. His privacy settings are so severe you'd think he was hiding a secret life as a Vegas drag queen. I can't even click on his profile picture to make it bigger, let alone see his personal information or posts.

Sipping the scalding coffee, I notice I only have two minutes left on the Wi-Fi. It's now or never.

Gesturing to the barista, I reopen the Erin tab. I flash him what I hope is a charming, noncreepy grin, and he responds with an equally overenthusiastic smile and starts to walk over, tray in hand.

Yeah, he's definitely attractive. I never thought bearded white guys with metal through their face were my type, but hey. There's something about the way his black apron hangs off his narrow hips, and the black T-shirt is tight around his arms.

"Hi." I smile before he's even reached me.

Smooth. Way to play it cool.

"Good morning, miss. Can I get you anything else? More Wi-Fi?"

I shake my head. He eyes the violet ombre at the bottom of my locks and something twinkles is his eye. "No, thank you. The coffee is great. I just wanted to ask a question . . . my friend, Erin, came in here recently. She mentioned a cute barista she wishes she'd asked out. Was it you? Do you recognize her?" I point to the screen, where I've maximized her profile picture.

I'm genuinely amazed how smoothly the lie glides off my tongue. Maybe I should play the role of flirty cappuccino drinker more often. I'm much less of a bumbling idiot.

He leans in and scrunches up his brow. "No, I don't think so. She is very beautiful. Not as beautiful as you, however . . ."

The stilted way he pronounces *beautiful* makes me almost sure he didn't mean to compliment me like that. Me? More beautiful than Erin? Yeah. And I can also talk to animals, don't you know?

I assume he's telling the truth about not recognizing her, although a small part of me wonders if he's seen her missing posters and doesn't want to get involved in this mess. I try to mask my disappointment. I had a whole list of questions I'd have asked if he'd seen her that day. Questions that would've made me look like a stalker, but I'm well past the point of caring.

Wait . . . a stalker. Would her potential stalker also have come in here asking for information about her?

I'm about to ask him whether anyone else has come looking for her when he points to the name on my other open tab.

"Andrijo Marković? He works here, too—maybe it was him she saw. Although he hasn't showed up for weeks."

Chapter Eighteen

August 3, Serbia

I LEAVE POVEZIVANJE with a home address and a trembling fist.

Andrijo was here. Erin was here. At the same time?

An unsent email, a crackling intensity between them in the midst of a thunderstorm. A missing girl, an enigmatic stranger. A connection—how deep?

There's a fizzing inside me, delicious satisfaction that my initial hunch had genuine weight, blended with the indescribable fear of what he could have done to my friend.

I have to to go to his house. Not ring the doorbell or look for trouble or anything crazy, but just to scope out the area. See if there's any sign of life in his apartment—the barista said he hadn't turned up for work in weeks. Since Erin vanished? Was taken? Again, it can't be a coincidence.

It was Andrijo. He was there that night at JUMP. He must have been.

This is the link I've been looking for. A link even the police missed.

There's a certainty in my gut I haven't felt since those very first interviews with Ilić, and it centers me like a sedative. Gives me renewed focus—calm, steady, sure. Now the rhythm of my thumping heart is fast, yes, but even. I'm getting somewhere. For the first time, I have a real lead.

I open my maps app, pull up his address. It's a few minutes' walk away. The rain has stopped now, and the sun is slicing through the gray clouds. Walking away from Povezivanje, away from the cute barista with the nice eyes and game-changing information, I stride quickly but assuredly, and trust me, assured is not what I feel 99.9 percent of the time.

As I round the corner at the street intersection, I look back up the cobbles, past the awnings and pavement tables and Serbian flags. And even though my eyesight isn't the best, I swear I see a uniformed man enter the café I just left.

ANDRIJO'S BUILDING IS an apartment block, but a very nice one. It looks like each flat takes up an entire floor. The exterior is mint green with big bay windows and hanging baskets of flowers, delicate drainpipes and glossy black doors. To be honest, though, the flowers and doors are not what I'm looking at.

I'm looking at the three police vans parked outside.

They're here for him?

They're here for him.

A crushing crescendo of satisfaction builds inside me. I knew. I knew from the start. Coal-black eyes and piercing intensity and unsettling conversations and nobody believed me, but now they are here for him.

What does this mean? Are they following the same lead I am, or do they have more?

A small throng of spectators has gathered, and one very junior officer is trying his damnedest to usher them away. A teenage girl in a school skirt takes pictures on a smartphone. I push through them, right up to Ilić. He's talking urgently into a phone, and looks more than a little irritated to see me standing in front of him, sopping wet hair drying into frizzy afro, coffee still lingering on my breath, hope wafting off my skin like a rancid smell.

He hangs up. Fixes a smile on his face, but not before I see his true feelings toward me. I'm too amped up to care. "Carina. What are you doing here?"

"I saw the vans and followed them. I was on the next street," I lie, not wanting him to know about my detective work in Povezivanje.

"Right. We're just following up on a lead. It's nothing to do with Erin's case," he says flippantly, but the final clause leaves me cold.

He's lying to my face.

It's not sinister. I know that. But he's said it before; he doesn't want to get my hopes up, doesn't want to have to explain himself, doesn't want to deal with the grief-stricken girl standing in front of him.

He's unaware that I know this apartment belongs to Andrijo.

Behind him, another detective loads a black bag marked *Evidence* into the back on the van. From the shape, it looks like a laptop case. Andrijo's? Am I making a leap? Another one?

Some of my leaps haven't been far off.

I swallow hard. "Okay."

A tight smile. "Go back to your hotel room. Relax. Spend time with Karen; she needs you. We'll be in touch if we need anything else."

I agree and walk away, knowing that back to the hotel is the last place I'm thinking of going right now.

MY HEAD SWIMS.

I'm in another internet café.

Andrijo. He's the crux of this case.

How?

Was it as sordidly simple as a rape-turned-murder?

Or was there something more?

How does it all tie together?

His alibi. What was it? His boss said he'd been at work. It struck me as odd at the time—Erin went missing on a Sunday. Could he have been working at Povezivanje?

I had looked up the café's opening hours before I flew back out to Belgrade. It's closed on Sundays, hence I waited until today to check it out.

"He hasn't showed up for weeks."

So he must have another job.

Where?

A half-formed thought floats to the surface of my mental cesspool.

Bastixair has a distribution center a few hundred yards from Povezivanje—and his apartment. Did he choose to live there because it's the perfect location for commuting to both jobs?

Hurriedly, I click through to the Bastixair homepage, then use the site's own search function to look for any reference to Andrijo Marković.

Nothing.

I don't let disappointment swallow me whole. I have nine minutes of Wi-Fi left.

A few more clicks take me to a list of Bastixair's key shareholders. None of the names ring any bells—they're all very Serbian. I'm about to click off the page, explore a different avenue, when the name right at the top catches my eye: Kristijan Kasun.

I frown. Why would I have heard of him? It's somewhere in the back of my mind, just out of reach.

His profile takes an eternity to load. When it does, I skim through pages and pages of information. Several phrases jump out at me: he's a parliamentary candidate for the Serbian Progressive Party whose son has Aubin's syndrome. His picture shows a balding white man in his forties, thin-rimmed glasses balancing on a narrow, pointed nose.

Pressing my eyes together, I try so hard to remember where I've heard his name that I nearly give myself an aneurism. Something appears, again half-formed. Tim, talking about Andrijo's alibi.

"He was at work with his boss. He's a respected figure in the area."

Respected like a parliamentary candidate?

I swear Tim mentioned a name, but I can't for the life of me remember what it was.

I look at the Wikipedia page for Kasun, as well as his official website and the news tab on Google. Nothing is jogging my memory, nothing is clicking into place. Six minutes left on the Wi-Fi.

For lack of anything better to research, I click on the images tab, crossing my fingers that by some miracle Andrijo and Kasun have been photographed together. That'd be perfectly neat, but far too easy. The first few pages bring up nothing interesting—lots of pictures of him making public speeches and running campaigns and visiting schools.

One does make me pause, though. A photo of him cutting a ribbon outside what looks like a clinic of some sort. I enlarge. A news story; yes, a clinic opening for sexual assault victims.

Sexual assault. Erin. Baby. Rape? Stalker?

Again, the leaps I'm taking are gargantuan, could take me from Jupiter to Neptune, but my hunch about Andrijo had something to it. Why can't this?

Five minutes left. I open the news article. The clinic, called Feminaid, is in Zrenjanin, the next city over from Novi Sad, and was opened nearly a decade ago to help sexual assault victims— both physically and psychologically. I see the word *abortion* and nausea churns in my gut. Erin's missing pregnancy test.

There's an image gallery at the bottom, and I scroll aimlessly through.

Aimless, that is, until I see him.

Not Andrijo Marković.

Tim Halsey.

THIS PICTURE WAS taken ten years ago. Tim Halsey was connected to Kristijan Kasun ten years ago.

Is this important?

Tim has never claimed not to know Kasun. It's never really come up in conversation—I had no idea who Kasun was until a few minutes ago. He might mean nothing in the grand scheme of this warped mystery. He's a parliamentary candidate, a shareholder in a pharmaceutical company and frequently attends local openings to show face and cut ribbons. That's all.

But this picture links Bastixair to Kasun, and Kasun to Tim, and Tim to Erin. And somewhere in the middle, Andrijo slots into place.

Brodie Breckenridge. She went missing eight years ago. Was she a sexual assault victim? Did she visit Feminaid?

I shake the thought away. She disappeared in Croatia, and this clinic is in Zrenjanin, northern Serbia.

Still, my stomach twists at the idea of Erin, pregnant and scared, going to a clinic like that in secret. But when could she? Up until she went missing, we were only ever separated for an hour or so at a time on this trip. Definitely not enough to travel to Zrenjanin, have an appointment and then get back to Novi Sad without anyone realizing she'd left.

Unless . . . while we slept? No. The opening hours, according to the clinic's website, are pretty standard.

Unless . . . she planned to go to the clinic at some point on the trip?

Two minutes left. I take some screenshots of the article, the clinic, the image of Kasun and Tim, of a map directing me to the Feminaid in Zrenjanin, and send them to myself. Now I have them on my phone once the Wi-Fi runs out.

I remember the police vans outside Andrijo's apartment block, the evidence bag, Ilić urging me to leave, lying about what they were doing. I try in vain to slot Povezivanje and Bastixair into the same picture. It's the game I never win. Abusive father and stalker? Bruise and Andrijo? Kasun and baby?

Pinning them down is impossible and I start to see why detectives in movies have those corkboards with pins representing different parts of the case, red string tying together the bits that are linked somehow.

One minute to go. I take a punt. Google Andrijo Marković again.

It was a long shot, and one that's not rewarded. There's just the usual Twitter account (an egg profile picture and no tweets), LinkedIn profile (which I can't see because I don't have my own) and another guy by the same name who's a respected lawyer in the south.

Zero minutes. I log out, thank the barista and send a message to Karen.

I won't be meeting her for lunch. I'm getting a bus to Zrenjanin.

Chapter Nineteen

August 3, Serbia

THE CLINIC LOOKS exactly the same as it did in the picture from ten years ago, with the exception of the fresh paint job outside— it's now duck-egg blue rather than peppermint green. A modern building, but there are only a few windows and you can't really tell what's inside from the street. A good thing, I guess. Its clients probably want to maintain confidentiality.

A sudden influx of sadness catches me off guard. I imagine Erin here: scared, ashamed, depressed. An unwanted child, a vulgar secret, a fear of the men around her. Smith, Andrijo, her father. Kieran Riddle. Kristijan Kasun. I touch my fingertips to the clasp of our bangle, not even trying to blink away the tears that've started to pour. I'm frustrated at my past self, too. For not paying enough attention to her, not reading between the lines of everything she said, not taking a second look at the flashes of fear in her eyes that I wrongly assumed to be of Lowe.

I came here on a whim. Bought a bus ticket, hoped that it'd

become clear what to do once I was here, once I was looking at the place. And it is clear. My gut is telling me to go inside.

Is that foolish? Will they know I'm a fraud? The website says they help victims emotionally and psychologically, not just physically. They can't force me to have a medical examination.

Or am I attaching too much significance to Feminaid, just because it's the place that ties together Kasun and Tim? In the context of Erin's pregnancy test, it seemed so crucial, so pivotal to her disappearance, but the more I look at this cheerfully sterile shopfront, I struggle to imagine why on earth she'd come here instead of visiting her local GP. We have free health care in the UK, through the National Health Service, and doctors are sworn to a little thing called the Hippocratic Oath, so word would never get out about her unwanted child. It makes no sense to travel to a random city in a random country to seek help.

Unless she was so far along that the NHS wouldn't let her abort. But I think of her still-petite frame and it seems unlikely.

Maybe she did have an abortion on the NHS, and she was coming here for counseling. I know waiting lists for the NHS mental health services are months and months and months long right now. Was she struggling so badly that she'd pay for a Serbian clinician to help her? But that doesn't make sense either. The original abortion would show up on her medical records, and the police would've known about it all along.

Which they could've. Would Ilić have told me? He's just lied to my face about Andrijo's apartment, and he's always stressing the importance of discretion. Has he ever told me anything concrete about the case? No. So why would he have told me this?

I'm standing on the street, letting pedestrians dodge around me as I sob quietly. I need to move, need to do something, but this is all so paralyzing, and it's becoming impossible to tell whether my million-miles-an-hour mind is a symptom of my anxiety, my obsession with finding Erin or if I'm actually on to something. I can't remember what it's like to have a quiet brain. I'm not sure I want to. The silence might cripple me.

For lack of anything better to do, I take a deep breath and go inside.

INSIDE IT SMELLS like bleach. The linoleum floors squeak as I walk over them. It's modern, like Povezivanje, but more toned down. A lot of white.

An impossibly slim, acne-scarred receptionist sits behind a white counter, staring at nothing. She's not flipping through a magazine, or tapping away on her phone under the desk, or clacking on a keyboard. She's doing nothing. And it's disconcerting. There's something so clinical about it. So devoid of . . . anything.

Before I can talk myself out of it, I approach her, and she snaps out of her trance with a polite smile, which I can tell she practices very hard. It's the perfect mix of unassuming and nonjudgmental and neutral.

"*Zdravo,*" she says, maintaining the smile as she speaks. It's an art form.

"Hi," I say, trying to mirror her placid grin. "English," I add apologetically.

"No problem. How may I help you today?"

My throat goes dry. "I, uh . . . I'd like to speak to someone. In private. About . . . about something that happened three weeks ago at JUMP."

She reads the subtext ultraprofessionally. "No problem. We have a counsellor available shortly. Were you looking to talk to someone right away? If you want to come back this afternoon, that's fine, too. Whatever works for you." Smile.

"Now is great. Thank you."

"No problem." Nothing is a problem for this woman. "Can I ask you to fill out this form while you wait?" She hands over a white clipboard with a questionnaire and a tiny biro attached. Gestures to the waiting room, where there are two other girls waiting. There are more potted plants than patients.

The chairs are hard, white plastic with a terrible ergonomic design. I have to slump over the clipboard to be able to write a single word. I fill it out as vaguely as I can, entering a fake name and date of birth, and don't declare my anxiety and depression when asked about preexisting medical conditions. One of the other girls, ghostly pale and beady-eyed, watches me with suspicion. She's very pregnant, resting a water bottle on her huge bump, but her limbs are tiny like they could snap between my fingers.

When I finish, I take the form back to the receptionist, who reiterates that it's not a problem and encourages me to relax in the waiting room. I down three cups of water from the cooler in the corner and take an uncomfortable seat. It's eerily silent.

I cannot imagine Erin here. It's too painful. Clutching her stomach—empty or not?—and eyeing the clock, wondering if she's made a mistake. Smith seemed genuinely shocked when I mentioned the possible pregnancy. But why? Why keep this from him? It's a question I've pondered several times since I collapsed onto him in the churchyard. He's arrogant, sure, and a little selfish. But what would compel her to keep this dark secret from her longtime partner? Especially if the baby's his . . . which I have briefly considered to be debatable, but I felt like a traitor as soon as the thought crossed my mind. Erin is not a cheater.

Unless she had no choice in the matter.

Nausea ripples through me so fast I bend at the waist, hanging my head between my legs and gasping for air. Nobody says a word. Not even the robot receptionist for whom nothing is a problem. She's seen it all before. She's seen rape and abortion and the grim aftermath. It's not a problem.

I pop a pill from my bag, and another, because even though my last overdose made me so drowsy I fell asleep on the floor, right now I'd give anything not to be awake.

I want to leave. Desperately. But I force myself to remember the link: Andrijo is connected to Kasun, and Feminaid links Kasun to Tim. Tim, who's looking less and less innocent as time goes on. Yet again, I find myself thinking of Brodie Breckenridge. Did she visit this place, too?

All my energy is focused on suppressing the vomit rising in my throat, so when the receptionist calls my name and asks me to go to room three, it takes me a few moments to rise. The other girls give me strange looks, but honestly, I've never cared less what other people think of me, and for a girl with crippling anxiety, that's not a good sign.

The clinic is small and looks like my GP's office back home. Desk and chairs and potted plants, an examination table covered in a fresh sterile sheet. Smiling medical professional with thick-rimmed glasses, sleek brunette bob and a tan so deep her skin is like leather.

"Hi, Carolina," she says, voice husky, accent stilted. "Please, come in. Take a seat."

I do, cheeks already burning, heart already racing, stomach already filling with self-loathing over the lie I'm about to tell. Real girls go through this every day. And I'm about to pretend I'm one of them.

"How can I help you today? Would you mind telling me why you're here?"

The three cups of water have done nothing to quench my dry throat. Remembering how to form words is easier said than done. "I'm . . . I'm here because I was raped. At JUMP, three and a half weeks ago. And . . ." I go all out. Try to see how they'd have treated Erin in the same situation. "I'm pregnant."

It's such a loaded statement, heavy with pain and darkness, and yet she barely reacts. Like I say, she sees this every day, multiple times a day. It's not uncommon. The nausea ripples again.

"I see. I'm sorry, Carolina. Is this the first time you've seen a medical professional since the incident?"

"Yes. I took a home test."

"And you didn't report the incident to the police." No judgment. She's as neutral as the receptionist.

"No."

She doesn't ask why, doesn't push for more details. Just makes a note on my chart. "So you haven't been checked for sexually transmitted diseases?"

"No," I reply, a little alarmed that her next question is a medical one. I kind of expected her to focus on the psychological trauma. Hastily, I add, "I'm not really looking for a physical examination or anything. I just wanted to . . . talk to someone. Is that all right?"

"Sure," she says, with no amount of certainty. "Although I'd really recommend having a medical professional determine whether you are, in fact, pregnant, and whether or not you've picked up any STIs. You don't want to leave these things undiagnosed for too long. Plus, for your own peace of mind, knowing is better than not knowing."

I purse my lips. "Not today. But I will, I promise."

"No problem." She lays down her pen, leans back in her chair. She's older than I first thought, maybe in her fifties. "How are you doing, Carolina? You can tell me anything, you know. Everything you say inside these four walls will be treated with the utmost discretion."

I smile, but I'm pretty sure it comes out as more of a wince. "Thank you."

She waits patiently for me to explain how I'm doing, but I'm drawing a blank. Regretting my ridiculous decision to go through with this. I'm no actress. She's bound to be able to tell that I'm lying. Who declines a medical examination so vehemently in this situation? What happens if she realizes I'm a fraud? Maybe she'll refer me to a real psychiatrist. What kind of psychopath fakes a rape? On behalf of every sexual assault victim in history, I despise myself.

"I'm sorry . . . I think this was a mistake," I mumble, rising from my seat.

"Carolina," she interrupts, her voice still perfectly calm and measured. "I know this is difficult for you. But running away isn't the answer. You need help. I can give you that." She notices my hesitation. "It is natural to feel afraid and alone. We need to work through that. Please, sit down. We can talk for as long as you need."

I find myself sitting.

"I met a guy at JUMP," I blurt out. "He was drunk, but so was I. He got too forceful, too full-on, and I tried to stop him. But we were back in his tent, and there was nowhere to run."

Shame. Deep, deep shame, larger than anything else.

"It wasn't your fault," she says.

Heat floods me. She's misreading my shame. "I didn't say it was."

"No. But it's natural in these situations to feel guilt for leading him on. It's what the world wants you to feel. Please don't. You told him to stop. That should've been enough."

"It wasn't."

"I'm sorry."

Don't be. Save your sympathy for someone who deserves it.

I stare at my feet.

"Have you had any thoughts about what you'll do about the baby?"

My neck snaps up at the change of pace. "Pardon?"

"Do you plan on keeping it? It must be a painful reminder of that night."

I narrow my eyes. "I'm not sure yet."

"Well, I'd be happy to talk through your options with you, if you like?"

I splutter. "I know my options. Keep it or don't."

Another smile, now so tranquil it's perverse. "I meant your options at Feminaid." She pulls a glossy leaflet from her top drawer. "You're still very early, so a termination wouldn't be overly traumatic, physically."

I stare at her. Is she trying to sell me an abortion? The calm pushiness on her face makes me wonder, only half-jokingly, if she's commission based. I look down at the leaflet she's pushing into my hands.

Pregnancy termination up to ten weeks: 250,000 dinar.

Pregnancy termination up to twenty weeks: 500,000 dinar.

"I thought abortion was only legal up to ten weeks in Serbia," I manage. I read that fact somewhere in the article about Feminaid— the one showing Kasun opening the Zrenjanin site ten years ago. The piece also said the country has one of the highest abortion rates in Europe. In 1989, sixty-eight percent of pregnancies were terminated.

"It is," she answers. "Unless you have medical documentation declaring mental or emotional instability." She looks at me meaningfully, and I find the subtext: she can give me that documentation.

Suddenly, painfully, I find myself praying this is not the rabbit hole Erin fell down.

"I have to go."

This time, grabbing the leaflet as proof, I make it to the door, through the white, white waiting room, past the calm smiles, bursting, gasping, onto the wet street.

ILIĆ'S NUMBER IS saved to my phone, and even though he's already dismissed me twice today, I need to talk to him. The voice in my head that something is wrong is growing louder—a scream, a yell, a roar—as I clutch the ugly leaflet in my hand.

"Jovan Ilić."

"It's Carina. I'm in Zrenjanin."

"Carina? Hold on." The background noise dims as he cups a hands over the mobile phone speaker, then again as he exits the street and goes inside. Inside where. Andrijo's apartment? Is he still there? He comes back on. "Carina? What's wrong? Did you say you're in Zrenjanin? Didn't I only see you a couple of hours ago?"

Dry, my throat is so dry I can barely swallow. "Yes. I, erm . . ."

Where do I start without sounding insane?

Fuck it. That ship sailed a long time ago.

"I came to see a Feminaid clinic I think Erin might've visited.

For sexual assault victims. She . . . I know she might have been pregnant, and . . . and it made sense. They offer abortions."

"What clinic?"

I tell him the name, the street. I'm met with silence.

"I know it sounds crazy," I continue hurriedly, desperate to keep his attention—the attention I don't deserve. "But Kristijan Kasun was Andrijo's alibi, right?" I take a stab in the dark. My whole theory rests on that being true. A respected figure in the area. His boss. "And you're searching Andrijo's apartment, so I know he's not clean. They worked together, him and Kasun. And Kasun is linked to Bastixair, and his son has Aubin's, and so did Erin's grandmother, and Kasun opened this clinic—with Tim Halsey. It's all connected. It all led me here. You know Tim was questioned as part of the Brodie Breckenridge case, right?"

I'm babbling, and it makes so little sense, and suddenly I've lost it. I've lost the train of thought I was on—the one that led me here. Was it really only a hunch? Did I really have so little to go on? It seemed so obvious at the time, but now, as I try and fail to land on the point of my story, I'm realizing how twisted my thinking has been over the last few hours. There's nothing. Nothing concrete. I want the pavement to swallow me whole; I want to go back five minutes and not dial this number, want to go back five years and not lose my mind.

But he doesn't dismiss me. "You say Kasun opened this clinic . . . and Halsey was there."

My heart skips a beat. He's listening. That means Kasun was Andrijo's alibi. "Y-yes."

Silence. He's considering. Does that mean I may actually be on to something? Maybe Erin really was pregnant. Maybe this makes sense in the context of what he knows.

What does he know?

I need the full picture. I don't have it, but I need it.

Maybe they're scared she went for an abortion, and she didn't make it out alive.

The nausea reaches a climax.

"Can you email me the address? We'll come and find you."

That's it. My heart stops dead. "You're coming here? To Zrenjanin?"

"Yes. What you've just told me makes sense in terms of something we just discovered in Marković's apartment. And, Carina?"

Chest thudding, I say, "Yeah?"

What the . . .

"Be careful." There's something like genuine concern in his voice. What the hell did he find? "Walk away from the clinic, go and get a coffee, and wait. I'll phone you when we make it to Zrenjanin."

I hang up, legs weak, stomach cramping. I'm about to do as he says, about to turn and walk away, far away from this white, white clinic with the robotic receptionist and the wholesale abortions for half a million dinar as long as you can prove you're as mental as me. But as I turn on my shaking heel, shoving my phone into the back pocket of my jeans, I collide straight into a sturdy figure. A sturdy figure I recognize all too well.

Short, stocky. Shaven head. Close-together eyes, a crooked nose. A smile that's anything but friendly.

Borko. Andrijo's friend.

Chapter Twenty

August 3, Serbia

IT TAKES US both a moment to react—him with rage, me with terror.

I want to turn and run, but I'm a split second too slow and he's grabbed my wrist before I can usher my legs into action.

"Borko? I . . ."

What do I say? What do I do? Plead ignorance? Insist on coincidence? Stick with the tent story?

He'll never buy it. Not after what happened to Erin.

And from the look on his face—shock and irritation combined with something darker—he isn't as clueless in the case as he claimed to the Serbian police.

"Let's talk inside," he mutters, but it's not a question, and I have no choice in the matter.

Tugging my wrist, tightly, painfully, he drags me back through the clinic door. Instead of turning right and entering the reception, he swipes a key fob to the door on the left. Some kind of storeroom. It's freezing, windowless and smells of chemicals and plastic.

He pulls out a cardboard box full of medical supplies, let's go of my wrist and pushes me down so I'm sitting on it. He towers above me, arms folded. I guess he does it to assert his authority over me—hard to do when you're a short guy.

I think that thought to try and make him less intimidating in my mind.

It doesn't work. I'm terrified.

"Be careful. Walk away from the clinic, go and get a coffee, and wait. I'll phone you when we make it to Zrenjanin."

What was Ilić so urgently telling me to walk away from?

"What are you doing here, Carina?" he says, calmly like the rest of the robots who work here.

My chest is tight, like there's an elastic band wrapped around it, and my breathing is shallow.

I try to mirror his eerily serene tone. "I came to talk to someone."

A frown, unfriendly. "I thought you went back to England."

"I did. I came back to Novi Sad with Erin's mother." I'm amazed how steady my voice sounds. "She had to fly out. I didn't want her to be alone."

Mind reeling, I think back over everything I just said, desperately trying to work out whether I referenced anything that might make him think I know about his involvement. If he suspected I'd spoken to the police just now, and they'd warned me away from this place . . . what might he do if he knew they were closing in on them? What might he do if he knew what I know?

Or what I don't. There's a black hole in my knowledge I still can't fill.

What did Andrijo do? Why? How was this place involved? How was Kasun, Borko?

"Why are you here? At this clinic?" he asks, brow cocked.

"I told you. I came to talk to someone about . . . something. Why shouldn't I be at this clinic?" I tilt my chin skyward, fixing defiance into my facial expression.

"Because there's an identical one in Novi Sad."

Crap.

"I didn't want Karen to see me. I haven't told anyone about what happened. Didn't seem important, after what happened to Erin."

Hopefully the beat I missed went unnoticed.

"What did happen?"

"To Erin?"

"To you." There's no sympathy in his voice.

Matching his iciness, I curtly respond, "That's between me and the clinician I spoke to ten minutes ago."

I'm instantly so relieved I've already told the lie, so relieved it's all on paper, in the brain of that counsellor, and he can't poke a hole in my story. I ran out of the appointment, panicked . . . sure. But that's plausible for a girl in my pretend situation.

Try telling that to my raging stomach. The nausea is cold, churning.

I leap on his silence. "What are you doing here? I thought you worked for the tourism board, and yet you've just stormed into a sexual assault clinic with a key fob."

His face purples, spit gathering around the corners of his mouth. "I did work for the tourism board. I don't anymore. How do you know that?"

"You told us. On the riverfront," I lie.

"No, I didn't." He stares, narrowed eyes bloodshot and bulging.

"Why are you so angry and defensive about my being here?" I ask. If I'm going for the sweet and innocent act, I have to commit to total ignorance. If I really knew nothing, I'd have no context for his paranoia, and would probably be questioning why I've been dragged to a random storage room far more than I currently am. For effect, I add, simperingly, "You're scaring me."

He studies me long and hard. "What are you really doing here, Carina?"

"I told you," I answer quickly, but my heart is pounding so fast a hand flutters instinctively to my chest. He eyes it with suspicion, this physical sign of my palpitations. I deflect the suspicion back on to him. "Why are you really so concerned about me being at this clinic?"

"Because it makes no sense. And I know you're lying to me."

"So are you." I regret it as soon as I've said it.

"What did you say?"

"Nothing."

"No. Not nothing." He drops his hands to his knees, hunches over so his face is inches from mine and I can taste the staleness of his breath. "What did you say to me?"

"You're lying."

Motionless like a statue of a hunchback, he stares at me so intently I swear he can read my soul. "What are you suggesting?"

I know I'm endangering myself right now. I know I've gone down the wrong road, pursued the wrong rabbit. I should've stuck with the scared and clueless act. But I couldn't resist. Probably because part of me, the most suspicious, terrified part of me, doesn't want to let this opportunity slip. I've spent weeks digging and digging, into Erin's mind and into her life, into the darkest corners of the darkest alleys of possibility, searching for answers, searching for anything that might lead me back to her. And now, standing right in front of me, is a key to a door I've been banging on for an eternity.

And even though I know it's stupid, even though I know I'm putting myself at risk, I don't care. The delicious sensation of nothingness is spreading through me—part depression, part drug-induced haze from my earlier double dose. Right now, in this game-changing moment, finding Erin seems more important than continuing to live through the blackness.

"I'm suggesting you're lying," I say, inching forward ever so slightly, showing that I'm not scared of him, that I won't back down just because he's using his testosterone to intimidate me.

A snarl, like a bulldog chewing a wasp. "What about?"

"Who you are. Where you work." A pause. "Why the police are currently searching Andrijo's apartment."

That's all it takes for him to snap; to see I know more than I should; to realize I've come here to look for answers.

That's all it takes for him to raise a fist and punch me square in the face.

My world goes black.

CUTTING THROUGH THE pain is the rumble of a vehicle in motion and the burn of rope around my wrists.

For a moment I can't work out if my eyes are open or not. The world around me is still dark.

I groan in pain. My nose throbs, agonizing, and my limbs protest against the rope binds around my wrists and ankles. I'm slumped in the back of what I assume is a windowless van, and we're driving, driving away from the clinic, driving toward my death.

Fear as cold as liquid nitrogen replaces the blood in my veins.

Is this how Erin felt in the moments before . . .

Before whatever happened to her?

A chilling thought pierces my brain like a fishing hook.

What if she died because of something she discovered?

The ropes around my wrists press my bangle into the bone.

If you are saved from the lion, do not be greedy and hunt it.

We've been chasing a beast of our own, and this wild animal knows no mercy.

I slide across the rough floor as we round a corner, slamming into the side of the van like a sack of potatoes. I can't move an inch because of the way I'm tied, wrists bound in front of me and ankles tight together, and my muscles quiver at the stress. I would cry if I weren't so terrified.

What's going to happen to me? Is he going to torture me, to find out what I know—and who else knows it? If he was going to kill me quickly, he would've by now. Why am I still alive? Where is he taking me?

I am alone in the back of the windowless van, alone with the shudder of flat tires against bumpy roads, alone with the smell of something stale and human, alone with the sound of the radio playing through the partition separating driver and cargo. Predator and prey.

Predator and prey and a lion, but who's leading this pride?

Breathing gets harder. He hasn't gagged me, but he might as well have.

Gasp. Gasp. Gasp. Quicker than my heart. Quicker than my brain.

Think, think, think.

How can I survive?

The backs of my eyes are painted with kaleidoscopic murals; I'm seeing stars, seeing the universe.

Spiraling, spiraling, endlessly, spaciously, to infinity.

I'm losing losing losing touch on reality.

Can't breathe.

An invisible knife stabs my chest repeatedly, but it's from the inside, it's hard, my heart piercing my chest in a bid for freedom.

Think, think, think.

How can I survive?

The more I think, the worse it gets. The less I think, the worse it gets.

I'm shaking, trembling, a flag flapping in the wind, a glass wobbling on the table of a fast moving train carriage. Faster, harder, shaking.

Think, Carina.

How can I survive?

Do I even want to survive?

Think.

Not about how to escape. That's bordering on impossible. But think about Borko—about how he slots into all of this. What do I know so far?

Andrijo is a suspect. They're searching his apartment. I previously thought he was a lone wolf, acting alone out of some carnal attraction toward Erin, a simple case of man pursuing his desires without care for the woman involved.

But Borko is here; Borko tied me up and loaded me into a van; Borko is driving me toward something resembling death.

Does he work for Kasun, too? What does the clinic have to do with it? Did Erin have an abortion? Did it go wrong? Why do these men care?

The bruise, the baby, the barbarians.

How are they connected?

Think.

Somehow, my breathing has slowed, my heart has retreated back into my rib cage.

It's a hollow curiosity now. Because I know even if I do magically figure it out, even if my overactive brain finally lands on the missing piece that'll tie this all together like my rope-bound appendices, I won't live for long enough to see justice exacted.

I'll never know if they find Erin alive or not.

We drive for so long that the adrenaline is eventually numbed again by my meds, and tiredness threatens to drag me under. A poem my English teacher used to read to us echoes through my foggy mind: "Do not go gentle into that good night."

I force myself to repeat it over and over, force myself to fight the exhaustion, force myself to keep breathing, even though I want nothing more than to succumb to the darkness.

Nothing about me is gentle, and nothing about this night is good.

I MUST HAVE fallen asleep anyway, because the harsh banging of van doors closing and opening jerks me awake. Light doesn't flood the back of the van as the rear doors are swung open—the sky is blacker than coal.

Struggling to prevent the whimper escaping my lips, I blink against the pain of my face. His punch was hard enough to break my nose, and I feel dried blood crusted around my mouth and cheeks. I can still breathe. Just.

"Silly girl," Borko mutters. "Why poke your head where it doesn't belong?"

Instincts scream futilely at me to press myself to the partition, as far away from Borko as possible, but I'm bound helplessly to myself and moving is impossible. Not to mention pointless. It'd only delay the inevitable.

Fear slams into me.

He unties my feet so I can walk, but leaves my hands bound in front of me. Hauling me up by the elbow, so harshly I'm amazed my shoulder doesn't dislocate, he drags me onto concrete ground and pulls me through huge, corrugated tin doors like the ones on farming sheds.

It's a warehouse, this single room big enough to fit my entire university campus inside. Forklifts and crates and rows and rows of shelves, brown cardboard boxes with complicated labels, strip lighting so bright it's almost UV, the smell of cold, of lifelessness.

What the hell is this? Does the warehouse belong to Feminaid? To Kasun? Bastixair? Are these medical supplies?

Borko said he doesn't work for the tourism board anymore. Does he work for Bastixair? Is that how he met Andrijo and Kasun, how he got involved in this twisted web of evil?

I want to crumple to the ground, to beg him to let me go, but my limbs are paralyzed and I stay obedient, allow myself to be dragged along next to him, thinking that maybe if I do everything he says I might live. Logic is a funny thing. When you have no hope, it kind of tricks you. Lets you believe there is, somehow, a way. Maybe the brain knows that true hopelessness is itself enough to kill a person.

My pathetic whimpers fall on deaf ears. Borko doesn't turn to look at me at any point, just focuses on getting me from A to B. I have no idea what B entails, but it's probably not a basket of kittens.

Think, I urge myself. *You're smart, hyperalert. If anyone can think themselves out of this, it's you.*

I frantically search the warehouse floor with my eyes, darting between boxes and trolleys, searching for anything I can use as a weapon. But we're moving too quickly, and my hands are out of action, and there's no way to grab anything.

My chest soars as I remember tucking my phone into the back pocket of my jeans, but as I rub my balled-up fist against my backside, the carpet's pulled from beneath me in one quick swish. He already took it. If Ilić tries to call back, he'll know immediately I told them about the clinic. He'll be even more inclined to hurt me. And deep down, I know Borko is too smart to stay on the line long enough for Ilić to trace the call back here. The phone will be smashed beneath a boot-clad heel within the hour.

Too soon we reach the far end of the warehouse, where steel-grated steps lead up to a mezzanine level. We clank up to the top, and from this elevated vantage point, the warehouse looks even more like a labyrinth of questions. Six doors lead off the balcony; I'm dragged to the farthest away.

It's a tiny storeroom. Empty. Cold. Rows and rows of blue metal shelves, coated in a layer of dust. Disused. Nobody will come looking for me here. Nobody. Panic rises in my chest. Breathing quickens, shallower than ever, leaving me light-headed. Black and purple spots dance across my vision; I'm losing it, losing consciousness, losing all hope of survival.

He throws me to the ground, and without my arms to steady me, I crash painfully into the rim of a shelf. All the wind is knocked from my lungs, and coupled with the panic attack, I feel my grip on the room slipping.

From a thousand miles away, he asks, "Are the police likely to be following you here?"

No. Novi Sad is over an hour away, and Ilić was only just leaving when we spoke. There's no way they got to the clinic in time to witness my abduction, and if they did, surely they'd have tailed the windowless van here, sirens blaring, high speed chase ensuing. My only hope is that the CCTV cameras somehow caught it.

"Yes," I say through blood-crusted teeth, fixing the last ounce of strength into my voice. I can't let him think he's won.

He swears and slams the door shut behind him. I'm plunged into darkness.

The last thing I hear before losing consciousness is the key turning in the lock, and his footsteps marching back down the steel-grated stairs.

Chapter Twenty-One

August 3, Serbia

As soon as I wake, I wish I hadn't.

Pain radiates across my face, through my skull, into my bones. My broken nose throbs, and my eyes feel swollen shut. The bottom of my ribs ache from where I collided with the shelf edge. There's a small amount of light creeping through the bottom of the doorframe and, even though it's pitch black outside, the slit of a window at the top of the back wall.

Strands of thoughts loop and swirl in my mind like a spider dancing through the air, weaving a web. Thoughts of escape, memories of Erin, threads of information relating to her disappearance . . . they're all so intricately spun together I can no longer separate them. Part of the same tapestry, the same masterpiece . . . a masterpiece I will never understand.

I'm concussed. Or just coming down from a panic attack of epic proportions.

Groaning with every inch, I pull myself upright and try to

adjust into a more comfortable position. I settle for leaning against the one bare wall, head tilted back against the cool plasterboard. The beginnings of a migraine pulses against my temples. I didn't drink a single drop of water today, and I'm suffering for it.

Water. I need water. There's no water.

Panic flutters through me again, waves from a bird's wings batting the air in my lungs. The palpitations start, and my first instinct is to bring my palm to my chest. When I can't, because of the absurdly tight rope binds, they kick in harder, faster. The sick part of my mind reminds me of an episode of a prison drama I watched as a kid, when my mum was too tired to force us to go to bed. One female inmate killed another by locking her in a cupboard, without air or water, for days and days.

What if they leave me here so long I run out of air?

There's no water and no air.

Of course, that knowledge makes breathing even harder. I frantically search for an air vent, or some other sign that I won't die from oxygen starvation, but in the darkness I find nothing.

Tears fall then. Reflexively, and for lack of anything better to do.

It's pathetic, but I want my mum. I want her to hold me in her arms, tell me it'll all be okay. I want to tell my brother I love him—I never do that—and spend a night on the sofa, just the three of us, no one staring at smartphones or video games. I want us to talk. I want us to laugh, to forget our various mental health problems and just be a family. I want it. I want it so badly it's as painful as the butt of a gun slammed into my heart.

Then, for the first time in so many years, I allow myself to think of my father.

Normally I suppress all thoughts of him—my psychiatrist thinks this is the root of my anxiety and depression. It's simply too painful to remember him, and remember the day he died. So I bury it. I bury it so far below the surface it cannot hurt me, despite the fact my body fights back with panic attacks and nervous breakdowns.

But I'm already in more pain than I've ever been in, physically and emotionally. I might as well feel it all. It might be the last time I do.

The fragments of my workaholic father left in my mind are dusty with neglect. Dark shards, like his absence as he worked seven days a week, and the sound of my mum wailing when the second heart attack took him. But shards of light, too—fairy stories in bed, all four of us, when we were young, him performing all the funny voices even though he was delirious with exhaustion.

The deterioration was rapid. Business was booming, but his health paid the price. Not enough sleep, not enough rest, not enough food. Too much booze, too much work, too much caffeine. Even the first heart attack, which had him hospitalized for a week, wasn't enough to slow him down.

The second one was more insistent. My mum came for Jake and me at morning break, took us to the hospital to say goodbye to a man clinging to life support. He was already dead, really, but we needed that goodbye.

Holding his cold hand as he slipped away was the defining moment of my adolescence. I grew up, in those sixty seconds. I came to understand that the world is deeply painful, deeply unfair, deeply devastating, and yet you're expected to continue on regardless.

Because the world kept spinning, and I couldn't cope with that. I needed it to stand still, stand still just for a few weeks, a few months, a few years, until somehow the heartache subsided.

But the world didn't stop, and my heart never repaired. The funeral came and went. My period started, my boobs grew, my body changed in every way, but all I wanted was for time to freeze.

That's when my anxiety started to manifest. My body, my life, was spinning out of control, like the earth was hinged on a different axis to my mind. My mother was deep in the ground, deep in a hole of depression my father dug for her, and I was drifting away in the air, carried by the gale of grief, trying desperately to find the ground, but never succeeding. I lost myself.

It took me a few years to realize how much less painful it is not to think of him at all, but by then the damage was done. Anxiety became as much a part of me as he ever was. I've lived with it for longer than I ever lived with him, and that's equal parts comforting and terrifying. My disorder belongs to me in a way he never did.

I still miss him like hell, though. It's a cold stone of emptiness in my heart.

Right now, sitting beaten and broken in a Serbian warehouse, defeated in the search for my friend, I feel a strange kind of peace. I don't believe in the afterlife, and I don't believe I'll ever see my father again. But I won't have to live in a world without him. And the absence of pain isn't all that different from happiness. At least not in my experience.

So, for the first time in my life, I breathe into it. I stop fighting the palpitations, the elastic band around my chest, the rushing thoughts in my mind and the prickling of my skin. I stop trying to beat the sparks of adrenaline and surges of fear. I simply succumb.

And just like that, it all melts away.

I'm left with a beautiful stillness, a simple clarity. It hurts now, but soon it won't.

It's going to be okay, even if it isn't.

My limbs fill with lead and helium; I'm both heavy with weariness and light with relief. The knot of pressure in my head that's been building for over a decade loosens, leaving only the physical symptoms of a broken nose and chronic dehydration.

I breathe.

I CAN'T TELL how much time has passed by the time I hear footsteps clanking back up the metal staircase and across the mezzanine. All I know is that, this time, there's more than one set.

I press my eyes closed. I just want it to be over, either way. I want to be released or killed. I'm tired of the in between.

That doesn't stop my gut from clenching, though.

Key turning in the lock. Muffled male voices on the other side of the door.

I know who's with Borko before I even see him.

Andrijo.

I blink against the light suddenly drenching the storeroom. When I finally adjust, I look up into his eyes—hard, black lumps of coal in a perfect face—and expect to see a number of things: anger, hatred, bloodthirst.

Instead I see fear.

I almost misread it for something else, at first. Shock, maybe, or mania. But it's unmistakably raw fear. And I don't know what to do with it.

It's surreal, seeing him up close after fixating on him for what's felt like a year but has actually only been a few weeks. A tight black T-shirt, gray jeans, beat-up Converse. Thick stubble, dark hair, a strong jaw. That indisputable intensity—rough, organic.

He's a wanted man. The police are searching his home, tracking him down, for whatever he did, or lied about doing. And here he is, right in front of me.

And I'm not afraid of him.

"Andrijo." My voice is small, but not scared. I'm proud of that.

He shakes his head slowly. "Why, Carina? Why did you come here?"

"Your friend knocked me unconscious, piled me in the back of a van and drove me here. I didn't have much say in the matter."

A tanned hand drags through his hair. "I mean to Zrenjanin. Serbia. Why did you come back? To the clinic?"

I keep my words measured. "I came with Karen. She had to come. For Erin." I put extra weight on her name, gauging his reaction. Something in his face twinges, but I can't read it. Guilt? Sadness? Regret? "The police are at your apartment."

"Yes." His face is frozen after his brief flash of emotion. Borko watches the exchange from just beyond the doorway, arms folded.

"Are you going to run forever?" I ask, genuinely curious. "What's your plan? Never return to your own life? You have to face what you did eventually, Andrijo."

Why am I not full of hatred? Why am I not convulsing with fury at the sight of him?

But I know why. It's that look in his eye. That fear I cannot place. More than any shred of evidence ever could, it makes me sure there's more to the story. It makes me sure I've missed something—misjudged him, the situation, the villain.

Right from the start, my gut told me he was involved. Now, that same gut is telling me it's not what I think.

"What do you think I did?" he asks, face still expressionless, eyes still betraying him.

I swallow. "The world thinks she was raped, left for dead in a ditch." I feel cruel when I add, "And now your apartment is being searched."

His Adam's apple bobs violently, his fist curls and uncurls. "What do you think I did?" he repeats.

Pause. Genuine. "I don't know. Why don't you enlighten me?"

He turns to Borko, one hand resting on the doorframe, shakes his head and turns back. Brow furrowed, staring at the ground. "You shouldn't have come here, Carina. You should've stayed away, stayed safe. You have no idea . . . no idea what you've got yourself involved in. Nobody was supposed to get hurt. Nobody . . ." He thumps the doorframe with a balled-up fist. "Just like nobody was supposed to find out."

Borko steps forward now, touches Andrijo's arm. Gently pushes him to one side as he enters the room beside him. Andrijo looks scared, like a bull approaching the slaughterhouse.

"We don't want to hurt you, Carina. But you know so much. We can't just . . ." He grits his teeth. "We can't just let you walk away. And we know the police aren't coming for you." He holds up my phone. It's switched off. "Not now." He doesn't look happy about it. He's not enjoying this, not enjoying the power trip like he was before.

I'm torn between wanting to throw myself at his feet, insist I know nothing, and begging him to let me live . . . or seeing how this pans out. Because the truth is . . . I don't know anything. Not really. But I want to. I so desperately need to understand what lion I've been hunting since the thirteenth of July.

"So you're going to kill me, just in case I know anything?" I tilt my chin upward to try and show some kind of defiance, but I know with a broken nose and blood crusted all over my face I look a mess. And honestly? I don't fucking care.

Progress.

Andrijo rubs both eyes furiously with his hands, pressing his fingertips hard against his eyelids. He mutters something to Borko in Serbian. Borko responds in rapid-fire, but Andrijo bites back, blinking against the spots he just created on his vision.

Borko shrugs, turning back to me. "It's not that we want to hurt you. Last thing we want is another missing foreigner drawing attention to the situation."

What situation? I want to scream, but I stay composed. "So what are you going to do?"

"We want you to tell us exactly how much you know," Borko says. "Then we can decide."

Self-preservation kicks in now. "I know nothing, I swear. Nothing."

"Why were you really at the clinic? We know you weren't really assaulted."

I tense my jaw. "How do you know that?"

"We know." He stares meaningfully at me. Is that where he's been all this time? Somehow checking where I really was on the first night at JUMP? Because I came back to the hotel early, dogged with exhaustion and social anxiety from the sheer weight of my fellow festival-goers. Could he somehow have found that out? Caught me in a lie?

I gulp. If he does know the truth, he knows I know more than I should about the clinic. How else can I explain my being there?

Maybe I don't have to explain. What's he going to do?

"I've told you why I was there. I can't make you believe me."

I make sure to hold eye contact, maintain steady body language from my crumpled position on the floor. I won't give him any more reason to doubt me.

He growls like a rabid wolf. "You're lying. If you don't start cooperating . . ."

"What? What are you going to do? I'm already your prisoner. You've already beaten me. Broken my nose. You're already considering killing me." The words taste like pure alcohol—sharp and painful and disorientating. Is this really happening? "Don't you think if I had something to hide, I'd have told you by now?"

More Serbian words are spat at Andrijo. His eyes widen, and he shakes his head, but not nearly defiantly enough. What did Borko just ask him to do? What's he afraid of doing to me? Borko snarls, steps toward me.

"Do you know you don't have a lock on your phone's photos? Everything else, yes. But anyone can access your pictures by swiping up the camera."

My blood runs cold, and now I realize exactly how he knows I'm lying.

The screenshots I sent myself.

The article and image linking Kasun and Tim to the clinic opening. He saw them saved to my camera.

He knows he's got me. Just a few inches from me now, he bends over and snatches my chin in his hand, gripping painfully tight. He forces me to look into his gray, too close together eyes, which betray nothing like the fear in Andrijo's. His breath is hot, sour. His hands rough against my face.

Don't whimper. Don't give him the satisfaction.

"I'll give you one more chance to answer me honestly before this starts to hurt. What do you know?"

There's nowhere to hide. He knows I already made the connection. Will he believe that's all I know? That I never filled in the bigger picture?

"I know there was a case eight years ago. Brodie Breckenridge. She was on a press trip with Tim when she vanished. He was clean, but I was suspicious. Then I found an empty pregnancy test packet in Erin's jacket back home. So when I found out a guy called Kasun opened a sexual assault and abortion clinic out here, and Tim was photographed next to him . . . I put two and two together. And came to see it for myself."

There's so much I left out. The idea of a stalker, my knowledge of Bastixair and Aubin's, the bruise on her arm, her imprisoned father. But he's not searching my face for that. Something I said has resonated on a level I wasn't expecting; his mouth drops open.

He drops my jaw like a hot coal, grabs his hand away. "Erin's pregnant?"

I swallow hard. "Maybe."

Both he and Andrijo stare at me in horror.

"Something worrying you, Andrijo?" I say, unable to resist the snipe. "Don't worry. Not yours. Timing doesn't work."

"I didn't rape her," he whispers, expression haunted. "I swear." He looks like he genuinely cares that I believe him.

I grit my teeth. The hard ridge of the metal shelf is pressing painfully into my back. "But you had a part in it. Whatever it is. Or the police wouldn't be at your apartment right now. Searching for . . . what? Evidence your alibi is bull crap? Her DNA on your clothes? Her blood on your shoes?"

He steps forward, ink-black eyes bottomless pits of conflicted emotions, but Borko throws his arm out to keep him from reaching me. As he twists to face Andrijo, I see the gun sticking out of his waistband and my blood turns to ice. "*Ne*, Andrijo." His accent makes the name sound like an insult. "*Ne*."

Biting fear is settling in again—I've never seen a gun up close before—but I don't fight it, just try to breathe through it. "What secret is so damning it's worth killing for?" I utter.

Borko's head snaps back to me, arm still outstretched. "What?"

"Well, you're so obsessed with figuring out how much I know that you're considering murdering me based on the answer. So I don't think it's a big stretch to say you're hiding something. Is what happened to my best friend the secret in itself, or did she die for uncovering it, too? Did Brodie? Who else has lost their lives over whatever you're hiding?" Andrijo's face is tortured now, and I know I'm hitting the mark. "Was it worth it? The first time? The second?"

He roars in frustration or something similar, half clenches his fists and swivels on his heel, walking slowly out the door. I hit a nerve. Hell, I hit a whole cluster of them. His footsteps pick up speed until I can hear him practically sprinting down the stairs.

Borko's face is beet-purple. He says nothing, just stares at me for a few more seconds, glances between me and the door and follows his partner out. The door slams shut behind him. The key clicks in the lock.

But not before I use the last of the light to pick out the exact location of the air vent.

Chapter Twenty-Two

August 4, Serbia

WAITING SEVERAL MINUTES after they've left to make my decision, I know what I have to do. The strip of night sky visible through the narrow horizontal window is dark navy with wisps of charcoal cloud; it must be nearing midnight, though I have no idea how long I've been unconscious for at various stages of the night.

I'm torn between putting it off until I know they're far enough away, and going for it right now in case they decide my fate and hurry back to find two legs hanging out of an air vent.

I choose the latter.

This could be my one chance at survival. I don't think of what happens if the vent leads nowhere.

Scaling the shelves is a nightmare with my hands tied, but I silently thank the universe that Borko didn't bind them behind me. I use the vertical railings joining the shelving together to hoist myself up, and after a couple of attempts I make it to the top shelf.

The air vent is small, a few feet wide and a few feet long, and as soon as I'm up close I realize I have no idea how to remove the grate. It doesn't really budge when I jiggle it around, nor when I pull down or shove upward. If it wasn't a matter of life or death, the lazy part of me would slump to the ground in a huff and give up, or descend into a tempest of anxious thoughts centric on the fact I am shit at everything in the world.

But I persevere.

I wriggle a few fingers around inside the edges where the grate meets the ceiling. My forefinger meets some kind of catch, which takes me a few seconds to maneuver, but eventually I unlatch the grate and push upward. After another logistical struggle, I'm up in the vent and closing the hatch behind me.

One victory down, seven thousand more to go.

It's a tight squeeze inside air vents. Nobody in the movies tells you that. It's dusty and claustrophobic and feels plain wrong, and also like you are likely to die in some kind of crushing incident. Every sound I make is amplified like I'm in the mouth of a tuba; my bangle clanks off the metal ground, my toes kick and thud as I shuffle along, and I'm fairly sure any Serbian with ears can hear what I'm currently trying to achieve.

Which is . . . I'm not sure. Find some sort of exit route, I guess? Do air vents even open out to the outside world, or just circle around the inside of the building? Why do I know so little about air vents?

After a few minutes of hapless shuffling, propelled by adrenaline and sheer bloody-mindedness, I reach another grate. I peer into the room below. It's an office—there's no light on inside, but a small square window in the door lets in enough that I can make out what's inside. Generic office fodder: a desk, desk chair, computer, filing cabinet, an old glass jar full of pens and pencils and a ruler. And . . .

A letter opener. A metal one, with one of those sharp ends.

A . . . weapon?

I flick the latch and lift the grate up. I have to be quick.

My sandals hit the top of the filing cabinet with an alarmingly loud clamor, and it wobbles under my weight. It can't be very full. I climb down to the ground as gracefully as I can manage with my hands bound, run to the desk and grab the letter opener. I use it to slice through the rope around my wrists, then shove it into my back pocket. There's a pocket USB drive in there, too, which I also grab for no real reason other than a one-in-a-million chance there's something on it. I pause and survey the room. Work out all the possible sources of damning evidence: the computer, the filing cabinet, the desk drawers.

I try the desk drawers. Locked. Course they are. There's no convenient key stuck underneath with tape either.

I shake the mouse and the computer whirs back into life. Password-protected. And I'm no hacker. I try obvious things like Bastixair and Feminaid, but when is life ever that easy? It blocks me out after three tries. Hopefully I'll have made it out of the warehouse by the time they return in the morning and realize someone's tried to break into their system.

The filing cabinet drawers are locked, too. I almost laugh. What do I think this is? A video game on the easy setting?

Positioning the desk chair next to the filing cabinet, I manage to clamber back up and into the vent, heart pounding and beads of sweat forming between my boobs. I only allow myself thirty seconds to catch my breath before moving on.

The next room I come to is an almost identical office, and the next a storeroom like the one I was held in. I remember the layout of the mezzanine level—six doors, equally spaced. I was in the sixth, and I've passed three more. Two more rooms to go, then hopefully . . . a way out? I'm on the first floor, not ground level, but I'd jump from the fifth if it meant getting away from those two men with fangs for teeth and empty cavities where their hearts should be.

Slowly but surely, I progress through the vent, coughing away dust and cringing at the echoes my body makes as it shuffles. Another storeroom. Another office, this one completely disused and empty of belongings. Not even a computer.

Only another twenty yards to the next grate, and then . . . what? All I can see right now is black in front of me. There's still no light, and I try not to panic. Surely, if it led to the world outside, there would be some kind of sky ahead. Nope.

My muscles ache, my face is killing me and I'm drenched in sweat now, but the only choice I have is to keep going. I reach the next grate, look down. Another storeroom, barely light enough to make out despite the strip window at the top. The shelves in this one are empty, too.

I'm about to move on, but something catches my eye as I turn my head away. An incongruous image I almost didn't register.

Dim night sky cast over a form on the floor.

A form so shadowed I nearly missed it. In fact, I would've . . . if it weren't for the white-blond hair catching the weak light.

Erin.

Chapter Twenty-Three

August 4, Serbia

FOR A MOMENT I'm paralyzed. Disbelieving, hopeful, scared.

She's not moving.

Forget the echoing in the tunnel; my heart pummeling my rib cage is deafening.

I almost don't want to look.

If she was alive, she'd have heard me coming.

Am I strong enough to drop down into a room containing my best friend's body?

Am I strong enough to survive the next minute of my life?

Right now, she's Schrödinger's cat. In this moment, she is both alive and dead.

I can't bear to open the box and confirm the latter.

And yet what's the alternative? Leave her here?

Shaking so hard I can barely grip, I lift the latch and tug the grate up into the vent shaft.

Drop down onto the top shelf, loudly.

She still doesn't hear. Doesn't move.

In the dim light, I can't tell whether or not her chest is rising or falling. She's curled limply in the fetal position, either in a last-ditch effort to give herself some kind of comfort, or because that's the position in which she was carried up the stairs and dumped on the storeroom floor.

There's a smell. Pungent, acidic, human.

A decomposing corpse?

I gag, both at the stench and at the idea of what it could be.

I look away from her flaccid form, and as my eyes adjust to the light, I spot a bucket in the corner of the room.

Waste. Human waste.

Which means . . . she's alive. Or at least, she has been until very recently.

The revelation gives me renewed hope. I awkwardly cling to the framework of the empty shelving and shuffle down to the ground like a burglar on a drainpipe. My feet hit the ground, but she doesn't stir. Flinching away from the smell, I dash over to her and crouch down. Rest both hands on her shoulder.

She's breathing.

"Erin?" I shake her, but so gently it's like she's made of glass and I'm scared of shattering her.

Ba-boom, ba-boom.

Every beat of my heart sounds like: "She's alive."

She doesn't stir.

"Erin," softly, softly.

Her eyelashes flutter. It's dark in the room; so dark she's just a shadow. I feel absence emanating from her, loss, a new void opened up. Everything missing from her, everything taken. I squeeze her bony shoulder, covered in a baggy gray hoodie; not the pink blouse from JUMP, not the murder victim smile. Lying frail and sense-less on the floor, empty, vacant. No red lipstick staining her teeth, no sparkly stud in her nose, no sailor's laugh or filthy innuendo, no fuck-you leather jacket. No animal howling or manic tears, no vivid blue eyes or razor-sharp wit.

There's no warmth emanating from her, no trademark Erin-ness. She's Erin but she's not.

My eyes burn. "Erin, please. It's me. It's me."

Then I realize she is awake. Her eyes have peeled open ever so slightly, and her hand, pale from three weeks without sunlight, has curled into a half-tight fist like a newborn baby. She's awake, but she doesn't want to be. Isn't trying hard enough to fight for consciousness.

"Erin," I say, and my voice cracks, and I hug her from behind like we're spooning. "Erin. I'm here. You're okay." The word is a falsehood. "But we have to get out of here. Before they come back."

She winces at "they," a tiny flicker of movement, and I wonder what they did to her.

"Can you move?" I urge, listening for footsteps on metal stairs and the murmur of low Serbian voices.

Eyelids droop again, unnaturally slow and heavy. The fist un-furls like a flower opening. She's loose, numb, cold. Did they drug her? Sedate her to keep her quiet?

Why is she here?

Did she find out the same thing I was on the cusp of uncovering?

"Erin, we can get out through an air vent. We can escape. You can live, you can survive. We can survive." Nothing. Despera-tion rising in my throat, I murmur, "Erin, you can see your mum again. She loves and misses you so much. And Annabel. Smith. Me. We love and need you. Please. Please. Open your eyes. Let me know you can hear me. Can you hear me?"

A shuddering breath I feel in my bones. But still nothing. Eyes, naked without their winged eyeliner, stay closed. I take her freezing hand in mine, lift up her arm ten centimeters. Release. It flops lifelessly back to her hip.

Smooth, hard dread like a pebble settles in my gut. I've found her, but I can't get her out. I have no phone to call for help.

And I still don't know why she's here.

Wow. It'd be so easy to have a panic attack right now.

"Erin," I whisper. "I can only ask you one more time before I have to think of another way. Can you move? Can you climb through the vent with me? Can you let the thought of seeing your family propel you?"

A tiny head shake, so slight it's almost imperceptible.

"Why?" I mutter, quietly so I don't frighten her even more. "Did they drug you?"

An even tinier nod, knocking the wind from my lungs. They drugged her. To keep her quiet but alive? Or in an attempt to kill her? Or because they wanted to get her addicted to drugs so that—

No. Stop being ridiculous. She isn't being trafficked. That no longer makes sense in the context of everything I know.

What does make sense?

That's the million-dollar question right now.

"Are you . . . pregnant?" I ask, the words delicate yet deadly between my lips.

She says nothing.

"I don't want to leave you, Erin," I almost plead. "But I need to go and get help. Can you stay alive for me? Keep breathing, keep fighting, don't do anything to anger them. Fight. Please. We need you to fight. Okay?"

A single tear slips down her cheek, pooling in the Cupid's bow of her perfect lips.

"Don't cry. Please. It's going to be okay. I'm here. I've found you. We're going to get out of here. I promise." I hug her again, a hug full of desperation and disbelief and fear. "It's nearly over."

Is it?

My mind reels as I clamber back up the shelving and back into the vent, pulling the hatch shut behind me. For a few moments, I don't start moving, don't opt for one direction over the other. What am I going to do? Should I try to escape anyway, and come back with the police?

But I have no idea how far I am from civilization, no idea how far I am from a town or a phone or the police. And by the time I reach someone or somewhere, Andrijo and Borko will have noticed me missing. What would they do to Erin then? Move her, knowing I'd be back with police? Worse?

I could try and search the offices to find the key to the storeroom she's being held in. Carry her out. But again, where would we go? We'd likely be caught before even making it to the doors. Then we'd both be in trouble.

I rack my brains. Lightning strikes. I could keep crawling around the air vents, keep looking for them. Try and find a location where I could listen in on their conversations, work out why I'm here and why they have Erin and what they're going to do about it.

The penny drops heavily.

They're Serbian. I'm not. The language barrier prevents any hope of eavesdropping.

Instinct is screaming at me to go back to my storeroom and figure it out. The last thing I want is for them to come up with a bucket for my waste, notice me gone and start searching the warehouse. Moving Erin. Or . . . worse.

I keep coming back to that word: *worse*.

Does such a thing even exist anymore?

For once in my life, I follow my gut, awkwardly turn around in the vent and go back in the direction of my storeroom.

SLEEP THREATENS TO swallow me, and soon I can no longer fight back.

It's the dark, and the warmth, and the silence, and the knowledge that my best friend is alive. Hunger aches in my tummy, and my bladder is full despite the lack of water. My throat burns with thirst. You don't realize how bad the physical discomfort can be when your basic needs aren't fulfilled.

So sleep, when it beckons, is easy to succumb to. My tired brain can no longer think of a solution to the Erin problem, and sooner or later, fear makes way for exhaustion. I curl up in the fetal position, exactly as Erin is less than a hundred yards away, and fall asleep knowing she's nearby.

I dream of Erin and of fire.

I'm back in the graveyard where I met Smith in the weeks after she disappeared. It's dusk, and the sky is dusty pink streaked with indigo clouds. The ancient oak trees are charcoal silhouettes shadowed by the towering church behind me, and the tombstones are crooked thumbs sticking out from the earth. Crows watch from the stone wall, embers reflecting in their eyes.

Everything in the graveyard is coated in ash, a thin layer of white-gray cinders catching the dying sun's rays. I run a finger slowly along the top of a tombstone. The ash is soft and powdery, already cold.

Somehow, I know what's happening behind me without turning to look. The church is ablaze, and Erin is standing before the stone steps leading up to the entrance, not flinching away from the licking flames. I turn to look at her. She's wearing the leather jacket.

"Erin," I call, but my voice is far away, both too quiet and too loud and vaguely ethereal.

The heat of the fire engulfing the building burns against my face, even from this distance. Erin's blood must be boiling in her veins, standing that close. I take a step toward her and the heat soars, but as soon as I do, she mirrors my movements, stepping even closer to the inferno.

I'm about to yell at her in my pseudo-distant voice, scream at her to step back, demand to know what she's doing and why, but as it so often does in dreams, the answer comes to me without words or explanation. It's a feeling, an abstract perception of her mindset. She's getting closer because she wants to. Because the flames make her feel alive. Because she's lived with the heat for so long she's terrified of its absence. Because the intensity lures her in like a mythical creature: coaxing, compelling, commanding.

She plays with fire because incandescence is her lifeblood.

Still convinced the heat is real, I wake up to a stiff, sweaty neck and the click of a key in a lock. The plan comes to me of its own accord: fully formed, terrifying, complete. I remain still, deathly still, stiller than even Erin in her sedated state.

I'm facing the shelf, curved back turned to the door, so when it swings open I don't know which lion it is; all I can gather is there's only one set of footsteps.

"Carina."

It's Borko, I think. Less gravel in the stilted voice.

I focus so hard on staying absolutely, completely rigid that my muscles are on the verge of shaking.

"Carina. I brought you water."

He brought me water? He mustn't be planning on killing me too imminently.

I remain still.

A sneaker squeaks against the floor as he moves closer to me. "Carina?"

I'd guess he's around a meter away. Not close enough. I tighten my grip.

The toe of a sneaker jabs at my kidneys; I suppress a gasp and allow myself to flop forward like I'm unconscious. He mutters something in Serbian. Another step forward, then the click of stiff knee joints as he crouches down on his haunches.

Now. I have to go now.

Not allowing myself the luxury of forethought, I swivel my entire body quickly to face him, grab his right shoulder and, before he has a chance to react, I slam the sharp end of the letter knife into the right side of his neck. The impact shudders up my arm and I let go.

Eyes wide, he tumbles forward, and I push the immediate and crippling guilt from my mind in time to slide out of the way before he collapses on top of me. Heart thudding, I wrench the letter knife from the deep stab wound, and the instant I do, I'm sprayed with a burst of warm blood. It gurgles and bubbles as it pulses from the gaping hole in his throat, flowing out of his body impossibly fast—a maroon river bursting its banks.

Squirming and moaning, he writhes on the floor for a few

moments before abruptly ceasing all movement, eyes still frozen open.

No.

He can't be dead already.

It can't have been that easy to take a life.

I'm numb. Why am I numb? Why did the jolt of shame only last an instant? Why am I not overcome with guilt looking at the corpse of a young man whose life I just stole from him?

Maybe because the image of Erin curled around herself just a hundred feet away, devoid of feeling and damaged beyond repair, burns hotter than my conscience can compete with.

Hand surprisingly steady, I wipe the now slightly bent letter knife on his black hoodie and tuck it back into my jeans pocket. His gun is still sticking out the top of his waistband, and so I snatch that, too. It's warm from his skin and smooth in my hand. I've never even seen one before, let alone held one, and it's heavier than it looks. I slide it into my waistband, the same place he kept it, double-checking the safety is on so I don't shoot myself in the ass.

Then I see it. The corner of my pink phone case sticking out of his back pocket.

Yes.

The relief is so instant it's almost overwhelming. Tears prick my eyes, hot and sharp. I grab it, wipe the dirty screen with my thumb. Hold down the on button.

In the few seconds that follow, I say a silent prayer, even though I've never been religious. Please, God, if you really do exist . . . please let my phone have been switched off manually. Please don't let it have run out of battery. I need this. I need to see the little white Apple icon light up the black screen. I need battery, I need reception. I need to survive.

Flicker.

The Apple icon.

Yes, yes, yes.

I clutch the phone to my chest, sob once, deeply, and sniff away the rest of the tears.

I eye the reception bar desperately.

Searching . . .

It searches for too many seconds. Minutes, hours, days, weeks. It searches for an eternity so vast and deep it gives me vertigo.

And then it connects.

The first thing I do is click on Maps and ask it to find my current location. My hands are shaking so hard it takes a few attempts, but it eventually drops a flag on a vast building in acres and acres of fields—we're in the middle of nowhere. I zoom out, out again . . . we're far north of Zrenjanin and Novi Sad, west of a city called Subotica, near the Hungarian border. Over one hundred and forty kilometers from the clinic. My stomach drops. Even though I'm sure they can send local police cars, it's going to take a while for Ilić to get here.

I dial his number—it's one of the most recent on my call log. He picks up after two rings.

"Carina! Where are you? Why has your phone been switched off? We tried to find you once we got to Zrenjanin, but—"

"Ilić," I interrupt. "I found Erin. She's alive, but not in good shape. She's been sedated."

I expect him to flip out, ask why I went looking for her, demand to know everything that's happened, chastise me for trying to play the hero. But he doesn't. He's the height of professionalism. I don't give him enough credit.

"Right. Where are you?"

I tell him what I saw on the map, and he guides me through the process of sending him my exact location using my phone.

"We're on our way. Are you in danger?"

I look at the corpse in front of me. There's a puddle of blood on the floor now, and my sandals are stained maroon. "I killed Borko," I say, measuredly, calmly, so he knows I'm not in an anxiety frenzy. "He attacked me, so I stabbed him in the neck with a letter opener." For a moment I worry there's not going to be enough evidence of his violence to justify self-defense, and they'll prosecute me for murder. Then I remember my bound hands and broken nose.

"All right. I don't want you to worry, Carina. You're not in any trouble. But now that we're on our way, I want you to start from the beginning. What happened?"

I tell him everything, from being dragged through the clinic and questioned to being punched in the face and loaded into a van. From being interrogated again by both Borko and Andrijo, to climbing through the vents and finding Erin.

"You say she's been sedated. Was she physically harmed?" Ilić asks. I hear sirens blaring down his end.

"Not that I could see. She'd lost weight, and her skin was pasty and dry. But no cuts or bruises. No blood."

I'm hit with a sudden surge of guilt for not being with her right now, instead remaining in a closet with a dead body and a whole lot of blood. I'm about to consider climbing through the vent again, until I remember the keys hanging in the door of my storeroom, a small loop most likely containing her key, too. I slip it from the lock and close the door as softly as possible.

Ilić is recounting something in Serbian, but I interrupt again. "Ilić, I'm going to see Erin now. Tell her you're on your way. Call me when you're here?"

"Wait, Carina. Stay on the line a few more minutes. I've put you on speakerphone in the car. Can you tell us why exactly you think Erin is being held there? Did you get any information out of Andrijo? Or Borko, before . . . ?"

Before I killed him.

The childish part of me wants to stomp my feet and demand he tell me everything he knows, because he's done nothing but keep things from me for weeks. But this isn't about me.

"I'm . . . I'm thinking she found out something she shouldn't have. Something about Kasun, or the clinics. Andrijo and Borko have been obsessed with figuring out what I know, too. There's a secret there. Something they're willing to abduct a young woman to protect. Something . . . something Brodie Breckenridge might have known, too."

"Have you got any idea what the secret could be?"

I strain my brain like I'm stretching a cramp out of a muscle. But I can't slot the pieces together. "No."

"All right. Go and see Erin. Call us if you need anything. We'll be there soon. And stay safe, okay? Once you get to her storeroom, lock yourselves inside and leave the key in the door so nobody can get in."

I swallow hard. "Right. Okay."

Mustering the courage to leave the room is almost impossible. I have no idea whether Andrijo—or anyone else involved in this scandal for that matter—is still on-site, and I don't know what they'd do if they saw me running from one room to another. They'd know I'd disarmed Borko. And the mezzanine is so exposed . . . I remember watching my brother play shooting games, and his entire tactic was staying away from exposed areas. He'd sneak around the perimeters, through abandoned trailers and behind oil drums, even if it took twice as long. His kill-to-death ratio was always stellar.

Maybe it's worth going through the air vent. It'll take three times as long, but I know for certain I won't be seen. And no matter how unpleasant the dusty surface and cramped space and the sensation of being crushed, I'm willing to bet being shot feels quite a bit worse.

Taking one last look at Borko's body—the wound still oozing thick blood, and the way his eyes are devoid of all light—is a mistake. I did that. I ended his life. I turned him from someone into nothing. Into a lifeless entity. He went from a person to not existing because of me.

Gulping in air as calmly as I can, something lead-like settles in my stomach. I remember how the thin handle of the letter knife reverberated in my hand immediately after the jarring sensation of metal through skin and muscle and flesh. I remember the horror, the shock, the panic on his face when he realized I'd hit an artery. I remember how quickly his soul left his body, how fast he made that transition from full to empty.

The invisible elastic band around my chest is pulled back and snapped against my skin. The pain is sharp, sharper than the letter knife. Guilt larger than anything screams in my ears.

I can never undo the murder I just committed.

So, through shame rather than fear, I clamber back up the shelves, arms wobbling like a plate of jelly, and climb back into the dusty air vent, leaving behind the evidence of the life I stole in order to save my own.

Tunnel vision.

I need to channel tunnel vision in order to save my friend. I need to leave my guilt in that storeroom with the dead body and focus on one thing and one thing only: getting us the hell out of here.

My movement through the vent is smoother this time. I slip off my sandals and leave them on the top shelf—I figure a quieter escape can't be a bad thing. I shuffle as efficiently as I can without thumping the metal too hard. I don't want Andrijo, or anyone else for that matter, to hear a commotion and come to check on us and Borko before the police arrive.

Passing the first office, then the second, I start to move quicker as the thought of telling Erin we're nearly safe propels me forward. I want it more than I've ever wanted anything, more than a successful journalism career or to be free of debt. None of it matters. All I want is to survive, with her, and live my life with a whole new appreciation for the people around me. For my broken family, my fucked-up friends.

And I want to understand. I want that delicious satisfaction of everything clicking into place: the bruise, the pregnancy test, the abusive father, the disease, the clinic. Tim, Andrijo, Borko, Kasun. Erin—who is she, really?

It's not until I'm within a few feet of the storeroom, sliding along silently on my knees, that I hear his voice.

Andrijo. He's in there with Erin.

Chapter Twenty-Four

August 4, Serbia

HE'S TALKING TO her in a tone I've never heard before. Guilt-ridden, which I recognize from the way I feel right now, and shame. Helplessness. But it's pierced with other emotions, too: desperation, care, longing.

Here's what I don't hear: malice, evil, aggression.

His voice is low and soft, but from just beside the grate I can make out what he's saying.

" . . . wanted to be a teacher. But my father . . . he is sick with Aubin's, and my mother is disabled and cannot work to support him. The government . . . they help out with money, but it's not enough. I am an only child. I need to take take care of my parents, and teachers' salaries . . . they're not enough. Borko . . . he knew I needed more money. For them. He gave me what he could from his own savings, but it still wasn't enough. So he got me the management job at Bastixair. It was great at first, you know? Lots of money, enough to live well and help my father, and the company

I worked for was on the cusp of a cure for the disease he's fallen prey to. When Borko told me he needed my help with something that could make our lives easier . . . I felt like I owed him. And . . . he's my cousin. He's family. And if you won't support your family, well . . . you of all people understand."

My blood freezes in my veins.

Borko and Andrijo are cousins.

Well, were.

Erin mumbles something inaudible.

"What?"

I peer through the cracks in the vent. The door is ajar, illuminating the scene. He's sitting on the floor opposite her, back against the shelves. He stares at her face, angled toward him. She's in exactly the same position as when I left her, wrapped in the baggy gray hoodie and a pair of sweatpants bunched around her narrow waist. Now there's more light, I see her greasy hair tied in a knot, her naked face washed clean of makeup, her bare feet tucked up to her backside.

She speaks louder, words slurred and flat. "Why are you telling me this? You said I already knew too much. Unless . . . unless you've already decided to kill me. And you just want me to die believing you're not as evil as you seem."

The creepiest thing is the lack of fear in her voice. Terror is replaced by resignation. Almost like she's known it's over for a while, and all she wants to do is give in to it.

No, Erin, I silently urge. It's the sedatives. You want to live. Please. Say you want to live.

Andrijo says nothing for a while, and the accusation hangs between them. "We've never wanted to hurt you. Never."

A groan of disbelief. Erin's face is twisted as she presses it into the floor, like all she wants is to not have to listen to him bullshit her. "No?"

"No!" He leans forward, staring at her with those intense black eyes, begging her to understand him. "When you came to me . . . I wanted to help you. I did."

My stomach falls through a trapdoor that's opened up somewhere south of my guts.

She came to him?

When? Why?

But my brain is working in overdrive trying to make sense of it, and a nugget of realization floats to the surface. A nugget with more clarity than any other I've produced so far.

Andrijo works for Bastixair. Bastixair makes an Aubin's drug, which isn't available in the UK.

She went to him for the drugs.

Racing through all the information I have, I try to work out how Erin could possibly have known how to contact Andrijo for the Aubin's drugs. Through Tim, perhaps? Did she do an online search, stumble into the depths of some dodgy forum and reach out there? It's a long shot.

No.

I have it.

"And if you won't support your family, well . . . you of all people understand."

She didn't need to find out who to contact herself. Because her father already knew.

He sent her here. He needed the drugs, because he, too, has Aubin's. And the only way to get them was on the black market.

Andrijo and Borko are the black market.

There's silence in the room below as I tuck this epiphany away, terrified of losing it again. Now the part I can't figure out is what went wrong. Why is she here in a random warehouse, drugged and defeated, at the mercy of two cousins who only wanted to help their struggling relatives, albeit by selling drugs illegally?

Andrijo wanted to help.

But . . . ?

Maybe the first part of my theory, the part I told the police, wasn't right. I told them I was abducted because they were afraid of what I knew, which is true, although it doesn't make sense in terms of Erin's case. Obviously she knows about the fact these drugs are being sold on the black market, but she's in no danger of exposing it to the police or press. She'd have kept it quiet forever if it kept her dad from suffering. So why is she here now?

It's one reach too far for my exhausted brain, and I fall short of the answer.

"So what are you going to do?" Erin murmurs. "You wanted to help me, but you're not going to. So what next? Am I going to live or die?"

His face contorts, betraying his indecision.

She sees it, too. "Can you do it? Can you really do it, Andrijo? Can you hold a gun to my head and pull the trigger, or smother me with a plastic bag, or slit my throat?" The slurred words are eerie, thick, heavy. "Watch the light in my eyes snuff out, feel my heart stop beating? Can you really take a life?"

Her words are stab wounds to my already crippled conscience.

I'm a monster. If we survive this, will anyone ever look at me the same again? Knowing I'm a killer?

Will I ever be able to look at myself and still believe I'm a good person?

"I want to believe you'd keep this quiet," Andrijo replies, voice hoarse. He runs a hand through his hair again. Nervously taps a foot on the floor over and over. "Even if Kasun lets you go. But once you're free, what's stopping you exposing this to the world?"

"Because no matter what happens now, my father will always need those drugs. And you're the only ones who can provide them. Why would I expose that?"

Andrijo nods slowly. "Right. It wouldn't make sense for you to tell the world."

"No." There's more force behind Erin's voice now. She can sense him backing down. The smallest shred of her survival instinct remains intact, and she's clinging to it now like a life raft at sea. She shuffles so she's facing him more head-on. "You and Borko won't go to jail. You can continue looking after your parents. Nothing would change."

Andrijo's eyebrows unknot slowly.

"I don't think it's bad, what you're doing. Giving Aubin's sufferers across Europe access to medicine to ease their symptoms. I don't disagree in theory, and I don't disagree in practice. But this? This is fucked up. Keeping me here, lifeless, wishing I was dead. This isn't good, or noble, or even making you money. This isn't you."

She's doing that Erin thing of making people believe she knows them, cares about them, more than anyone else. And it's working.

He climbs slowly to his feet, like a just-born baby deer. When I first met him, he seemed so tough, so resilient. Now he just looks tired.

Why is Erin here? I want to scream at them both. The answer is there, just beyond my grasp, and I know I probably have all the information needed to answer it. Unless she directly threatened to expose them, there must be more to it than the simple need to protect their drug trafficking secret. Why Erin? Why now?

I don't have time to ponder the answer, because Andrijo is on the move.

Rubbing his jaw tiredly, he says, "Try and get some sleep, okay?"

A girlish murmur. "Andrijo?"

He pauses. "Yes?" There it is again. That trace of something like compassion in his voice. Does he actually care about her?

"Even if you do have to kill me . . . promise you'll leave Carina alone? Let her go. She knows nothing. And even if she did . . . she wouldn't say anything. I know her. She wouldn't."

He stops in the doorway before bowing his head and pulling the door closed behind him. He locks it—of course he does—and much to my dismay, there's no keyhole on the inside. Not only can we not get out, but we also can't keep him out by leaving the key in the lock. Shit.

What'll happen when he finds his cousin's murdered corpse in the farthest away storeroom? Will he come racing back in here? Unleash his wrath and grief on Erin? Kill us both on sight?

I cross my fingers that he'll search the rest of the warehouse first. Perhaps Andrijo wasn't supposed to come here and talk to his hostage. Maybe he'll go back downstairs and wait for Borko to resurface. Maybe we have plenty of time to figure this out.

Or maybe we have no time at all.

I drop into the room, and Erin visibly reacts with a sharp inhalation and a jerking movement. She's far more alert than when I saw her, and, from what I've just heard, capable of speech. She stares at me disbelievingly with renewed wonder. Does she even remember me being here earlier in the night?

"Carina! What are you—"

"Borko's dead," I say flatly. "I killed him. We have to get out of here."

"He's . . . you . . . what?!"

"I'll explain as soon as we're out of here, I promise. Can you walk? Climb up into the vent?"

She frowns, deep in concentration, and I see her attempt to tense her muscles enough to move her body. Propping herself up on her elbow requires so much energy that she promptly collapses back to the ground with a whimper. "No. Shit. What are we going to do?" The bags under her eyes are dark purple, like bruises.

"The police are on their way," I say. "But I have to find a way to keep you safe until they get here. Andrijo could discover Borko's body and come back any minute now. And I'm willing to bet he'll have changed his mind on letting us live when he does. This door doesn't lock or unlock on the inside, so even though we have the key we can't get out—or keep him from getting in. I have a gun, but I don't want to have to kill him. Once was bad enough."

I rack my brains for a solution. She's staring at me with some kind of newfound respect. The Carina she knew three weeks ago was hopeless, the worst person you'd want in an emergency, but now I'm overcoming my anxiety and taking charge. It'd feel good if I wasn't in mortal danger. And I hadn't just killed a man.

I push a stray lock of hair out of my eyes. "Okay. I'm going to use the air vent to go back to the storeroom they were holding me in. The door's closed, but not locked. I'm hoping Andrijo won't be on the mezzanine, he'll be waiting for Borko downstairs. I'll slip out and . . ." A bolt of inspiration strikes like lightning. "And I'll grab one of the crate pull carts from downstairs. Then I can come up and unlock you, load you onto it and we can escape."

Fear is written all over her naked face. Bloodshot eyes, pale skin, a sheen of cold sweat. "Wouldn't it be safer just to wait in here until the police arrive?"

"Yeah." I nod. "If I hadn't just killed his cousin. Next time he's back in this room, he isn't going to be whispering sweet nothings in your ear."

She recoils like I've slapped her. "You think something happened between Andrijo and me?"

I'm about to retract my ugly words, pull them back inside myself, when I stop. A difficult truth crystallizes. "You left the fortress with him, Erin. Voluntarily. There's no way he could've abducted you without someone noticing. You . . . you wanted to be with him. You didn't know then that he was bad news."

Now her cheeks flush red. "Carina, I . . ."

"Why?" I whisper. "You have a boyfriend."

"I . . . Smith . . . he's not a good man, Carina. I haven't loved him for a long time, but I can't leave him. I don't know what he'd do." I read the subtext: *I don't know if he's violent like my father.* "He was spying on me."

"What?" I ask, although I think I know where this is going.

"He created a fake Facebook profile to check up on me." She presses her eyes closed. She looks so tiny in that huge gray hoodie. Frail. Breakable. "He started flirting, pretending to be some other hot guy. Was so sure I was unfaithful to him, and wanted to catch me in the act."

"Kieran Riddle?" I guess.

Her eyes ping open. "How did you—"

"We've been looking for you pretty hard, Erin. You'd be surprised what we know."

She swallows so hard I see her neck muscles ripple. "Andrijo was just . . . he's so . . ."

"I know," I interject. "Erin, I know." I try to soften my voice, but it's laced with impatience and fear. Fear of what'll happen if I don't start moving. "But we don't have time for this now. I have to get us out of here."

I start moving toward the shelves to climb up to the vent, hating myself for the irrational anger I suddenly feel toward my best friend. I should hate the men that drove us here: Smith, Andrijo, Kasun, her violent father. The men who made her so terrified of the world that she lost her way.

Maybe I'm furious with them, too. And maybe I'm angry with us for not fighting back harder.

Maybe all my rage is just wrapped into one.

"Carina . . ."

Her voice is tiny, ashamed, like a child who's wet the bed.

I stop, like Andrijo did in the doorway just a few moments ago. "Yeah?"

"Please don't hate me."

I swivel to face her. A lump rises in my throat. "I don't hate you, Erin. Nobody does. We love you, and need you home safe. Let me rescue you, okay?"

She nods once, a minuscule motion I almost miss.

And then I turn back, climb up into the vent and pray that's not the last time I see her alive.

THE ROOM CONTAINING Borko's body is as empty as it was when I left it. Andrijo is nowhere to be seen.

Stepping over the body, I fumble with the doorknob and open it a sliver.

Empty. The whole mezzanine floor is deserted. No Andrijo, no other people. Not even the cardboard boxes that were stacked adjacent to my doorway—they've been moved, too.

I'm scared. So scared. Rooted to the spot, obsessing over all the ways this could go wrong. If Borko had a gun, Andrijo probably does, too. If he sees—or hears, because even though I'm barefoot I'm still not silent—me running down the stairs, he may just shoot me on sight, knowing something has gone terribly wrong with Borko's visit to my storeroom.

I strain my ears for sirens—sirens that would allow me to sit and wait instead of taking action.

Nothing.

And so I take a deep breath, forbid myself from thinking too much about what I'm about to do and run.

The crack of gunshots and pinging of bullets on metal stairs never comes; there's just the sound of my bare feet padding along the cool surface. It takes me twenty seconds to reach the stair-case, then I'm sprinting down them, trying to pretend the soft thumping isn't audible to anyone but me. I leap down the final three steps, landing quietly on the cold concrete floor, and with a pounding chest I dash over to the nearest stack of crates and crouch behind it.

First leg: complete.

Can't I just stop now?

I survey the area. It's like the warehouse at the end of IKEA where you pick up all the flat-packed furniture you've spotted wandering through the showroom. High shelving laid out in narrow aisles, lined with white cardboard boxes neatly labeled with information on whatever drugs they contain. When Borko first dragged me through this warehouse, that's where I saw the forklifts and crate pull carts—the latter I need right now, but from here I can't see any.

Poking my head out the side of the stack, I quickly scan the room. Still empty of people; Andrijo is nowhere to be seen. This makes me feel worse rather than better. He could appear around a corner at any second, grab me by the throat, hold a gun to my head. I think I'd die of fright rather than grievous bodily harm.

Go.

I make for the closest aisle, relishing the feel of the air rushing past my face after hours of being trapped in a tiny storeroom. I run halfway down the aisle before realizing there's no trolley here. I dive into an open space on a bottom shelf, crouching into a tight ball, breathing hard.

There's no time for this, Carina.

No time to catch my breath when my best friend is in danger and the police are still miles away.

Go again. I jog down to the far end of the aisle, farthest away from the bottom of the stairs, and steer around the end. I cast a quick glance up to the mezzanine—no sign of life. No sign of our captor.

I'm not sure what I expected. I suspect that as soon as Andrijo stumbles over Borko's body, they'll hear the roar in Belgrade. There's still time.

The door to my storeroom is ajar. Did I leave it ajar?

Fuck fuck fuck.

Is he in there now?

I have to move.

Two, three, four aisles pass by in a blur until my side is pierced by a ripping stitch, but finally I find a trolley. One of the wheels sticks and wobbles as I drag it noisily along the concrete, back across the open space of the warehouse—no point in trying to hide behind crates and boxes now—until I'm at the foot of the stairs and suddenly panicking about how the hell I'm going to carry it up when I already feel so weak.

My mistake is not looking up.

"You killed my cousin."

Chapter Twenty-Five

August 4, Serbia

HIS VOICE IS cold, full of hatred that drips off his words like icicles. He doesn't shout, but it echoes around the warehouse regardless.

I drop the handle of the trolley. Look up. He's standing in the middle of the mezzanine, hands by his side, one drenched in blood. Did he try to stem Borko's wound? Did desperation make him think he could still save Borko?

There's a gun in the other.

Reflexively I step back. It's pointed at the ground, not at me, but somehow that's no solace. "Andrijo . . ."

"You killed my cousin," he repeats, as if reminding himself of the fact. Maybe he is. Maybe the last thing he wants to do is murder me, but again and again he remembers what I've done in an attempt to give himself the courage.

Because I see it in his eyes. He doesn't want to kill me. He's not a murderer by nature. I saw him with Erin, conflicted, caring, trying desperately to think of a solution that didn't involve slitting her throat. He wants this all to be over as much as we do.

But now his cousin is dead. Because of me.

"Your cousin was going to kill me," I say, steadily as I can. The strip lighting reflects off the gun. It's all I can look at. "I had no choice. I . . . I didn't want to die."

He grits his teeth so hard I hear it from the bottom of the stairs. The air is cold, so cold, and I shiver. Why do I feel like I'm lying? I didn't want to die. I wanted to live. I still do.

Maybe because I don't know that Borko was going to kill me. He could've just been coming to check on me.

I chase the thought away. There was no happy ending for me or Erin until I got that phone.

He just stares at me, in shock, or a daze, or something more psychotic.

I tilt my chin up. Force myself to look at him, not the gun. "The police are on their way. It's over. There's no reason to kill either me or Erin. Your best bet? Run."

Maybe I was trying too hard to be manipulative, because I didn't think it through—I know immediately I've said the wrong thing. His face thunders, and a pit of fear settles in my chest. What I've basically just told him is this: "The police are on their way, and unless you kill us both, we're going to tell them everything we know. We're going to implicate you. And your parents will be left to suffer alone."

Instantly I attempt to backtrack. "But I already told them everything. Killing us now, enforcing our silence, won't buy your freedom. They already know. They've already been to your apartment. They know. Why make it worse by murdering two innocent girls? You'll get a life sentence. But if you cooperate now . . . maybe they'll be lenient. Strike a deal."

His expression darkens. Shit. I can't play people with my words the way Erin can. I can't replicate that feeling, that "I truly care about you in every way" vibe she sends everyone's way.

What he says next catches me completely off guard. "You have something that belongs to me."

"I . . . what?" I take another step back from the foot of the stairs. Try to glance around quickly as I do. Suss out the best direction to run in. I feel incredibly vulnerable with him staring me down from a height. Everyone knows high ground is the safest. Right now, I am anything but safe.

Blood drips from the tip of his forefinger to the ground. "You were in my office."

The confusion on my face is real. Does he mean the letter knife?

Then I remember. I feel it in my front pocket—smooth and firm and rectangular.

The USB stick.

Keep your cool.

"I don't know what you're talking about."

Meet his eye. Don't look down, or up, or sideways. He'll know you're lying.

He takes a step toward me, nearing the top of the stairs, and I hate myself for flinching backward three more steps. "What did you use to stab my cousin in the neck?"

I bite my lip. "A letter knife. It was left on the top shelf in the storeroom." Slowly, I pull it out of my back pocket, hold it up for him to see, then drop it on the ground in front of me.

Another step toward me. This time I stand my ground. "You have something else. I know you do. You're lying—you were in my office."

I narrow my eyes. "How the fuck would I have got into your

office? I've been locked in a storeroom for hours. And don't you think if I had managed to escape, I'd have left the warehouse without looking back, rather than gone rummaging around in your office drawers?"

That makes him pause. I'm torn between using the hesitation to run for my life, or trying to talk him around.

They're both flawed. I sprint, he knows I'm lying and he puts that gun in his hand to use. I talk, he could poke another hole in my story and use the gun anyway.

So I choose the former. Elongating my words as much as possible, I murmur, "I don't have anything to hide from you, Andrijo. But I've told you. I don't want to die. And I don't think you want to kill me."

And then, leaping over the letter knife and dodging the crates to my right, I run.

It takes ten seconds for the gunfire to start—enough time for me to reach the nearest aisle. The noise isn't as harsh as it seems on TV. More a tat-tat-tat than sharp cracks of exploding gunpowder. Still fucking terrifying.

I make it to the far end of the aisle before he fully descends the stairs, and I duck behind the stocked end-cap before pulling out my own gun.

How is this happening?

There's no time to dwell on the absurdity of the situation. I fumble with the safety on the gun, weigh it up in my hand. I don't want to use it; although I've already taken a life, pulling a trigger at another man's head seems like too big a leap, like a line within myself I could never uncross.

So I keep running.

He's halfway to the first aisle now, bullets pinging off the shelves and bursting the boxes. I sprint past several more end-caps, hoping he's as inexperienced with a gun as I am. The erratic spraying of bullets seems to suggest so. He doesn't even have a clear shot and he's already using up his round.

Terror starts to kick in as I take a sharp left and dart down a different aisle, hoping he can't make out where I am. Blood roars in my ears, electrifying adrenaline shoots through my veins. Pure, raw fear like I've never felt before, not even in my worst panic attack. I could die. I could die in the next few seconds.

I'm halfway down the aisle when I realize I have no plan. I can't keep simply running away from him until the police arrive; he's leaner than me, faster, and he wants to kill me more than he wants himself to survive. Because survival means prison, and that kind of nothing-to-lose determination is impossible to outrun.

No plan. The keys to Erin's room still press into my hip, but even if I could get up there uninjured, what then? Why pull her from a trench just to throw her onto the front line?

My bare feet pound the concrete painfully. I'm nearing the end of the aisle. He's drawing closer.

I have to shoot. Maybe not to kill, but to slow him down . . . or bring him to a stop. Then I can get Erin out of the warehouse in the crate pull trolley and hide in another building, or out in the dark fields where he'll never find us, until the police arrive.

The realization gives me focus. Momentum.

When I reach the end of the aisle, I make a last-second decision. And I swing left, running back in the direction I came from—in the direction of Andrijo, who's down one of these aisles I'm about to run past.

For my first shot, I have the element of surprise: he doesn't know I have Borko's gun. I plan to keep this card close to my chest until the last possible second.

Thump, thump, thump. My bare footsteps are muffled, but not enough. He'll still hear me coming.

One aisle, two. Nothing.

Three.

Crack.

The bullet misses me, but I kick myself for not being quick enough. I need to get a shot in fast.

I double up the fourth aisle while he lingers in the third. Duck down as he fires aimlessly into the middle shelf between us, sending boxes cascading down around me.

I keep forgetting to breathe.

He's peering through the shelves; he sees me, but doesn't have an angle.

Go.

I continue to sprint down the aisle, loop around the end-cap and quickly fire into his aisle.

The gun shakes in my hand and two, three, four bullets spray wide of Andrijo.

I don't react fast enough.

Turning my side to the aisle, I start to run, but he's anticipating the movement.

A bullet thuds into my shoulder, and I cry out in pain and shock.

In that moment, everything else fades.

Fuuuuuuu—

I stumble forward, force myself to keep tripping one foot in front of the other, but the warehouse swims around me. Pain, fear, shock. Dizzy. Swirling shelves and boxes and concrete.

All I can see, all I can hear, all I can feel, all I can taste, all I can smell: the bullet wound.

It fucking hurts.

He's catching up with me. I pass two, three more aisles and dive down the next, gasping, sprinting as far down as I can, then spinning on my heel to face the entrance where he'll appear in three seconds.

Two.

One.

Breathe. I drop to the ground. It's the last place he'll expect me to be when he swivels and shoots, and it'll give me the split second advantage I need.

He appears, fires, bullets sailing a meter above my head. In the same moment, I take aim and fire four, five, six bullets at his legs.

One hits its mark and he collapses to the ground, roaring in pain, clutching his shin. He lets his gun clatter to the concrete.

I could shoot again, but I don't. I turn and run.

Dizzy, dizzy, I'm so dizzy, so breathless as my shoulder wound sears and bleeds and pulses.

Stairs. Just make it to the stairs.

Five years later, I get there. He's not following.

Hauling the pull trolley, I emit a wail so piercing it comes from miles away. The motion tugs my shoulder, shifting the bullet and causing a jolt of fresh pain.

The warehouse whooshes and dives and whirls.

Don't pass out. You'll never wake up again.

I have to leave it.

Two at a time I dash up the stairs, begging my brain to stay conscious. From the top of the mezzanine I can see Andrijo still crumpled on the ground below, not even attempting to climb to his feet and pursue me.

Shaking and wheezing, it takes me a few attempts to jam the keys in Erin's lock and twist. Click.

She must've drifted out of consciousness again, because when the door slams open, she jolts awake from her curled-up position on the floor. Her eyes go straight to the blood gurgling down my arm. Widen, gape.

"What the fu—"

"No time. I can't carry you downstairs. You have to walk, or crawl if you must. There's a trolley at the bottom. If we don't go now, we'll both be shot."

Steely resolve fixes on her face. Maybe it's the sight of my bullet wound—she realizes she's not the only one in physical pain. "Okay."

Unsteadily she pulls herself up using the shelves.

"Once we get to the stairs, you can lean on the bannister. Until then, use my arm." I offer her the crook of my uninjured elbow. "Faster, Erin."

Swallowing the last of her hesitation, she grips me tight and we start making our way across the mezzanine.

That's when I realize Andrijo is no longer in the aisle. All that remains is a pool of his blood, smear marks where he's climbed to his feet and a patchy trail that stops halfway down the aisle—he must've stemmed the bleeding after that.

Shit.

Trying not to spook Erin into halting, I subtly scan the warehouse for any sign of movement.

Nada.

Where the fuck is he?

I was in Erin's storeroom less than a minute. He can't have gotten far.

And yet he has.

Shit, shit, shit.

We wobble down the stairs, both of us hovering treacherously on the verge of collapse.

Adrenaline is the only thing keeping me moving. Survival instinct. Fight or flight.

My shoulder is killing me. Literally.

Throb, step, throb, step. The rhythm is painful, intoxicating.

I'm still holding the gun. It's covered in my own blood.

The silence of the warehouse is lethal, and my muscles tense, my body anticipating the imminent patter of gunshots as Andrijo takes aim from wherever he's hiding.

We make it to the bottom of the stairs without fire cracking through the quiet. Maybe he's out of bullets, I hypothesize hopefully, foolishly, desperately.

Or maybe his gun's range isn't long enough, and he's waiting for us to draw closer before he buries the final bullets in our brains.

Erin collapses into the crate trolley. Surveying the warehouse one last time, I fix my eyes on the nearest door, just to the west of the aisles, and go. Push her in front of me, angle myself so I'm ready to drop down the second he shoots, make sure the gun is firmly in my grasp.

One hundred fifty yards away. One hundred twenty-five. One hundred.

My eyes stream, my vision dances. Erin's crouched as low as she can.

The farther we get from the stairs on the wall, the more of an open target we become. There's a dartboard on my back, and he's taking aim. I can feel it. Feel his eyes on me, feel the barrel of a gun burning between my shoulder blades.

Seventy-five. Fifty.

I'm almost disbelieving as the huge sliding doors, corrugated iron and dull gray, draw closer.

Might we really survive this?

Twenty-five.

I start thinking about the next steps. Will the ground outside be hard enough to push Erin through a field on a trolley?

Will the police be here?

I imagine the relief of sirens blaring and blue and red lights lighting up the night sky.

Ten. Five.

We're there.

Erin doesn't know how much of a miracle this is because she's blissfully ignorant of the fact Andrijo is not where I left him.

"Hold this," I mutter to her, handing her the loaded gun, not reacting to her horrified stare. I'm dizzy and in a lot of pain, and my aim is bound to be even worse than before. And she's going to be harder to push across open field in the trolley. "Safety's off. Be careful."

Thud.

Somewhere nearby, terrifyingly nearby, a cardboard box shifts and thumps to the ground.

We both recoil in shock, her swinging to face the offending shelf just ten yards away.

The next second lasts an hour.

No shadow shifts behind the boxes, no labored breathing can be heard over the silence of the warehouse.

Moving as quickly as possible, I haul the sliding door to the side, whimpering at the effort of tugging a heavy sheet of iron with a wounded shoulder.

Without looking back toward the aisle, I shove Erin in her trolley out onto the concrete forecourt. A floodlight illuminates the area—it's motion sensitive. We're outside. Queasiness tears through my abdomen, and the rays of light wobble across my pupils.

Blood loss. I think I'm going into shock.

It's warm and sticky down my arm, beginning to clot.

The nausea is searing. I almost double over.

Can't.

Push, Carina.

I try breathing through the agony in my shoulder. How is it possible for something to hurt this much? If I survive this, I'm never complaining of a migraine again. My skin is cold and clammy, and my pulse and breathing are quickening alarmingly. I'm so weak my head keeps drooping onto my chest, because the effort required to hold it up feels intolerable.

Definitely shock.

Think.

Keep thinking.

As long as you think, you're still alive.

And Erin needs you alive.

A few sheafs stick out of the neatly stacked pile of papers in my head. The clinic. How does that fit in? Perhaps it's just coincidence that Tim and Kasun were photographed there together all those years ago, but . . . no. Borko was there, outside. It has to be connected. And Brodie Breckenridge . . . is she relevant, or another coincidence?

Something prods into my hip: the thing Andrijo was willing to shoot me for.

Do the contents of this USB stick somehow link all this together?

There are blips and jerks in my consciousness, skipped moments like a broken tape.

I can't get a grip on the world. I'm losing my foothold.

Part of me is floating above myself. The other part is nearly empty. I stop pushing the cart.

"Erin . . ."

"Yes?"

"I love you, you know that?"

From behind us, words slice through the moment: low, cold, final.

"Well, isn't that touching."

Andrijo.

He's right behind me, and the barrel of a gun is pressed against my skull.

Erin whimpers. "Please, Andrijo, please don't shoot—"

I hear the snarl without seeing it. "She killed my cousin."

"Please," Erin begs again. "Please don't do this. All we want to do is go home and forget this ever happened. We wouldn't tell a soul, I swear. We wouldn't—"

The gun shifts slightly against my scalp.

A click. Safety off.

It's too late. I'm already fading . . .

In the distance, a faint wailing.

Is it . . . sirens?

Less faint.

Erin's head jerks to one side, listening.

Sirens.

I'm sure the sky is alight with blue and red flashes, but my world goes black. I'm succumbing.

They're too late. The police are too late.

The last thing I hear before I slip away is Erin's piercing scream and a gunshot cutting through the night.

Chapter Twenty-Six

August 5, Serbia

I COME TO in the ambulance.

The rattle of medical equipment. The blare of a siren.

Cold, so cold. I've never been so cold in my life.

Opening my eyes is like lifting a box twice my bodyweight: heavy, hopeless.

I'm lying on a stretcher, but my legs seem to be elevated. Covered in blankets, but still so cold.

I can't even feel my shoulder.

Fade again.

WHEELING DOWN THE corridor in what sounds like a hospital.

Strip lighting in broken lines like road markings, whizzing overhead.

The smack of doors flapping open, the smell of disinfectant, someone sobbing.

Cold, so cold.

THE NEXT TIME my eyes peel open, it's an altogether calmer affair. I'm warm, albeit woozy, and in a hospital bed with extra blankets. The ward is small, with only one other woman—elderly—sleeping in the bed opposite me. It's light outside.

My limbs are filled with lead, but there's no pain in my shoulder.

A short, blond nurse pads through, sees I'm awake and smiles. "Miss Carina. How are you feeling?"

"N-yerrgh?" My throat is parched, my voice box lazy.

"Oh, dear." She chuckles good-naturedly. Her English is flawless, and her rotund build and kind face make me feel at ease. "The anesthesia will still be wearing off from your surgery."

Surgery?

The bullet, I suppose. They can't just leave it in there. The sadistic part of me wants to try and lift my arm, see how it feels, but I'm too foggy and, to be honest, too scared.

I make another incoherent noise. The nurse smiles.

"I'll get the doctor. He won't be a moment."

As she leaves, I let my eyes flutter closed again, purely because it's easier than keeping them open.

I must drift off again, because I awaken to a cold stethoscope on my bare chest. The idiot in me blushes at the intimacy.

The doctor is young and handsome, dark hair and a deep tan. Like Andrijo minus the intensity.

Andrijo.

What happened?

Where's Erin?

Is Andrijo in custody?

The gunshot in the hedge. Who was hit? Who fired?

Andrijo at Erin? Erin at Andrijo?

The scream, shudderingly high, replays in my mind.

Pain, or fear?

The doctor senses my panic. "Miss Carina. Please, try to relax. I'm Dr. Petrović. First, how are you feeling?"

More murmurings. I'm getting a bit pissed off at my inability to vocalize my thoughts.

"I must say, I'm surprised at how quickly you've woken up. You've only been out of surgery for a couple of hours. You were in quite severe shock when you arrived, but you should be feeling better now. We managed to remove the bullet from your wound— you're lucky the shooter wasn't closer to you, or it might have gone all the way through to your heart."

Speaking of my heart, I suddenly realize I cannot feel it beating. That might sound ridiculous, but as someone who deals with palpitations almost constantly, the absence of feeling is disturbing.

"Whurrr-n?"

I think that was supposed to be "Where's Erin?"

He's leafing through my chart and doesn't respond. He checks my vitals one more time, jots down a few things, then says, "Detective Ilić came by with a few questions for you, but I asked him to return later. You need to rest, okay?"

Drawing together all the energy I have, I focus really hard, and eventually manage, "Whereserin?"

A sigh, but it's not impatient. Just weary. "Please, Miss Carina. Try to rest. Everything else, it can wait. Your health cannot."

Like hell I'm going to rest.

After everything I've been through in the last twenty-four hours—hell, the last three weeks—I'm not going to lie down and sleep without knowing what happened to the best friend I fought so hard to save.

I try to push myself up then, prop myself onto my elbows in protest, and it's a mistake. Pain shoots through my shoulder, up and down my arm, so sharp it takes my breath away and I collapse back down.

"All right, all right," he concedes. "You have a couple of visitors waiting outside. They know you're fine, and we were going to wait until visiting hours, but . . . you don't seem like you're going to do as I ask until you get answers." A smile I try and fail to analyze. Is he . . . pitying? Bearer of bad news? The guy should play poker. I have no idea who's about to walk through the door. Or what they're about to tell me.

My mum and brother? Would they have flown out at the news, or frugally considered it a waste of money because they know I'm safe?

Or do they?

Ilić and Danijel? Come to conduct a debrief? Ask about the final moments of Erin's life?

Dr. Petrović helps me take a few sips of water, which helps my speech a little, then exits the room. But unlike when the nurse departed, I'm too nervous to fall back asleep. My shoulder continues to throb in protest at my foolish attempts to move.

The door takes an eternity to open again, but when it does, I almost collapse in tears.

Forget almost. I do.

Erin and Karen.

Karen pushes Erin in a wheelchair. Erin is ashen-faced and frail, but alive. They both burst into tears when they see me.

Hot, thick, fast, all the motions of the last few weeks come pouring out. Erin reaches the bed, and her hand grips mine— warm and bony, no trademark jewelry. For a second all we can do is cry and hold each other.

"You're not wearing your rings," I observe, for lack of anything better to say. "Normally you're like fucking Saturn."

She laughs then, not a fake girlish giggle, but her signature sailor laugh. Coupled with the tears of relief, it's the best thing I've ever heard. Karen drops into the plastic chair to the side of the bed. Her eyes are red and swollen, her skin dry and puffy. She wraps her cardigan tightly around herself and lets the tears flow without any effort to stop them.

"We're alive," Erin whispers, disbelieving. "We're actually alive. I thought . . ."

Her voice catches, and I squeeze her hand back. "I know."

Our eyes meet, and so much is left unsaid in that moment. Endless thank-yous, a thousand are-you-okays, a million descriptions of how scared we were. We stay quiet, communicating with our eyes—everything I feel, I see in her, too. Relief. Lingering fear. An unprecedented gratitude for the fact we're still breathing. Voicing these thoughts would cheapen them somehow.

Karen watches us, not wanting to interrupt the moment, and for a long time the three of us sit there in perfect silence.

Then Erin breaks it, her voice still rough and hoarse. "So . . ." Something new flickers in her oceanic iris. "We're both killers now."

It's the least funny thing in the world, but exhaustion and delirium and residual adrenaline force the laughter from me, melting together with my tears. "You shot him?"

She nods. "You collapsed. Lifeless. Even though there was no sound, I genuinely believed that he'd shot you. And in that moment . . . I was so angry, Carina. And scared. For what he'd done to me, and what I thought he'd done to you. So I raised the gun you gave me and shot into the hedge. Three, four, five times, until there were no bullets left."

"He's dead," I say, trying out the phrase. The words aren't as loaded as they should be.

Nod. "They both are."

Karen clears her throat, although she's still sobbing. I wonder if she's stopped since Erin was returned to her. "Is it strange to tell you both how proud I am of you?"

"For being murderers?" Erin snarks, smiling cheekily, and seeing her familiar sass is the best thing ever. I worried three weeks in hell might have buried her personality forever.

"For fighting for your lives. No matter what you had to do."

I swallow hard, trying to forget the shudder of the letter knife plunging into a muscular neck and draining it of life. Fleetingly, almost as a reflexively anxious reaction, I wonder what the elderly woman across the ward thinks of this conversation, but the thought is so minuscule, so insignificant in comparison to everything that's happened, that it's almost laughable.

Karen looks at us in turn, then says, "I'll leave you two alone." She leaves quietly.

"Erin," I begin softly. "Why were you here? What . . . what happened?"

"My dad . . ." she murmurs, staring at her hands. "He's showing symptoms of Aubin's. And there's nothing the doctors in the UK can do. Especially not the ambivalent arseholes who deal with prisoners. So when I went to visit my dad a couple months ago, he begged me to help him. He got so urgent he grabbed my arms—" she gestures to the bruise on her arm "—and the guards nearly had to get involved.

"He'd been illegally buying the Aubin's medicine from Bastixair for years . . . through Tim. With the help of Andrijo and Borko, Tim traffics the drug all over Europe—it's not approved

by most of the national food and drug standards agencies—and
nobody bats an eyelid at his excessive flying because he's always
traveling for press trips anyway. But the drug isn't cheap, and
Dad owed Tim a lot of money for my grandma's medication. And
I mean a lot. Which meant he owed Kasun a lot of money, and
Kasun doesn't forget debts that big. So when Dad put me in touch
with Tim, and I came here . . . they . . . they kidnapped me so they
could blackmail my dad into paying up once he got out of jail. 'My
money for your daughter.'"

It clicks into place.

*"When Simon's mum got really sick, he couldn't cope. Turned
to drink. Simon adored that woman, and he couldn't cope with her
demise. Then the financial crash happened, and we just about survived, but that sense of stability was gone. He started drinking even
more. And the drink, coupled with the grief, is what ruined him."*

The economic recession wasn't just a vague contributor in
Simon's decline. It was the main catalyst. He ran out of money,
but desperation and love for his mother made him keep illicitly
buying the drug regardless. And he got into debt. A lot of debt.
Enough to inspire Kasun to kidnap his daughter in order to get
his money back.

I'm filled with hatred for Tim. "Andrijo said . . ." Tears slide
down Erin's cheeks now. "Kasun would've been willing to forgive
the debts if Dad had gone to him and explained. Kasun's son has
early onset Aubin's. He knows how brutal it is to watch someone
you love suffer like that. But after he heard my dad had gone to
prison for domestic abuse . . . I guess his sympathy ran out. He
said my dad must never have truly loved his family, or he'd never
have wanted to hurt them. Never."

"I'm sorry, Erin," I whisper. "I'm sorry about what he did to you." She shrugs miserably. "Why did you . . . ?" I can't finish. But she knows.

"Why did I help him? Even after what he did? What he became?" She sighs so deeply I'm amazed there's any air left in her lungs. "He's still my dad. I couldn't bear to see him in pain. No matter how badly he deserved it."

There's something I want to say, something I need to say, something burning so hot in my throat that I can't bear to swallow it because it'll scorch me from the inside out. Something that started growing when I first saw her grab-mark bruise, and manifested into a monster when I tied that piece of the puzzle to her imprisoned father.

"I just . . . I hope you didn't help your dad because . . . you're afraid of him, you know?" I work hard to remove any trace of accusation from my tone. "I hope you're not . . . scared of your own father. The Erin I know is too fierce for that." I try for a small smile, but it falls flat on the ground.

Her brow knots, and another tear drips onto her upper lip. "Aren't you scared? Doesn't every single man in this world scare you? What they can do . . . what they can take from you. Don't you carry that fear with you everywhere you go?"

I swallow hard. "Yes." And it's true. It's not something I've ever articulated, but it's true.

"We're so much smaller than them, so much weaker. Once they decide to do something, most of us don't have a hope in hell of stopping it from happening. The whole world is our dark alley at midnight," she murmurs, entranced by a speck of dirt on the floor. "So how do you separate it from the men you love? Isn't every girl just a little bit frightened of her uncles, her lovers, her brother's friends?" A pause, so loaded the air between us is dense with her unease. "A handsome stranger at a music festival? Her boyfriend? Her father?"

We're silent a few moments, the bleep of hospital equipment and the faint sound of sneakers squeaking through hallways in the background. The weight of it all is starting to press down on my shoulders.

"Kasun's been taken into custody," Erin says after taking a deep breath and recomposing herself. "Though he claims he had no idea what Andrijo and Borko were doing in order to relinquish his money. The money my dad owed him."

Something slots into place. Erin's grandmother died not long after Simon was sentenced. Initially we speculated that it was the shame that killed her in the end, but what if it was more than that? What if the only thing keeping her alive, the only thing giving her hope, was the drugs Bastixair were developing? The medication Simon illegally imported just eased the symptoms, yes, but once her access to them was taken away, maybe she knew she'd never live to see a cure. So she gave up.

"There's something else," she adds, as though unsure whether to continue. Unsure whether I'm strong enough to hear it. "The police found something in your pocket . . . the object they believe Andrijo was willing to kill you to protect."

Of course.

The USB stick. In the emotion of our reunion, I'd almost forgotten.

"I'll leave Ilić to explain the details, but . . . this all goes so much deeper than one grieving son from the North East of England, and his missing daughter. It's . . . it's huge, Carina. And you uncovered it."

I face her full-on now. "It's like you've just shown me a trailer for an epic movie, but are making me wait an eternity to see the real thing."

"The clinics. Feminaid. They're corrupt."

"Okay . . ." I frown. "But how does that—"

"How does that fit in?" Erin asks. I nod. "It took me a while to make sense of it, too. But basically, Kasun owns the clinics. Most people knew he was an advocate—he's pro-choice, fights for women's rights, protects the mental health of sexual assault victims—but through a lead they found in Andrijo's apartment, the police managed to trace Feminaid to a parent company, registered to a fake name. Funds from this parent company had been transferred to and from an offshore bank account, owned by none other than . . . Marija Kasun. His wife."

"Right. What does that mean?" Maybe I'm still foggy from the anesthesia, but it's still not making sense.

"Nothing, until you found that USB. For over a decade, the Kasuns have been embezzling money from the clinics, below the radar, and donating it to Bastixair . . . to fund Aubin's research."

I stare at her. "The USB proved that?"

"No, it was password-protected," Erin explains. "But not very sophisticatedly. Once the police managed to hack it, they uncovered a spreadsheet of more passwords—for online banking, cloud accounts, the Feminaid records . . . everything."

The words feel significant, but I'm really struggling to process them. "I still don't get it. How did they find evidence of the embezzlement?"

Erin wavers. "That's where it's a little complicated. They did it by cross-referencing the clinic records, the bank statements and Bastixair's donations, Ilić told me. In the beginning, Kasun tested the waters with tiny amounts, but over the last couple of years it's been pretty substantial. Ten-million-dinar-a-day kind of substantial."

I gape at her. "How the hell did they get away with that for so long? Weren't they audited?"

She shrugs. "Sure, but on the surface their financial records were pristine. That's what the USB gave the police access to—databases stored on the cloud, detailing the real transactions. So someone went in for an abortion, right? Paid their fee, and that was declared in all the official ways. To the tax man, to the auditors, to the shareholders. Enough to turn a profit, but not a suspiciously high one. But these databases showed the truth. The girls were also charged for nonoptional extras—aftercare, painkillers, longer stays in the inpatient facilities if they needed them. None of those transactions were processed officially."

Holy shit.

How did an anxiety-ridden girl from northern England stumble on a conspiracy so massive? All I wanted to do was save my friend, and now I've helped the Serbian police bring down one of the biggest scandals of the decade—just by grabbing a USB from a desk? Sure, the aspiring journalist in me sunk my teeth into the case more than your average best friend might've, but still.

Holy shit.

A flaw in the reasoning is bugging me. "Why did these girls pay so exorbitantly for abortions? Why go to a private clinic at all? Doesn't the Serbian health service offer them?"

Erin's voice is still wobbly when she answers. "Of course. The legal limit is ten weeks, but in cases of rape, incest and psychological trauma, they're available until the twentieth week." She looks at me meaningfully.

I remember how unquestioningly the clinician I saw accepted

my sexual assault claims. "So Feminaid are much more liberal with their late abortions? Meaning . . . girls who exceed the legal gestation period use these private clinics as plan B."

"Yep."

This is huge.

We chat for a while longer. Part of me is terrified to stop talking to Erin, for fear of waking up and realizing this was all a dream and she's still missing. But sleep is begging me to succumb, and my eyelids droop. It's not until Dr. Petrović appears in the doorway that she finally says her goodbyes.

Erin climbs gingerly from her wheelchair, bends over my bed and gives me a gentle hug. She's fragile, but clean and warm and safe, and even though she may struggle mentally to overcome this horrific experience, physically she's on the mend.

I'm about to slip away into slumber once again when my eyes drift to the bedside table.

My silver bangle.

If you are saved from the lion, do not be greedy and hunt it.

This whole time, I thought the lion was a man. Simon, Andrijo, Kasun. Now I think the real lion is Aubin's, a disease so ruthless it drives people over the edge of their own morality. Not the sufferers. For them it's hideous, sure. But for those around them—friends, family, loved ones—it's a living hell, seeing those they care about descend into the shadows, lose themselves to the vicious clutches of their condition. It's enough to make them forget themselves. They see only pain, and they'll do anything to make it stop.

Seeing a loved one suffer is enough to turn even the timidest sheep into a cruel lion capable of anything.

Simon's mother had Aubin's, and he became a version of himself not even he could recognize. Violent to the women around him, his wife and his daughters, and to himself—with alcohol. Falling into acres of debt for the drugs his mother so badly needed, illegal in the United Kingdom, and leaving his family to pay the ultimate price.

Andrijo's father has Aubin's, and he allowed himself to be dragged into a dark circle of drug trafficking and abduction and blackmail so his income—the one keeping his family alive— wouldn't be compromised. His love for his parents, his desire to save them, drove him to unspeakable things, to pointing a gun at two innocent women and pulling the trigger.

Kasun's son has Aubin's, and he exploited thousands of vulnerable women in sexual assault clinics in order to fund research into a cure. He embezzled their money—their hard-earned pennies scraped together from double shifts and dodgy loans—and funneled it into his own agenda. His love for his son turned him into a monster.

It's not that I'm making excuses for the horrific acts of these men. There are no excuses for abuse. Not grief, not intoxication, not stress. Not fear, or hope, or love. It's just that I'm slowly realizing they aren't at the top of the food chain.

Aubin's is.

Chapter Twenty-Seven

May 6, England

THE FUCK-YOU LEATHER jacket is back.

Earlier this week, Erin was promoted from fashion assistant to fashion editor, and now she has an intern of her own to bring her Starbucks every morning.

Since we moved into a small quayside flat together, our relationship has gone from friendship to almost-sisterhood. We share victories and losses, pizza and movies, laughter and tears, sarcasm and gossip. We share it all.

I can't help but think she's becoming a mini-Lowe, and strangely that isn't the insult I once imagined it to be. Lowe is a force, yes, and a terrifying one at that. But she's also fiercely independent, passionate about her career, loving and maternal when the occasion calls for it, and she doesn't take shit from anyone. Erin could find worse role models.

I don't tell Erin that, of course. I simply say, "Check you out, you superstar. You're going to be the next Anna Wintour."

She laughs her sailor laugh, lips once again painted siren red, and replies, "I don't want to be the next Anna Wintour. I want to be the original Erin Baxter."

God help anyone who stands in her way.

Tonight, we're meeting for celebratory Friday night cocktails, and the iconic leather jacket is making a comeback. She broke up with Smith as soon as we got back to England, and I can't say I was too devastated. He's a selfish stalker, a closet misogynist, and he didn't deserve her for a second. Like I say, I can't say I was too devastated. Nor was she.

Her dad got out of jail a few weeks after we got home. Moved into a council flat across the River Tyne. Karen, Erin and Annabel will never forget what he did to them, never forgive the damage he caused, but they're supportive of his rehabilitation. Karen filed for divorce, but she's helping him find work, making sure he has the care he needs for his Aubin's. Not out of obligation, but because she's allowing her daughters to make their own decisions on whether or not they want him in their lives. And if they decide on the former, she wants him to be more than an empty shell. For them.

She'll always love the man he once was, but she'll never be able to forgive the man he became.

Kasun's trial is now under way with more charges listed than I can even remember. And last week, it was leaked that he accidentally implicated Tim Halsey in the murder of Brodie Breckenridge, a young reporter who figured out exactly where Bastixair's funds were coming from. Kasun paid him to quiet her forever. I shudder when I think of the gelato we shared in Danube Park, back when I was convinced Erin was the victim of a Liam Neeson movie plot, not the man sitting next to me on the bench.

Erin has come a long way in six months. Her emotional recovery has been tumultuous, and she's been seeking treatment for PTSD—and, with typical Erin panache, completely bossing it. She's not hiding from the psychological aftereffects of three weeks in hell. She's staring them in the face and saying, "I see you, and I respect you, but I will not let you define me."

The way she's dealing with her mental health—ferociously, openly, without fear of discussing it—is a constant source of inspiration for me. I'm still taking my meds, albeit a lower dose, and I still have my moments. But they're few and far between, compared to how regularly I used to succumb to the savage panic attacks and long stretches of depression. What helps more than anything is having someone to talk to about it—not a medical professional, but someone who really cares, who'll always be there. Someone who'll listen to me talk about my dad without filing the gaps with empty condolences and pointless platitudes. She just . . . listens. She's just there.

It's sad that I don't have that in my mum, but she's fighting her own battles.

I did eventually write my piece on Serbia, although it took a slightly different angle than my original draft back in that Serbian hotel room. Less history, less travel and quite a lot more focus on the way an innocent press trip to a celebrated music festival escalated into the holiday from hell—and ended in a warehouse shootout and the ultimate exposure of a national scandal that's gone unnoticed for decades.

My first-person account of the entire experience sold to a national newspaper. Enough to land me a second-chance interview at the *Daily Standard*.

This time, I nailed it. I've been a junior crime reporter for six months, and I'm loving every minute.

Every single day, I think of what Erin said to me in that hospital room in Serbia, both of us hurting, both of us unsure whether we were going to survive the next few minutes:

"Aren't you scared? Doesn't every single man in this world scare you? What they can do . . . what they can take from you. Don't you carry that fear with you everywhere you go? We're so much smaller than them, so much weaker. Once they decide to do something, most of us don't have a hope in hell of stopping it from happening."

The whole world is our dark alley at midnight.

We are all hunted by something, or by someone. We are all prey. But that doesn't mean we can't fight back.

Acknowledgments

PERFECT PREY WOULD not be a book without the amazing team of publishing professionals supporting me. The whole New Leaf team (Suzie, Sara, Joanna et al) plus the inimitable Jess Dallow have been in my corner since day one, and I couldn't be more grateful. At HarperCollins, my editor, Emily Krump; cover designer, Gail Winston; and copyeditor, Christine Langone (you're the unsung hero of the publishing process, and I apologize sincerely for my semi-colon-based issues) are the champs who brought this story to life. Thank you all for not realizing I am an imposter.

Countless eyes have been cast over this story at various stages of the drafting process. Huge shout-out to James Bateman, the real-life detective who provided infinite notes on this kind of investigation and how it would realistically unfold, and to Carly Ahmed and Al Ehm, who made sure my first-person portrayal of a POC was dealt with sensitively and accurately. I also drew on interviews with several anxiety sufferers when working on Carina's mental health journey, so thank you to Sadishika, Becca, Danaella, and Maren for your candid answers to some pretty deep questions. When I started out with this manuscript, I wanted to make the plot and characters as authentic as possible, and there's no doubt in my mind that this wouldn't have been possible without these wonderful individuals. And a big writerly group hug to the NAC (the most incredible support system when publishing feels like an uphill battle), to Scarlett Cole, and to Rebecca McLaughlin, who started as my PitchWars mentee and soon became a valued critique partner (and awesome friend who sends me delicious American candy from across the pond). Thank you all for helping me feel like less of an imposter.

Then there's the array of nutters who support me on a day-to-day basis, and do not shun me when I do things like accidentally throw the keys to my entire life in a street dumpster—my champagne-addled family (the Milnes, the Allens, the Paxtons, and, of course, the Stevens) and my extremely entertaining friends, including but not limited to Toria, Millie, Heather, and Lucy (a.k.a. the Coven), Nic, Hannah, Lauren, Amy, John (who I met on a real-life press trip to Serbia in 2014), Steve, Spike, and my ultimate favorite human, Louis. Thank you all for accepting the fact that I am an imposter and being (reasonably) nice to me anyway.

About the Author

LAURA SALTERS is a twenty-something magazine journalist from the northernmost town in England. *Run Away* was her first novel.

Discover great authors, exclusive offers, and more at hc.com.

www.laurasalters.com